FROM THE YONDER

A Collection of Horror from Around the World

Volume V

War Monkey Publications, LLC
Orem, Utah

©2025 War Monkey Publications, LLC

First Print, 2025

Edited by Joshua P. Sorensen

Cover Art by LaVonna Moore

ISBN 978-1-954043-12-1 (Paperback Cover)
ISBN 978-1-954043-13-8 (ePub)

www.warmonkeypublications.com

AUTHOR COPYRIGHTS

TABLE OF CONTENTS

<u>A NOTE FROM THE EDITOR</u>

This anthology has been a challenge. My schedule and responsibilities became extremely busy. It got to the point where cancelling the project all together became a real possibility.

But there are so many incredible stories and hard work by the enclosed authors that I could not in good faith let the project languish.

Luckily, several other personnel were able to join in and assist with the initial editing. And the anthology came together.

I would like to thank the patience and work of everyone involved towards the success of this publication.

Sincerely,

Joshua P. Sorensen

AUTHOR BIOS

DEREK DES ANGES - Derek Des Anges is a multigenre author and press-cutter living in London, UK, but originally from Dartmoor, where his story is loosely set. His work has also appeared in publications from Flame Tree Publishing, Trollbreath Magazine, and Ghoulish Books, among others. A full catalog of his work can be found at https://derekdesanges.wordpress.com/books

GRANT BALFOUR - Grant Balfour graduated from New College of Florida with a degree in herrneneutics, then spent time as a writer and editor for the tabloid papers *Sun* (famous for the 2001 anthrax attacks) and *Weekly World News* (famous for Bat Boy), ensuring that America got vital information about Roswell, Nostradamus, and apple cider vinegar cures. His byline has appeared in other publications as diverse as *Kung Fu/Tai Chi Magazine*, *New York Post*, *Porthole Cruise and Travel*, and *Cordite*. He has also helped create indie films and regularly releases sad songs about current research on GuildOfScientificTroubadours.com.

SUE BARNARD - Sue Barnard is a British novelist and award-winning poet whose family background is far stranger than any work of fiction. She would write a book about it if she thought anybody would believe her.

Sue was born in North Wales some time during the last millennium. She speaks French like a Belgian, German like a schoolgirl, and Italian and Portuguese like an Englishwoman abroad. Her mind is so warped that she has appeared on BBC TV's *Only Connect* quiz show, and she has also compiled questions for BBC Radio 4's fiendishly difficult *Round Britain Quiz*. This once caused one of her sons to describe her as "professionally weird". The label has stuck.

She now lives in Cheshire, UK, with her extremely patient husband and a large collection of unfinished scribblings.

MAUREEN BOWDEN - Maureen Bowden is a Liverpudlian, living in Wales. She has had 217 stories and poems accepted by paying markets including Third Flatiron, Water Dragon Publishing, Allegory and many others. She was nominated for the 2015 Pushcart Prize and in 2019 Hiraeth Books published an anthology of her stories, 'Whispers of Magic.' She also writes song lyrics, mostly comic political satire, set to traditional melodies. Her musician husband has performed them in folk music clubs throughout the UK. She loves her family and friends, rock 'n' roll, Shakespeare, and cats.

SAMANTHA BROOKE - Samantha has been writing horror for over a decade, ever since completing a writing course in 2012. Since that time, she has had stories published in both England and America. When not writing herself, she is also a judge for Reedsy Prompts. She lives in Yorkshire, England.

STEVE BURFORD - Steve is a former English and Drama teacher who left academia a couple of years ago to become a full time writer, focussing mainly on his "Summerskill and Lyon" police procedural novels, but also writing at least one Christmas ghost story a year for his friends and fellow MR James enthusiasts. "Malvhina" is set in his beautiful hometown of Malvern, England, famous for its hills, wells and C.S. Lewis inspiring lampposts. The locations described in the story are real. Some of the events are not.

SADIE CARDENAS - Sadie Cardenas lives in Seal Beach attending Orange Coast College as a Liberal Studies major. She has had her work published in BlazeVOX Journal, Cathartic Lit Magazine, Transfer Magazine, and her first short story feature in War Monkey Publications.

C.J. CARTER-STEPHENSON - C.J. Carter-Stephenson is a British writer, who was born in the county of Essex and currently lives on the Isle of Wight. He holds an MA in Creative Writing from the University of Southampton, has been a Writers of the Future finalist, and has had three books published. Other publication credits include stories and/or poems in *HWA Poetry Showcase X, Aesthetica, Speculative North, Dark Horizons, Radon Journal, Utopia Science Fiction* and *AE: The Canadian Science Fiction Review*. He is also the narrator of *Back of the Bookshelf*, a monthly podcast of classic genre fiction, and gives regular readers theatre performances of his work. Find him online at https://www.carter-stephenson.co.uk/.

VALERIE CHATINDO - Valerie Tendai Chatindo is a biochemistry graduate, writer and communications consultant. She's a regular contributor for The Kalahari Review, Enthuse Magazine, The Diplomat Zimbabwe and EarGround. Her work has also appeared in Pink Disco Magazine, Creepy Pod, Agbowo, Argyl Literary Magazine, The Afterpast Review, Whisper House Press, Omenana, Efiko Magazine, Writer's Space, and Literary Yard. Her short story "Sheba," was shortlisted for the African Cradle African Heroines literary prize, and her pieces were featured in Povo Afrika's Nehanda Reimagined anthology. Her debut novel Mono: Tales of The Tapa Kingdom is shortlisted for the Iskanchi Book Prize. The thirty-year-old resides in Harare, Zimbabwe with her cat, Muffins. She runs her own Literary Platform, Shumba Literary Magazine.

JAMES R. COFFEY - A graduate of University of South Florida (USF), James has degrees in Psychology and Anthropology and currently lives in Florida. He is a life-long musician and multimedia writer whose work appears regularly in numerous journals and magazines including Journal of Compressed Creative Arts, AntipodeanSF, Red Cap Publishing anthology, History Defined, Salvo Magazine, and Mystic Owl.

SARAH DAS GUPTA - Sarah Das Gupta is a writer from Cambridge UK who has taught English in India, Tanzania, and UK. Her work has been published in over twenty countries from New Zealand to Kazakhstan, in journals and anthologies. She has recently been nominated for Best of the Net and a Dwarf Star. She has won and been shortlisted in poetry and prose competitions including in 'The Fairy Tale Magazine', 'The Bermuda Truiangle Poetry Contest', and in 'Magnets and Ladders'.

J. D. HARLOCK - J. D. Harlock is an Eisner Award-nominated American writer, researcher, editor, and academic pursuing a doctoral degree at the University of St. Andrews, whose writing has been featured in Strange Horizons, Nightmare Magazine, The Griffith Review, Queen's Quarterly, and New York University's Library of Arabic Literature. You can find him on Bluesky, Facebook, Instagram, LinkedIn, & Twitter.

STEVE HIDE - S J Hide lives and works in Bogotá, capital of Colombia, a South American country which lile La Muelona is both beautiful and deadly, but never boring.

ZIAUL MOID KHAN - Ziaul Moid Khan (born 14 August 1985) in an aristocratic Nawab's family in the countryside, Johri of Western Utter Pradesh. His mother Ansar Fatima is a religious woman; while his father Abdul Moid Khan, a renowned scholar in Baghpat, was an Urdu author, who died when Zia was four. Among his six siblings, he's the youngest son. Despite his entire education in Hindi medium, he trained himself hard to write in English. He lives in Jaipur, Rajasthan with his wife Khushboo and their son Brahmaand Cosmos. His fiction can be read in *Bards* *and Sages Quarterly, NiftyLi, The Fifth Di…, The Society of Misfit Stories,* and others.

TOM LARSEN - Tom Larsen is the author of six novels in the crime fiction genre.

Tom's short fiction has appeared in *Alfred Hitchcock Mystery Magazine, Ellery Queen Mystery Magazine, Mystery Tribune, Black Cat Mystery Magazine, and Black Cat Weekly.*

2025 marks the third year that one of Tom's stories appear in the anthology *Best Mystery Stories of the Year* from Mysterious Press.

NICOLA LOMBARDI - Nicola Lombardi is an active participant in the Horror Writers Association. He has published in Italy the novels *The* Gypsy *Spiders, Black Mother, Night Calls, The Red Bed, The Tank* and *Strigarium,* and seven collections of stories. In addition, he has published novelizations from the films of Dario Argento (*Profondo Rosso* and *Suspiria*) and translated works by Jack Ketchum, Seabury Quinn, F.B.Long and many others for the Italian market. Many of his stories have appeared in English, and in 2021 Tartarus Press published his collection *The Gypsy Spiders and Other Tales of Italian Horror.* Full bibliography at www.nicolalombardi.com.

J. WEINTRAUB – (translator for Nicola Lomdardi) J. Weintraub has published fiction, essays, and poetry in all sorts of literary places. A member of the Dramatists Guild, he has had one-act plays produced throughout the world. As a translator he has introduced the Italian and Swiss horror writers, Nicola Lombardi and Davide Staffiero to the English-speaking public. His collection of speculative fiction, *A Visit to the Catacombs*, is scheduled for publication later in 2025. More at https://jweintraub.weebly.com/

SERGIO 'ENTE PER ENTE' PALUMBO - Sergio 'ente per ente' Palumbo is an Italian public servant who graduated from Law School working in the public real estate branch, who published a Fantasy RolePlaying illustrated Manual, WarBlades, of more than 700 pages. Some of his short- stories have been published on American Aphelion Webzine, WeirdYear, Quantum Muse, Antipodean SF, Schlock!Webzine, SQ Mag, etc.,and in print inside 90 American Horror/Sci-fi/Fantasy/Steampunk Anthologies, 60 British Horror/Sci-Fi Anthologies, 2 Canadian Urban Fantasy/Horror Anthology, 7 Indian Anthologies, and 4 Australian Sci-Fi Anthology by various publishers, and 16 more to follow in 2025/2026. He was also a co-Editor, together with Mrs. Michele DUTCHER, of the Steampunk

Anthology "Steam-powered Dream Engines", published by Rogue Planet Press, an Imprint of British Horrified Press, of the Fantasy/Sci-Fi Anthology "Fantastical Savannahs and Jungles", of the Horror/Sci-Fi Anthology "Xenobiology – Stranger Creatures", by the same British Publisher, of the Sci-Fi/Fantasy/Horror Anthology "Bleakest Towers" by the same Publisher and "Of Poets, Spies and Unearthliness - Otherworldly tales in the times of Shakespeare and Marlowe" - Anthology, of the Urban Fantasy/Horror/Sci-Fi Anthology " Dickensiana Steamfantasy - A very different 1800s " and of the Sci-Fi/Horror/Grimdark Anthology "Exomoons- Natural and Unnatural Astronomical Bodies Orbiting Strange Planets".

He is also a scale modeler who likes to build mostly Science Fiction and Real Space models.

The internet site of his Scale Model Club "La Centuria": www.lacenturia.it

SHANE PILLAY - Shane Pillay lives in the Netherlands and works in music, film, and literature. His short stories have been published by multiple journals, including Hawaii Pacific Review, Kalahari Review, Nthanda Review and Fiction Magazines. His adult novella, "Affairs of the Dick" was published by The Little French Books (2018), while his horror novella, "The Knocking", was published by indie publisher Alban Publishing (2019).

He has produced animation films, as well as worked with musical artists from the USA, Ireland, Indonesia, and Australia.

Visit his website: shanepillay.com

EDWARD ROSICK - Edward R. Rosick is a writer living in the urban wilds of Michigan. His diverse works of dark speculative fiction, from the sublime to surreal, have appeared in numerous award-winning magazines and anthologies including *Pulphouse, The Half That You See,* and *Monstrous Tales Vol. 2 & 3.* His first collection of dark speculative fiction stories, WHERE THE GRASS DON'T GROW AND VULTURES SING, was published earlier in 2025 by Baynam Books Press. When he's not reading, writing, or working, Rosick enjoys spending time exercising, doing martial arts, and being outdoors with his family, friends, and canine companion. More info can be found on his website: www.edrosick.net.

VALERIYA SALT - Valeriya Salt is a sci-fi/thriller author from Sheffield (UK). She studied history and earned her Master's Degree in Art Expertise at St. Petersburg University of Culture and Arts. Born in Belarus, she'd lived for many years in different corners of Eastern Europe before settling down in the north of England.

Her short stories, essays, and reviews have appeared in anthologies and magazines, and won an Honourable Mention in the Writers of the Future Contest in 2022. Her debut novel Dive Beyond Eternity was published by Northodox Press (UK).

Facebook: www.facebook.com/saltandnovels

Twitter: https://twitter.com/LSalt1

Instagram:
https://www.instagram.com/valeriyasalt_author

Blog/site: www.saltandnovels.wordpress.com

J BENJAMIN SANDERS JR - J Benjamin Sanders Jr is a freelance writer in Richardson, Texas and a Marine Corps Vet and a compulsive story teller. He lives with his wife, Rosemary, a pair of loving Airedales called Fiona and Angus Og, as well as a pair of rescued feral cats called Loki and Thor. He's a longtime member of the Dallas Fort Worth Writer's Workshop where he rubs elbows with several noted authors. An eclectic reader, since the age of six, with a special life-long love of pulp fiction and thirties noir.

His Short stories have appeared in such anthologies as M is for Medical, L is for Lycans,K is for kidnap, Night in New Orleans, Enter the aftermath, Nigtmare whispers, Terrors in the Toybox, Goblin Souk, Eights, Aces, and Unmarked Graves, and many other. His Texas Noir novel, Mexicanos Hustle was released July of 2024 by Fawkes Press and won the Judges top pick at the Killer Nashville Conference.

CHARLES SARTORIUS - An ostensibly MBA corporate type with an artist's soul, Charles Sartorius makes time to write both short stories and music lyrics. His *The Missing Case of the Missing Case* and *Boo Hag* have been published in respective crime and horror anthologies. Two other creations, *Shadowed* and *Riven*, were recently featured online at MetaStellar. Several tales of terror have appeared in various horror zines as well. His songs can be found on conventional venues such as Amazon, Apple Music, and Spotify, including the powerfully raw *Actuality*. Another tune, *Circus Politico*, won first place (Rock/Alt) in the Great American Song Contest.

PAUL STANSBURY - Paul Stansbury is the author of the five volume *Inversion* short story collection, *Down By the Creek – Ripples and Reflections*, and *Under the Faerie Moon,* an illustrated poetry collection. Over one hundred forty of his stories and poems have been published in print anthologies as well as online publications. He is a Kentucky Monthly Penned winner. His short play, *Nana Toby*, was selected for the Festival of New Plays at Union Commonwealth University. He is Scheduling Coordinator for The Jeanne Penn Lane Celebration of Kentucky Writers. He is the owner of Sheppard Press. Now retired, he lives in Danville, Kentucky.

P.S. TRAUM - P. S. Traum is an unusual presence in the exciting underground genre scene, writing escapist speculative fiction in a wide range of styles, tones and subjects, with a fresh voice and perspective. Subtle or extreme, macabre or melancholy, PST is a devoted acolyte of all things Horror, with occasional forays into dark Fantasy/Sci-Fi. As an author, the mercurial Traum prefers to remain invisible, so that the unique storylines and compelling characters remain interesting and interpretive, unburdened by any external distractions or preconceived perceptions. Readers deserve a fun imaginative experience that feels real, personal and entertaining, even when it might be scary, spooky, or creepy!

In 2025, Baynam Books published PST's short story collection, *Hellish Hotblooded Horrors*. P.S. Traum has had more than three dozen short stories published.

DJ TYRER - DJ Tyrer is the person behind *Atlantean Publishing* and has been widely published in

anthologies and magazines around the world, such
as *Alone in the Borderland* (Belanger Books), *Chilling
Horror Short Stories* (Flame Tree), *All The Petty
Myths* (18th Wall), *Steampunk Cthulhu* (Chaosium),
What Dwells Below (Sirens Call), *The Horror Zine's
Book of Ghost Stories* (Hellbound Books), and *EOM:
Equal Opportunity Madness* (Otter Libris), and issues
of *Sirens Call*, *Hypnos*, *Occult Detective
Magazine*, *parABnormal*, and *Weirdbook*, and in
addition, has a novella available in paperback and on
the Kindle, *The Yellow House* (Dunhams Manor).
DJ Tyrer's website is at https://djtyrer.blogspot.co.uk/
DJ Tyrer's Facebook page is
at https://www.facebook.com/DJTyrerwriter/
The Atlantean Publishing website is
at https://atlanteanpublishing.wordpress.com/

K. J. WATSON - K. J. Watson's stories and poems
have appeared on the radio; in magazines, comics, and
anthologies; and online.

CHUPACABRACADABRA

by P.S. Traum

"All of us here at The Cynical Debunker are absolutely mystified." The stocky man adjusted his Lennon-esque spectacles and stared out at the audience.

"When the local authorities sent the video to our office, we were intrigued, and, ultimately, shocked. We decided the best course of action in this particular case was immediate action and full disclosure. Now, normally we wouldn't broadcast what some are hysterically calling a 'snuff film,' but I have to say, I'm still not entirely convinced what you are about to watch is genuine and real. Admittedly, the footage is extremely convincing, and the...encounter showcases what are surely the most spectacular special effects outside of Hollywood."

The frowning man rubbed his shaved head. "The fact is, this isn't simply a case of misidentification or questionable testimonials. There are only two possibilities here. One, this is a highly impressive, albeit cruel and distasteful, hoax. The other... Well, I don't have to tell you what it means if this video is authentic. But in any case, the fact remains that two prepubescent boys remain missing. Even if these middle-schoolers have indeed perpetrated an elaborate hoax, their parents and families are understandably very concerned. Our sympathies go out to them, and we all pray that the boys are in fact alive and well. Against our better judgment, and our normal broadcast policies, we now share with you this video, in the hopes that someone out there knows something that can help bring these kids safely home to their worried families...”

*****

The dark-haired boy stepped over a fallen log, his skinny legs struggling to find balance amidst the branches. Behind him was a small farm at the edge of a sparse forest.

“Dude, I really don’t think a Cucaracha killed your dog.” He kicked at a broken pinon tree until a pinecone fell. Finding nothing inside, he threw it, shaking his head.

“*Chupacabra*. I showed you the evidence, Ramon. It all fits.”

“Whose camera is that anyway? It looks like a toy.” Ramon thrust his face close to the lens and shook his tongue and rolled his eyes. “Hi Malachi! Say hi to your sister for me!” He waved.

“Dude! Your ugly face is going to break the lens.” Malachi wiped it. “It’s digital, I borrowed it from—”

“And you really think that just because you brought a camera, you’ll magically catch something no one’s ever seen that doesn’t even exist? Surrrrrrre.... What are the odds?” Ramon rolled his finger near his temple in the customary "you're cuckoo" gesture. "Ladies and gentlemen...Malachi and his invisible movie star monster, the Candelabra!"

"Chupacabra. Yes, we do have a very good chance! We're in the right place, at the right time of day and no one's around."

"Whatever..."

Malachi poked a soggy cardboard box with a wooden staff. He struck it until it collapsed. "This stick is pretty strong. And see how Sodajerk even carved some symbols and designs on it? I should be nicer to him, but I am grateful."

"But not grateful enough to LARP with the dork, are you?"

"Dude, his roleplaying games are silly enough as it is. I'm not about to dress up and act them out too. Would you?"

"If it was normal D&D I might. But he has some dumb ideas." Ramon grinned at Malachi. "Almost as dumb as your little monster hunt! Listen, don't they also call it a 'goat-sucker' or something? You do realize your dog wasn't a goat, right? So why would a Chimichanga mess with it?"

"*Chupacabra.* Actually, it makes perfect sense, if they really are weird mutated dogs, right?" Malachi leaped at some bushes, bringing his staff down on them as he held the camera high. A mangy cat ran out, yowling.

"I don't know, dude, that chick in the old TV show said it looked like a little green spiky goblin, didn't she?" The tan preteen pulled some berries off a bush and popped them in his mouth. "Some of that artwork looked cool, though. Maybe your Chichona really is an alien."

"*Chupacabra*, you idiot!" Malachi threw a dirt clod at his friend. It exploded on impact with the orange Kennedy Middle School windbreaker, striking the cougar printed on the back.

"Asshole!" Ramon threw one back, hitting the lanky boy in the rear when he tried to dodge. "I know what the stupid thing is called! No duh! I'm just messing with you because this is a waste of time. I'm bored as hell."

"Look at these tracks! I can't identify them, can you? You're the one who spent all that time in the Butt Scouts." Malachi pulled some pictures out of his jacket pocket. "So check it out, Ramon. Here in the Southwest, there's like three different kinds, I guess. Like those skinned dogs are mostly down in Texas, but why not here? This photo is in Los Lunas...see? It's like a shaved blue coyote or something."

"I still kind of like the little green lizard-monkey thing. It's kind of cute."

"Yeah, but that one's in Cuba or Puerto Rico or something. One crackpot doesn't speak for all chupacabras. She was probably drunk, or ate some bad tacos or something."

"I think that's probably racist."

"How?"

"Hell if I know... Somehow." Ramon slapped his friend's shoulder. "Dude, you didn't even like that dog. So who cares? Let's go to that balloon fiesta. We still have time. You can't live in New Mexico and not go up in a hot air balloon at least once. Or are you chicken?" He flapped his arms and made clucking noises. "Hey! You're a chickacabra!"

Malachi shoved his friend. "Marty's dad said he saw something chasing his goats. And we're already here. There's the goats." He pointed to the field behind the wire fence. "I'm checking it out. I don't like mysteries! It bugs the hell out of me! I want answers! What drains blood out of a dog? Or a goat or cow or whatever? It's just weird."

"I think the only animals that suck out your blood are vampire bats. And mosquitoes. Oh, and leeches." Ramon looked at Malachi slyly, edging away slowly. "And your sister!"

"Ha, ha, so funny I forgot to laugh. You little turd." He lunged at Ramon, who tried to jump back but tripped and fell. Malachi laughed. "Serves you right. Fell on your ass right into some chupacaca."

Ramon held up his hand. "Whoa, dude! Look!" He waved his fingers, blood dripping off of them. He wiped them in the dirt.

"See? I told you we were close. You know, none of those animals literally drain out blood. Nothing has hollow teeth like a hypodermic needle." Malachi pointed the camera up at the clouds. There was no rain in sight, but it was gradually getting darker.

"I think snakes do, you know, like for the venom, right?" Ramon scanned the ground. "I hate snakes." He held his jacket out like a cape, and then made the Dracula pose with his elbow up. "Vampires leave two little fang holes too."

"But my mom says nothing sucks all the blood out of an animal. How would it all fit? Even you couldn't hold that much. She said it's just regular animal bites, and the blood leaks out and soaks into the ground." He faced his friend. "But...you saw the dog. No blood under it. No bite marks. Just that little slit on the neck. And she was all dried up and light. But she was fine that morning! It was sudden! And why all dried up the same day? How?"

"Yeah. I know, dude, that's why I'm going along with this crap." Ramon shrugged. "Maybe it's a big microwave or something?"

"Maybe it's like those UFO cattle mutilations, I guess. Like, maybe it's some asshole alien doing experiments. Like a mad scientist alien sticking tubes in them or something."

"Well, aliens do like to probe people." He glanced sidelong at Malachi. "I bet they've probed your sister..."

"Damn, you really have a thing for her, don't you? She's in high school, dude! You're like, a baby, compared to her. And she's pretty! She'd never in a million years want anything to do with you." Malachi patted his friend on the back.

"Hey! Maybe if you were cool for once, you could use your chupacamera to make me a video—you could hide and film her the next time she's—"

"Whoa! Look!" Malachi whispered excitedly, poking his friend.

The boys watched a small brown shape leap out of a ravine. It darted into the tall grass the goats wandered in. A chorus of strange goat-noise rang out as the furry blur joined the flock.

"Come on! Let's get a closer look." Malachi adjusted the camera's focus. Ramon was already jumping the low fence.

"Aw, dude...it was just another goat. Look. All goats." Ramon leaned down, imitating the beasts' odd calls, annoying the one nearest him.

"It sure could jump, though! It looked funny, too. I don't know..."

The boys moved back and sat on a pile of old railroad ties. Ramon wiggled a rusty spike, trying to pry it out of the oily wood.

"Hey! Check it out," Malachi said quietly, gesturing to the far edge of the little herd. "Are they trying to mate?"

They watched a shaggy brown goat put its front hooves onto a small tan and white goat's back, not in a mounting position, but at its side, perpendicular.

"Huh. Stupid goat doesn't know how to hump. He—" Ramon jumped up. "Whoa! Did you see that?"

Malachi stood up as well. The lanky goat had shot its tongue out like an anteater, right into the smaller goat's neck. He zoomed in on the mouth. The tongue was too long and too thin. It was embedded in the throat, straight and stiff.

"What the hell?" Malachi crept closer as Ramon followed. "Look!"

The tongue was also translucent, red fluid could now be seen flowing into it. Blood. The goat's blood.

"A vampire goat? It really is a goat-sucker!" Ramon laughed.

"No, that's not a vampire or a goat. Look carefully."

The small goat collapsed to the ground, bleating helplessly as the creature's dark claws pierced its back and ribs, jutting out from between split, cloven hooves. The skin on the goat's face suddenly stretched tight over its skull, pulled thin against the bone as its fluids drained away.

"Holy crap!" Ramon yelled.

The creature turned to him, its tongue still firmly lodged in the little goat's throat, pulled against the creature's right cheek. The thing's eyes narrowed as it frowned.

"Dude!" Ramon cried.

The goat-creature retracted its tongue and bared its teeth at the boys, hissing. Its weird Kermit-the-Frog goat eyes bugged out of its head, extending on sinewy stalks. It screeched loudly and leapt at Ramon.

"Hell no!" Ramon yelled as the beast landed on him. It shot its tongue out like a piston, grazing the boy's tender neck. Ramon dodged as the tongue made a second attempt. The tip punctured his throat next to his trachea. Ramon pushed the creature hard. "Get it!"

Malachi jumped forward with his staff—the camera now dangling from the strap around his neck—and threw it like a javelin at the creature. It hit the ground in front of the beast, twisting. The side struck the beast's legs.

"Dammit!"

The creature reared up and screeched eerily at Malachi. The unholy sound filled the air and made the boy's knees go weak. It glared at him with accusatory eyes and an indignant sneer.

"I think you just pissed it off, dude! Kick it or something!" Ramon yelled, holding his palm against his wounded neck.

The angered creature screeched again, then bounded off into the grass. It disappeared into the ravine. Malachi started to follow, holding the camera up at arm's length.

"Dude! Get me to a hospital!" Ramon grabbed Malachi's arm.

"But it'll get away! And no one will ever believe us!"

"Dude! I'm bleeding to death!"

Malachi pulled Ramon's hand away. "It didn't even hit a vein or anything! You're barely bleeding!"

"Are you kidding me?! To hell with that thing! Just help me already!" He shook his friend.

Malachi stared at the ravine and sighed. "Yeah, I guess it's gone, anyway. Damn..." He shook his head. "We're never going to find it. Not if it's that fast, and can just blend in with other goats. Damn."

Ramon shakily pointed to the bleating flock. "Forget that one. First, I think we better, um, check out those other goats! You know, one minute just a stupid goat, then 'ABBA-Cadaver' and it's a goddamn monster!"

"Uh...I think you meant 'abracadabra'..."

Ramon plopped back down onto the ground. "Yeah, man...sorry... Duh! I think – uh, maybe...I was thinking of...that, uh, Voldemort bullshit..." He held his head and quietly moaned.

"Yeah, and you got that one all wrong, too!" Malachi squeezed his friend's shoulder. "Hey...you okay, Ramon?"

"Probably...blood loss...didn't I...uh, tell you— I'm...bleeding to death!"

"There's hardly any blood! Geez, dude... Just rest a minute, okay? Let me check out that little dead goat then we'll split." Malachi ruffled the boy's hair as Ramon turned away.

Malachi walked over to the fallen beige goat. The other goats were wandering away from it. "Okay, let's check you out, kid..." He reached out to turn the body over.

As his hand touched its spine, the goat suddenly twisted and flipped itself over. It reared up, screeching frantically.

"Holy crap!" Malachi jumped back.

The newly mutated goat-creature wavered, as it stood upright on its wobbly hind legs. Its strange-pupiled eyes popped out of the orbits on tendrils as the first monster's had, as it shook its upper hooves at the boy as if in admonition. Claws sprouted out from the cloven centers. The beast reared up at the sky, kicking its legs like a whinnying horse.

"Ramon! You see that shit?!" Malachi ran to his friend, forgetting to grab his staff. He pulled at the boy's shoulder. "We're out of here, dude!"

Ramon struggled to stand, shaking violently. He spun around, his enlarged, distorted eyes bulging out of the sockets obscenely. He screeched shrilly at Malachi, piercing his ears. Malachi screamed back.

The heavily drooling Ramon-creature shook, its face twitching hideously. It grabbed Malachi with black claws that sprouted from its fingertips, splitting the fingernails. They dug into the soft flesh of the boy's bleeding shoulders. The camera shook as his hands trembled. The thing screeched again, spraying viscous yellowed spittle into the boy's face.

Malachi had only a split-second to see the sharp tubular tongue shoot into his right eye and penetrate his brain, before everything went dark.

The digital camera fell to the dirt with a clattering sound as the lens and casing shattered. The image filled with static, and faded to black.

BRIBING THE BARON

by Paul Stansbury

"Look, Chwal. Who this be coming down the street?" Baron Cimitière asked with a thick Haitian-Creole accent. He gazed down the long, narrow avenue of shabby buildings. As the sun set, shadows crept across the cobblestone pavement. Cimitière sat in a tall wicker armchair between tall columns on the elaborate stone porch of his mansion.

Chwal, a large black stallion, dressed in a red brocade waistcoat, raised his head and nickered.

"Yes, that be Diogo," said Cimitière. "Been expecting that scoundrel sooner or later. No doubt about it. He be up to no good, I tell you true. Look there," he said, pointing his gold handled walking stick at the thin brown man wearing a wedding shirt and palm hat. "What that be he carry with him?"

Chwal bobbed his head and stomped his hoof twice. His iron shoes sent sparks flying.

"Be careful, my friend," said Cimitière. "We would not want to scare him off. I think he has important business to conduct."

The stallion flicked his tail and whinnied.

"Ah yes," Cimitière continued, "you be right. That be a pouch hanging on his shoulder and he got a pail in his hand. Wonder what they might be for?"

Chwal raised his head and neighed.

A deep bass laugh rumbled up from Cimitière's lungs, careening along the narrow dead-end street. "Mebbe so. We will ask him when he gets here."

Diogo shuddered under the cold weight of Cimitière's laugh. Moving slowly, he was careful not to slosh the contents of the pail. The strap of his pouch dug into his shoulder. The aptly named Rue du Défunt was deserted, running straight to Cimitière's front steps. His gleaming white mansion filled the end of the alley, standing in stark contrast to the crumbling plank and stucco buildings.

As Diogo approached, Cimitière arose, adjusting his black top hat and straightening his purple satin gentleman's tailcoat over his bare chest. His mahogany skin glowed in the light from two massive carriage lamps on the porch columns. "Look sharp, Chwal. I think Diogo be a trickster. Let's see what he have to say." They waited patiently while the man walked toward them.

Diogo stopped a few steps away. "Good evening, boss," he said. Lowering the pouch from his shoulder, he set the pail on the ground, then removed his hat, bowing. "I pray you be Baron Cimitière, for I bring gifts and have a favor to ask."

"I see," said Cimitière. Chwal shook his head and snorted. "Whoa, not now," chided Cimitière.

Diogo backed away, head still lowered. "I hope I have not said something to offend."

"No, no," said Cimitière. "Chwal still be a bit peeved over a bet he lost."

"I am sorry to hear that," said Diogo.

"Why you be sorry?" asked Cimitière. "Would you wish misfortune on me? It is I to whom he lost the bet. Fair and square."

Diogo bowed his head even lower. "Oh no, boss. I wish no misfortune for anyone. Please forgive my unfortunate statement."

"You see," said Cimitière, patting his trouser fly, "him and I had a bet on who had the more pleasing *pati gason*."

Diogo looked up, eyes growing wide. "Pati gason?"

"Yes, and he lost."

"Him?" gasped Diogo, pointing at Chwal.

"You look surprised," said Cimitière.

"But he is a stallion."

"But I am Baron Cimitière. Care to judge for yourself?" Cimitière reached for his belt buckle.

"No, no boss, I will take your word for it."

Another deep bass laugh boomed from Baron Cimitière. "I thought you would. Now, you spoke of gifts. Tell me, what things have you brought?"

Diogo picked up the pail. "First, I offer this pail of Prestige beer to your horse. Perhaps it will cool the sting of the bet he lost." Chwal nickered. Cimitière motioned Diogo forward. He placed the pail at the horse's feet. Chwal lowered his head, sniffing at its contents. He snorted once, then began to lap up the mellow golden brew.

"It is apparent Chwal be pleased with your gift," said Cimitière. "Now, it is time to see what you have brought for me."

"Ah yes, I have something special for you, boss," said Diogo. He rooted around in the sack before producing a bottle of liquor and a large cigar. He placed the bottle on the mahogany and gold drink table next to Cimitière's chair. "Boukman Botanical Rhum, boss," he said. "Very pleasing to the taste." Then he held out the cigar. "And while you enjoy your sip, perhaps you would like to savor a Bohekio Robusto, Haiti's finest."

Cimitière took the cigar, rolling it in his fingers. He passed it under his nose, inhaling its aroma. He held it out to Chwal to sniff. "What you think?" The horse bobbed his head. "I agree," said Cimitière.

He looked at Diogo. "Chwal approves." He lit the cigar and took a deep draw, allowing blue smoke to roll out between his lips. "Now for the rum." He poured a measure into a small silver tumbler, swirling it once before taking a drink. "Try making that out of a cola nut," he laughed.

Diogo waited patiently while Chwal finished his beer and Cimitière puffed on his cigar and sipped rum. Even though a cooling dusk had seeped between the tattered buildings lining the Rue du Défunt, beads of sweat formed on Diogo's forehead.

Finally, Cimitière said. "Now down to business, Diogo. You mentioned a favor?"

"Yes, boss, indeed, I seek a favor."

"Know this, friend Diogo, favors are a serious matter with the Guédé. So what is it you think Baron Cimitière can do for you? I am simply the doorman between the world of the living and the afterlife, the guardian of the cemetery, protecting its graves. I keep the dead in and the living out."

"But that is precisely what I seek."

"Seek what?"

"Soon, someone's spirit will be arriving. I would be most happy for you to kindly see that her spirit be locked in the graveyard."

"*Her*?"

"Yes."

"Who be this *her*?"

"She be my woman, Lucrèce."

"And she be coming here?"

"If I be here, she be coming here looking for me."

"When that be?"

"Soon, I expect."

Cimitière turned to his equine companion. "Tell me Chawl, why do you think she be coming here looking for our friend Diogo?" Chwal stomped his hoof on the stone patio, sending sparks flying again.

Cowering, Diogo stepped back.

"Yes, I too think some unfortunate thing happen to this Lucrèce," said Cimitière. "Perhaps you know what happened, Diogo?"

He lowered his eyes and whispered, "Bad rum."

"Bad rum? What do you mean, bad rum?" Cimitière stared at the bottle Diogo had given him.

"Oh no, boss," said Diogo. "Not so much bad rum as something *bad* in her rum."

"Ahh, you mean *red* rum. Well, you had better tell me all about this, Diogo. And don't be lying to a Guédé. If you do, it will not be a pleasant experience."

"My Lucrèce, you see, she be one very mean woman. Been married to her for ten years now, and she get meaner each year. Just could not live with that woman no more."

Cimitière turned to Chwal. "I think there be something that makes her so mean. What you think?" Chwal snorted and shook his head sideways. "Okay. Chwal says you know why, Diogo."

"Well boss, could be anything." said Diogo. "Who can know what goes on in the mind of a jealous woman?"

"Jealous woman?"

"Boss, you know how it is with a man. Got to have his diversions."

"So who be this diversion?" asked Cimitière.

"That be the beautiful Emelia," answered Diogo, sporting a broad smile. "She be a hostess at the Pijon Ble."

"I see. And what does this have to do with something bad in Lucrèce's rum?" Diogo pursed his lips and shrugged, to which Cimitière shouted, "Don't worry boy! I'm not your priest. I'm a Guédé — a spirit of the dead." Cimitière's eyes flashed. "I'm not here to make you say the Rosary. I care not about the petty intrigues of the living, But I will know the truth. Now, tell me what happened."

Diogo bowed his head. "Sorry boss, truth is Emelia say she not going to share me with no other woman, so I put some poison in Lucrèce's rum and she be dead for sure by now."

"Tell me this," said Cimitière. "Why not just leave this Lucrèce?"

"But she got all the money. I could not leave that behind."

"Ah, I see. She die and you get all her money."

Their conversation was interrupted by a woman calling in the distance. "Diogo. Where are you?"

Diogo jerked his head around, looking wildly down Rue du Défunt. He turned back to Cimitière. "Please. That be Lucrèce. She be coming."

The voice grew louder, echoing down the street. "Diogo, you cannot hide. I will find you."

Cimitière poured another drink and took a sip. "What is it you would have me do?"

"Please, boss. She comes to haunt me. You say you are the doorman, the guardian of the graveyard, keeping the living out and the dead within. She cannot be haunting me if you lock her away."

"Diogo, this be serious business," Cimitière said, shaking his head slowly. He looked at Chwal then pointed toward the open end of the street. "You think that be the famous Lucrèce come to haunt our friend Diogo?"

Chwal whinnied, nodding his head vigorously.

Cimitière smiled. "I think so, too."

Diogo whirled around, eyes fixed on the narrow street's opening. He shuddered. "That be her for sure."

A dark speck in the fading light, Lucrèce called out, "Diogo! You cannot escape from me."

Diogo turned back. "Please, Baron Cimitière. Please hide me," he whimpered, falling to his knees. "Please, you must hide me."

"Diogo. Diogo. I know you are here." Lucrèce's cries grew louder as she approached.

"Chwal, shall we help out our poor friend, Diogo?" asked Cimitière.

The horse bobbed his head in agreement.

"Come now, Diogo," said Cimitière. "You best be getting up. You can hide inside my mansion while I tend to the matters at hand."

Diogo scrambled to his feet. "Your mansion? You are most gracious. Thank you, boss."

Cimitière gestured with his right hand and the grand white door behind him swung open. "In you go. Chwal, you stand guard."

Diogo scampered through the opening.

Cimitière followed, saying, "Now, this be a fine place for you to hide." In the dimly lit foyer, Diogo could see only the Guédé's smiling face.

Outside, Lucrèce's wail grew louder. "Diogo. Diogo. You cannot hide from me."

"Please close the door," pleaded Diogo.

Cimitière snapped his fingers and the door whisked shut. He led Diogo down a long, dimly lit hall and into a small room.

"Will you not go and fetch Lucrèce to the graveyard?" Diogo asked.

"I think she know her way. Now, look out the window," said Cimitière. Diogo spied Lucrèce in the distance lurking outside the great iron cemetery gate.

Trembling, eyes wide in terror, Diogo screamed. "You have deceived me."

"I deceive no one. As you requested, I am to make sure the spirit of your dead wife be locked in the graveyard." Cimitière pointed his walking stick at the gate. "See, she enters now."

Lucrèce screamed, "Diogo, you cannot escape me now," then swirled through the iron bars.

"Thing is," whispered Cimitière, "it seems Lucrèce came to see me yesterday. She also wanted a favor."

Diogo's knees buckled. "No."

"She wanted to make sure a certain party, who was soon to die, made his way into the graveyard with no problems." Diogo dropped to his knees, sobbing. Cimitière continued, "She also offered something in return for this favor. And what possible gift could she offer?" Cimitière sneered, patting his trouser fly. "Diogo, my friend, she judged the bet between myself and Chwal." He paused. "So tell me Diogo, did you enjoy the joumou Lucrèce made for you this evening?"

Diogo buried his face in trembling hands. "I don't want to talk about the soup I had for dinner." He exhaled a ragged breath. "This cannot be happening."

Cimitière's soul-freezing laugh welled up one last time. "Oh, but it can. No accounting for a jealous woman. Seems she added a little something to your soup. As you would say: something bad."

"But…"

"But when Baron Cimitière grants a favor, he always follows through." He swept his arm in a wide arc, then snapped his fingers. The mansion evaporated, leaving Diogo standing among a chaotic assembly of garishly decorated tombs and semi-collapsed mausoleums. "I bid you adieu," said Cimitière, as Lucrèce charged toward Diogo.

Cimitière rejoined Chwal at the cemetery's front gate as Lucrèce and Diogo's screams echoed through the cemetery. "Know what I think, my friend?" asked Cimitière. "I think we go down to the

Pijon Ble and see if the beautiful Emelia needs a favor."

End

THE VOID PEOPLE

by Valeriya Salt

Theo stared into the void, motionless and silent, and the void's black nothingness stared back at him. It beckoned him in and wouldn't let go. He closed his eyes for a few seconds and exhaled, as if he was readying himself to take a step forward into the beckoning chasm.

"Mr. Jung?" Petar's heavily accented voice sounded behind him. "Mr. Jung? Are you okay?"

"Ah? Ah, yes. I'm fine, fine." Theo waved him off. "It's just this terrible smell and stuffy air in the vault." The last thing he wanted right now was for his foreman to think that Theo had decided to give up on the castle and the whole project all together.

"The local folk tell stories about the gates to hell under the castle's keep." Petar shrugged. "No wonder it stinks here." He chuckled.

Theo took a few steps away from the half-collapsed vault's floor. His torch's light crisscrossed the low ceiling and the bare stone walls of the underground space. He brushed away a cobweb from his face and turned to the foreman, "When I bought this property, my agent recommended you as a skilled civil engineer, not a folklorist. Could you and your team finally investigate why the water is coming to the surface and how to fix this mess to stop it once and for all?" He gestured to the void. "The tourist season is just eight months away. I need this place to be fully rebuilt and ready for the first guests."

Petar looked unimpressed and uninterested, as he usually did, though. "There's no water source nearby, that's for sure." He shrugged. "We need to call a land surveyor."

"And I need to pay again and wait?" Theo exploded. "I need to attend a few important meetings in London next month. I can't babysit all of you here and control your every step."

"Well, if you don't want your boutique hotel to stink of stale water, you need a land surveyor. I'm capable to look after them."

"How long will it take? The survey?"

Petar shook his head; his black eyes shone in the dusk of the vault. "Not sure. All decent surveyors I know are busy now. There's lots of construction work going on in the area nowadays, you know. Besides—"

"Will you find me a specialist or not?" Theo snapped.

"We're talking a month or two of waiting."

"Bring the machinery down and fix the hole or you and your guys may start to look for another job." Theo turned away and, without saying goodbye, walked back to the ladder to climb his way up from the vault to the surface.

*****

Theo left the castle and headed to the hunting lodge, the only habitable building on the property. He could've probably booked a guesthouse in the nearest village, but even "the nearest" meant a forty-minute drive up the mountains on a road which… well, looked more like a logging track.

The last few days of September brought rains and chills from the sea, but today the sun, still bright and stubborn, warmed up the midday air. Autumn crawled slowly to this part of the Balkans, leaving the trees and shrubs still green.

A muddy path led Theo uphill, and he stopped to catch his breath. Hours in the gym, tennis or golf almost every weekend helped him to keep fit, and yet, his age caught up with him. Theo sighed and ran his hand over his receding grey hair. He turned around, shot a glance at the castle, and smirked.

What was proudly called "Veliko Vadanovo Castle" in the property purchase forms comprised just a few partly collapsed walls with empty eye sockets of windows, a mighty keep, and lots of contractual issues. Surrounded by a dense forest and mountains, the property covered almost twenty acres with the ruins of the castle, the hunting lodge, and other derelict structures. Petar's team of builders brought all kinds of heavy machinery, turning the sleepy ruins into a busy construction site. The project kept on stalling as the castle threw one problem after another at the team.

"Veliko Vadanovo is an ideal investment, trust me," Theo's real estate agent in Eastern Europe had said to him before the auction. "It's a real bargain. Just what you need to expand your property portfolio. It needs a lot of work? So what? You're buying it cheaply. Besides, the castle is unique. A real hidden gem of Bulgaria. Its architecture, its dramatic past, all the stories about the gates to hell… Honestly, Theo! British and American tourists will flock there every season. No doubt about it. They'll love it even more if you make it nice and comfortable."

Theo shook his head, recalling his agent's words. *I've been conned.* He'd been in the real estate business for over twenty years but couldn't remember a more troublesome project. The agent played on his desperate desire for expansion and setting his foot on such a promising region like the Balkans before his rivals.

A branch cracked behind Theo, making him jump and turn around.

An elderly gentleman, dressed in a shabby leather jacket and high boots, stood a few paces in front of him where the steep path forked. A double-barrelled shotgun hung from his shoulder. The man raised his faded cap in a greeting. "*Dobar den,*" he said with a shy smile.

Theo frowned. "What are you doing here? This is private land."

The man shook his head.

"English? Do you speak English?" Theo raised his voice as most people did, trying to explain something to a foreigner. "You're trespassing on private property. You can't walk here without permission, let alone to hunt." He pointed to the man's shotgun. "No trespassing, no hunting."

"No, no English." The man shook his head again. "Bulgarian? Deutsch? No English."

"Ah, so you speak German. Good." Theo nodded and continued in German. "My name is Theo Jung. I'm a new owner of this property. You can't wander around without permission. Did you see the signpost on the fence?"

"The fence? No, there was nothing there." The man shrugged. "I walked through the gap like I always do." He paused.

Oh, that slob Petar hasn't fixed the fence yet and, of course, he completely forgot about the signposts. Theo sighed but said nothing.

"My name is Vasil, by the way. Vasil Nikolov. I live in the village." The man attempted to smile again. "Are you from Germany?"

"No. I'm from London. My father was from Germany, hence, the German name." Theo squinted. "Anyway, what are you doing here?"

"Hunting, berry and mushroom picking. I've got a hunting licence. If you want to have a look—"

Theo waved him off. "Your licence is not valid on private property. I ask you to leave. Please."

"But I've been hunting in these woods all my life. Quails, pheasants, wood pigeons – nothing bigger than that. It's all covered in my licence. This path leads to my hunting shack in the wood. It's the shortest way, and if I can spot something on the way then—"

"I'm sorry, but from now on, you'll need to take a longer route to your shack, I'm afraid," Theo snapped. *Old man, you're wasting my time. Just get off my land!* He turned to the left at the path's fork, ready to go.

Vasil shook his grey head and mumbled to himself, "Some additional forty-fifty minutes of hiking uphill and downhill at seventy-six is not an easy task."

"I'm sorry, but it's not my problem. You need to leave. Now." Theo shrugged. *I should stay tough with the locals. Otherwise, the whole village will be wandering around the castle soon.*

"I guess I need to get used to long walks or maybe even forget about hunting and picking at all," Vasil continued with a deep sigh. "If your castle is rebuilt into a hotel, then there'll be nothing to hunt.

First, the builders, then tourists. They'll scare all the birds off."

"What do you mean *if*? You mean *when* the castle is rebuilt. The opening of the hotel is scheduled for the beginning of the high season next year."

Vasil smirked. "The castle doesn't want anybody on this land, let alone tourists. Since the market crashed in 2008, it has changed God knows how many owners. Nobody could last long enough to restore it. It should've stayed nationalised, but our government has no money to sustain our national heritage."

"Hah! If you mean all the stories about the gates to hell, monsters, and people going crazy here, then trust me, I'm going to make a fortune out of it. Tourists will be flocking to the "haunted castle" from all over the world."

"Well, good luck with it." Vasil bowed in farewell, ready to turn back.

Theo didn't reply, just watched the old man struggling on the steep path, then resumed his walk to the lodge.

*****

After a quick meal, Theo threw some more logs into the fireplace, poured some whiskey, and made himself cosy on a low sofa in front of the crackling fire. He switched on his laptop and stared outside the window.

The days were getting shorter, and dusk had already started to crawl around, surrounding the lodge. The thick fog descended from the mountains, making the neighbouring hills look dark and solemn.

The hunting lodge was the latest addition to the property. Built in the late eighteenth century in the so-called National Revival style, it had two floors with the first floor being much larger than the cold and damp ground floor. Petar's team did some work on cleaning and restoring the upstairs rooms ready for Theo's arrival, but nothing could help against the autumnal chill, damp, and absence of central heating.

Theo shivered under his woollen quilt, even whiskey didn't help. He opened his inbox and started to read through emails. Bank statements, invoices to sign, calendar invites to online meetings, insurance papers, a couple of emails from Petar, requesting a repair of an excavator and a bulldozer... Theo sighed. *The third breakdown in a week. The equipment is crap. All I do is pay for the repairs.* On the other hand, what was he supposed to do? Drag all the heavy machinery from London?

The second email from Petar was about one of his builders, who fell from a ladder a few days ago and broke his collarbone. The guy claimed that some unknown force pulled him down. He was sent to the nearest hospital. The attached sick note gave him a month's break from work.

Theo swore. *Unknown force? Damn! They're taking me for an idiot. Now, we're one man down.* He rubbed his eyes and opened the next email.

It was from his ex-wife's lawyer. It had been dragging on for three years, five even, together with the divorce, but she or rather her father, who was also her legal guardian, didn't want to accept defeat and let Theo and the money go.

Theo shut the laptop without even reading the email and glanced outside.

The fog had thickened and covered the lodge completely. It brought deep, desperate sadness which flooded Theo's soul like the evening dusk flooded the room.

He closed his eyes. The void, dark and beckoning, opened in front of him. He saw Petar, the old hunter he met today, his ex-wife, and other people, known and unknown, surrounding him and pushing closer and closer to the gaping nothingness below. He wanted to shout and push them back, but they all had turned into ghostly shadows, swarming and dragging him into the void. Then, he fell.

He jerked and opened his eyes. His mobile phone had been ringing, buzzing on the wooden coffee table.

"Yes," Theo barked when picked it up.

"Mr. Jung, are you okay? I've been trying to call you, but…" Petar's voice sounded worried.

"I've been busy. A video call with my accountants," he mumbled, "what's the emergency?"

"I was going to go home when… How can I put it?"

"Don't tell me something broke again."

"Oh, no, no. It's just… This gentleman has appeared out of the blue." Petar sounded more and more agitated. "He wants to talk to you in person. Immediately."

"What do you mean "appeared out of the blue"? Trespassing is not allowed on my property, you know that."

"He wasn't trespassing. He came out of the keep."

Theo sighed. "Petar, are you drunk?"

"I swear to God and my guys can confirm that. The man came out of the keep," Petar almost shouted. "He claims he knows you very well. I can pass him a phone."

"Okay. What's the name of this gentleman?"

"He's name is Simon. Simon Green. He claims he's your business partner."

"What?!" Theo jumped on his sofa. "I'm not sure how you know about my former business partner Simon Green, but he's dead," he screamed. "Dead. Do you understand?"

"I'm happy to hear you too, Theo," a painfully familiar voice sounded from the speaker.

****

Theo was driving down the dark path – the shortest route to the castle. His hands were shaking.

Simon, his friend, business partner, the man who introduced him to the real estate business, was dead. Dead! He died almost three years ago in a car crash. Theo attended his funeral, saw his coffin, mourned together with other colleagues and friends, but today… What was it today? Somebody's stupid joke? But he recognised the voice. He would've recognised this low baritone after hundreds of years.

The path curled, making a semi-loop. A massive white shadow flew into the car's front window, almost hitting it and making Theo swear and duck down.

"Damn owl!" Theo gritted his teeth and clenched the steering wheel.

In a couple of minutes, his car reached the car park at the southern entrance to the castle.

Theo turned the engine off and got out.

There was no wind, no sounds of wildlife in the still air – nothing. The night had covered the valley, and only the dark silhouettes of the castle's towers loomed against the sky. The only source of light was the static caravan park, which Theo organised for Petar and his builders who lived on the site.

He saw Petar, accompanied by another man, tall and large, emerging from his caravan. Theo stared at the large man.

Simon Green hadn't changed at all. Everything was the same, down to the same clothes he wore during the accident.

Theo swallowed his shock and kept staring at his former business partner.

The two men came closer. Simon stared back at him. His eyes, the two dark voids, made Theo's heart skip a beat.

"Good evening, Mr. Jung. I'm sorry to bother you so late." Petar started with an apologetic half-smile. "Mr. Green doesn't want to wait until tomorrow to speak with you."

"Thank you." Theo nodded to his foreman. "You can go back to your caravan. I'll take care of my guest."

"Guest?!" Simon chuckled. His voice, deep and low, sounded like a drum in the stillness of the night. "You don't want to admit that you screwed up in front of your foreman?"

Petar shifted from one foot to another, clearly unwilling to witness the conversation. "My shift finished long ago. Good night." With that said, he almost ran back to his caravan.

"Simon, how did you get here?" Theo mumbled.

"By plane and then by taxi from the airport." He shrugged. "I wanted to rent a car, but they didn't have anything suitable in their pool. So I paid double for the taxi to crawl all the way up and down the mountains. Anyway." He waved. "Don't try to avoid the subject. What the fuck is going on, Theo? Since when are you buying property without consulting me first? I'm still an International Property Director and senior member of the board as far as I know."

Theo shook his head. *How is it possible? Who are you? What about the crash?* "I must admit I didn't expect you to come to the site, especially after the accident," he started. "In your long absence, I obtained the agreement from other members. Henrietta, Krishan, Jean-Luc – they all agreed it was a good investment."

"Ah, the accident, yes," Simon barked. "Four months in hospital, not even a call from you. Your personal assistant sent me flowers with a "Feel better soon" card. That was it. Then, another two months of rehabilitation at home. Again, nothing from you. You were busy, constantly abroad. And what did I find out on my first day back to work? Theo has wasted our money on this." He gestured to the ruins.

"It's a great building. You don't understand." Theo backed away and wondered how quiet and miserable his voice sounded.

"Theo, get real. Could you, please, explain how we are supposed to rebuild it in eight months? Why do we need it at all? There're no roads, no infrastructure, no sea. What draws tourists there?"

Theo wiped the cold sweat from his forehead. "I'm sure many tourists enjoy the scenery and the mountains," he mumbled.

"The mountains? There aren't even any ski slopes around here. The mountains are too low for a ski resort. How are we supposed to make money out of it? The scenery? There's nothing to see here apart from the dense forest." Simon shook his head. "Castles are normally built on a hilltop. This one is in the valley. The defensive walls and the towers, or what's left of them, are facing inward not outward like in all castles. The whole building is just preposterous."

Theo exhaled. "You'll have a good look at the property tomorrow. I'll show you around the land. I'm sure that in broad daylight you'll appreciate the beauty of the place and agree that it's a fantastic investment."

"Okay." Simon waved, annoyed. "It's late and dark, and I feel tired after the flight. We'll see what you have in store for me tomorrow."

He turned to the caravans without saying goodbye.

"Where are you going?"

"Don't worry about me now. Petar said I could stay in the caravan, occupied by one of his builders. The guy fell from the ladder or something and ended up on sick leave."

"Good night, Simon," Theo mumbled.

*****

Theo circled the living room. The fire had extinguished, and the burned throat of the fireplace gaped wide open. He didn't bother about the cold and damp, though. He must be some kind of imposter. It's not possible, but so much was impossible to fake. And why would someone do this? He squeezed his head with his hands.

At first, Theo wanted to call his board members and confirm what Simon said, but on second thought, he refused this idea. *They'll think I'm drunk or mad.* He called his foreman instead.

"Hello," Petar's voice sounded through the loud chewing.

"Sorry to interrupt your dinner, but the matter is urgent," Theo started.

"Well, never mind."

"This gentleman, Simon Green, you said you met him near the keep. Did you see a taxi bringing him in?"

"No. Nobody entered the keep." Petar stopped chewing. "The bricklayer and I had been assessing and measuring the keep's walls for about an hour before finishing the shift. There was nobody around the grounds. The man came out of the keep as if he'd been there all the time."

Theo frowned. Were they lost in translation? "What do you mean "he'd been there all the time"?"

"How would you explain that we didn't see him approaching the keep?"

"I don't know. What did he say? Did he show you some ID?"

"No. No ID." Petar sounded annoyed. "The bricklayer left, and I'd been collecting the equipment, ready to go when the guy appeared on the keep's doorstep. He carried only a small briefcase with him. He introduced himself as Simon Green, your business partner from London. He wanted to see you immediately, sounded rather pushy and agitated. I called you straight away."

Theo bit his lower lip. "Okay. Can I have a look at the CCTV cameras around the keep?"

"We don't have them. You said they were too expensive, remember?"

He cursed. "We still have cameras around the outer fence, right? They should record all vehicles, coming and leaving the property."

"Yes. I can send you the evening recordings."

"That would be great."

Petar kept silent, and Theo was going to say goodbye and hang up.

"You said over the phone that your business partner died." The foreman broke the pause first. "He might be one of the Void People then."

"What are you talking about?"

"You still may not believe it, but doppelgangers and all sorts of doubles have been seen around this land. They come out of the Void. The gates to hell." Petar sounded as if they discussed a routine business matter.

"What do they want, these doppelgangers?"

"Who knows? You'd better ask local folks from the village, especially the elderly ones. They know all this stuff."

"Okay." Theo grunted. "Just send me the CCTV recordings, please."

"No problem."

They said goodbye, and Theo hung up.

*****

Theo spent a couple of hours going through the cameras' recordings but couldn't find anything. Heavy trucks, contractors, and vehicles of all types arrived and departed during the evening, but none of them was the taxi that brought Simon from the airport.

Theo shut down the laptop and covered his tired eyes with his hands. *What if Simon survived the crash?* Theo swallowed his emotions back. A cold chill ran down his spine. *Then, he knows everything. No, it can't be. Besides, why would he reappear now? There's some time missing for him. He speaks as if he hasn't been absent for three years.* Theo rose from the chair, ready to take a shower. He desperately needed a rest, but after everything that happened, he knew he would struggle to fall asleep.

He stood under the hot water jets, closed his eyes and tried to relax, to free his mind, but the memories flooded him. He was again in his house in Berkshire. The party was about to finish, and the guests started to depart. Simon was a bit tipsy, but he insisted on driving back home. He took the final sip of his drink and put his jacket on. Theo saw him off.

"Stay safe, buddy," he had told Simon on the doorstep.

Fifteen to twenty-five minutes, and it should be all over. Simon was a big guy. Maybe he would've lasted thirty. Just enough time to turn to the motorway and pick up the speed. With his first degree in chemistry, Theo knew exactly the right dosage and the right time for the deadly mixture of alcohol and the drug to start working.

The water stopped and Theo opened his eyes. The whole room vibrated. Theo tried to catch himself, but it was too late. The floor's tiles collapsed inwardly, sucking Theo into the black void. He screamed, trying to clench the sink but slipped and fell.

*****

The rays of the low, autumnal sun penetrated through the worn off curtains, leaving light patches on the dark wooden floorboards.

Theo turned his head and found himself on the sofa in the living room. *How the hell did I get here?* He rubbed his head but couldn't remember anything after the fall.

His musing was interrupted by plates rattling in the kitchenette. A familiar female voice sang quietly.

Theo got up, put his dressing gown on, and peered around the corner in the kitchenette.

"Priya?!" He mumbled in shock. "But how? Why are you here?"

"Ah, you finally woke up." His ex-wife turned from the pan with pancakes. "Good morning. Or should I say almost afternoon?"

"Do you feel better now?" Simon stared at her. *No wheelchair, no breathing apparatus, a carer is nowhere to be seen. How on earth is it possible? Who are you?* He was ready to scream but bit his tongue.

"Meaning?" Priya frowned. "I feel amazing. The clean mountain air and fresh food from the village. I've never felt better. It was the right decision to come and spend some time here with you. And you? You look so pale." She came closer and touched his forehead. "Oh, you have a fever."

Her palm was soft and delicate but gravely cold. She looked the same as he remembered her before the accident, before the divorce – looking much younger than her age, with the huge brown eyes and glossy ringlets of black hair.

"Ah, I'm fine." He squeezed a smile, trying to sound as natural as possible. "And your father? Where's he?"

"He and Mum went to Florida yesterday as they normally do around this time of the year. You know it. Why are you asking?"

But Mr. Laghari had sold his Florida house long before our divorce to sort out his financial issues. So, we're still not divorced, and she's here, and I'm trapped. "I need to go," he said finally.

"Won't even have coffee?"

"No, no. I have too many things planned for today. I've overslept. I need to catch up."

"I'm sure Simon and Petar are capable of dealing with construction issues without your constant presence." She waved him off. "They don't need babysitting."

Theo swallowed a lump in his throat. A spasm in his stomach made him cringe. "I need to discuss a few things with them. In person."

"Are you sure you feel well? Simon told me about your weird behaviour yesterday. You shouted at Petar over the phone something about Simon being dead or something." She touched his cheek and stared at him without a blink.

Her eyes mesmerised him, making his heart quiver, bringing deep, heavy sadness, the same terrifying sadness which he felt in the evening mist, which didn't let him fall asleep, which had been following him in his nightmares.

"Don't worry. I'm fine." He kissed her cold hand.

"At least, take coffee and pancakes with you. Share with the guys." She turned back to her cooking. "I'll pack everything for you while you take a shower."

"Thank you, angel. That would be nice." He backed away into the living room.

*****

Theo's car jumped all over the place on the rough, bumpy path, the only road which led to the village, but he didn't want to slow down. His head was spinning, and he clenched tighter to the steering wheel.

His ex-wife had been paralysed and spent the last few years in a wheelchair. His business partner was dead. Now, that all seemed to have changed. The cold darkness of the void was closing on Theo.

"He might be one of the Void People then." Petar's words sounded in his mind repeatedly. "Ask local folks from the village."

Vasil, the hunter, definitely knows something. Yesterday's conversation emerged in Theo's memory. *If I allow him to use the path to his shack in exchange for information, he may help.*

Soon, he reached the outskirts of the village. Traditional houses perched on the mountain's slope, an ancient wooden church in the middle, and a couple of small businesses. The village was tiny.

It didn't take Theo too long to find Vasil. Apparently, he was a respected elder here.

"Ah, Mr. Jung? Please, come in." Vasil greeted him from the high porch in German as if he had been expecting him.

"Hi. I need to talk to you about some events in the castle," Theo mumbled, unsure where to start.

Vasil stared at him for a few seconds. His pale eyes studied him. "Please, come inside."

Theo didn't oppose. The last thing he needed was some nosey neighbour overhearing their conversation, even if they didn't understand German.

"Please, take a seat. I've just finished my lunch, but the coffee is still hot." Vasil guided him through the tiny corridor where Theo left his shoes and jacket to the living room. In the far corner, he noticed Vasil's shotgun.

Traditionally built, like all houses in the village, Vasil's dwelling met Theo with the smells of the open fire, strong coffee, and freshly baked bread.

"Thank you, but I don't have much time." He said, occupying a wide armchair.

"So, what is the urgency?"

"Let me put it this way: some people came to the castle, the people from my past, who're not supposed to be there," Theo started, weighing his every word.

"Well, tell them there's no trespassing allowed." Vasil chuckled, taking a seat on the sofa in front of the fireplace. "I'm not sure how I can help you with it."

"They're not trespassers." Theo exhaled. "The man I met yesterday was my former business partner who tragically died three years ago. Today in the morning, my ex-wife appeared in the lodge out of the blue."

"Is she also dead?"

"No, but she has a certain health condition. She's paralysed. Today, I saw her fluttering around the kitchenette, cooking breakfast and chatting away, while she should be thousands of miles away, in London.”

Vasil eyed him with concern but said nothing.

“I’m not drunk or on drugs,” Theo fired out. “Petar, my foreman, saw my former business partner too. He talked to him.”

Vasil stood up and came to the small window, staring outside at the misty mountains.

“Tell me what you know about the castle. Please. You can use the path to your hunting shack any time. In fact,” Theo clapped his hands. “You can stay in the castle when it opens. Relax, use the spa, all-inclusive.”

“And what makes you think I can help you?” Vasil turned to him with a smirk.

“You said that the castle didn’t want anybody around.”

“You said you didn’t believe in old stories.”

“Petar told me something about the Void People. He said that people in the village know about them. The only person I can ask is you.”

Vasil frowned. “Go back to London,” he said finally. “Right now. Drive to the airport and buy a ticket to the first available flight.”

“What? No, I can’t. What about the project?”

"Forget about it. Just go."

"No." Theo shook his head. "I'm not going anywhere, at least, not without answers." He raised his head to Vasil. "Who are the Void People? What do they want from me? Why?"

Vasil kept silent, then sat back on the sofa. "My father died many years ago. He would've told you lots of interesting things about them and the castle."

"Did he see them too?"

"He and other officers and soldiers had numerous encounters with them. They drove them crazy. A couple of soldiers committed suicide, others just ran."

Theo squinted. "Your father was German, wasn't he? I read about the castle during the Second World War. The SS used it as storage for stolen books and art treasures, as an archive, so to speak."

"That's true. My father was a librarian and a scholar, fluent in several Slavic languages, including Bulgarian. He was sent to the castle to look after the collections."

"Your father worked for the SS?" Theo grimaced but pulled himself together. It was too late, though. Vasil had noticed his contempt.

"He was just a scholar. He didn't kill anybody." He sighed. "When the Soviet Army started approaching, the archives were evacuated from the castle. The Germans retreated, but my father decided to stay. It was risky, but he made it. He took a local name, a local faith, a local wife, and erased his German past. If the Void People left him alone, the Soviets wouldn't touch him either."

Theo couldn't hold a smirk. "He got away with it all right, eh?"

"Who are you, Mr. Jung, to judge him?" Vasil snapped. "He didn't kill people. He was a librarian, working for the SS. He passed his "test". What about you?" He squinted.

"What do you mean?"

"There's a reason why the Void People are here. Perhaps to test or to avenge. Look into your heart and ask yourself what they want from you. I'm sure you'll find the answer."

"I'm not sure I'm following." Theo grimaced.

"Try harder. It must be something that brought them to your life. Your business partner. How did he die?" Vasil stared at him without a blink. His eyes scrutinised him, making his heart skip a beat.

"In a car crash. It was an accident. He was drunk."

"Are you sure it was just an accident?" Vasil's quiet voice echoed all over the room, reflecting from the walls and ceiling. His pale eyes turned black.

Theo's stomach cringed, his head spun. "He was an asshole." A wave of nausea made him stop. "He wanted to sell the business cheaply. I couldn't allow it to happen. He'd made so many wrong decisions, almost bankrupting the company. I saved it." He struggled to catch his breath.

Vasil's eyes pierced him. "And your ex-wife?" The voice rang in Theo's ears. "What happened to her? Another "accident", I guess."

Theo jumped from the chair, but the unbearable headache stopped him, and he sunk back into the wide seat. "We argued. She wanted not only a divorce; she also wanted all her father's money back," he whispered. "It was a dirty trick. Her family played dirty. I told her that, I told her she wouldn't see the money, I told her to piss off." Theo's hands trembled. "She slapped me, I pushed her back, and she fell from the top of the stairs. It wasn't my fault."

"Perhaps not, but you divorced her after the accident. You left her when she needed you the most." Vasil shook his head, his voice quiet, his eyes pale again. "And you dare to judge me for my father's mistakes?"

"It's not real." Theo rose from the sofa again. "They are not real. They won't harm me."

"Oh, I wouldn't be so sure, if I were you."

Theo remembered the shotgun. He ran out of the room to the corridor, grabbing the shotgun as he left.

"Mr. Jung, Mr. Jung," Vasil called him from the house, unable to catch up with him. "Please, come back. You're making a terrible mistake." His last words drowned in the roaring of Theo's car engine.

*****

Theo got out of his car at the castle, clenching Vasil's shotgun at the ready. The headache and nausea didn't go, but nothing could stop him now. He headed to the main entrance.

The construction work was in full swing, but Theo realised straight away something was wrong. The builders dropped their tools and stared at him. A bulldozer's driver stopped the vehicle and jumped out, blessing herself with a cross. A few people ran to the woods screaming in panic.

"*Kakvo po dyavolite?*" Petar appeared from the keep and stopped, petrified. "Who the hell are you?" He shouted at Theo.

"Pardon?" Theo frowned. "What's going on here, Petar?"

"You look exactly like my boss." Petar backed away to the keep. "But…"

"I am your boss. I am Theo Jung." Theo grabbed the foreman's sleeve and shook him. "What's wrong with you?"

"Mr. Jung is in the crypt, together with Mr. Green. I just came from there," Petar whispered, his face turned pale.

"Let have a look what this Mr. Jung is made of," Theo hissed and ran to the keep, then down the spiral stairs to the ladder which led underground.

He descended into the bowel of the crypt. His eyes slowly adapted to the darkness, and he could distinguish light at the end of the long corridor. Two shadows moved around in the yellowish light of the torch, discussing something in low voices. He aimed the shotgun and cocked the hammer, ready to fire. He came closer. "Hands up! Don't move!"

Two men turned, and Theo faced Simon and the copy of himself. Even his clothes were identical.

"What the hell?!" Simon screamed and raised his hands. "Who're you?"

"That's what I need to ask you," Theo snapped. "I'm Theo Jung. The real Theo Jung and you're going to tell me what's going on here." He pointed the weapon at his double's head.

"I am Theo Jung." The man backed away to the void. "Whoever you are, I'm going to call the police and let them deal with you."

"Don't fucking move!" Theo yelled. The sound of his voice was unbearable. Reverberating from the vaulted ceiling and the walls, it amplified. His head was about to explode. He squeezed the trigger. Time began to slow.

Simon grabbed the gun's barrel. Theo pulled the trigger. The loud bang echoed in the crypt, and Theo saw Simon's heavy body start to sag. Theo wrestled with his doppelganger when a powerful force pushed Theo off his feet, and he fell. A second of a free fall, then nothingness…

*****

"He took my shotgun and ran." Vasil almost cried, trying to explain to Petar what happened. "He's insane. In such a condition, he's going to kill somebody. With my gun."

"We can't go inside. It's better to wait here." Petar put his hand on Vasil's shoulder. "It's not in our power to help him now. You know it better than I do. He's on his own."

A gunshot made the two men jump and turned to the keep.

"It's happening," Vasil mumbled.

"We need to wait."

A minute passed, another one. No birds singing, no insects buzzing, all work around the castle had stopped. The autumnal air was still and quiet.

Petar saw his workers, running uphill and disappearing into the forest.

Vasil squinted, noticing a tall, slim figure emerging from the keep. "It's done."

"Mr. Jung," Petar asked, coming closer, "is everything okay? We heard a gunshot." He studied the man's face for a second. "Do we need to call an ambulance?"

"Everything is okay." Mr. Jung smiled his polite smile, then turned to Vasil. "Thank you very much for your help." He handed him the gun. "You're very welcome to hunt on these lands." He turned away and walked to his car.

"What do you think?" Petar turned to Vasil. "Which one of the two is this one?"

Vasil shrugged. "Whatever he's now, I'm sure he's the right one."

A LETTER TO DESHAUN

by Edward R. Rosick

The scene plays out in my mind over and over, a nightmare I can never forget:

A pitch-black night in the desert.

The stench of rotting meat left out in a sweltering summer sun.

And a *thing* from a mad man's dream.

But it wasn't a nightmare.

It was a *monster*.

*****

I watched the sun die over the Western horizon, the air in the cramped eighth story room of the Jasmine Hotel humid and stale. Looking out a cracked window, Detroit appeared old and tired, a caricature of American industrial might turned impotent.

Matters such as those didn't mean much to me anymore. They didn't mean anything to the long-limbed, red-haired, 20-year-old army private still dressed in fatigues sprawled dead on the floor, lying in a pile of his own intestines.

We met earlier at a riverfront jazz concert after I had gotten back into town. He was getting ready to muster out for his second tour in Syria. He saw me as a kindred soul, a man who could understand—unlike his friends and family—why he was going back to that caldron of war. It wasn't because he was a rabid patriot, or filled with some sense of greater destiny; it was because that's where his brothers and sisters were—his *real* family. After half a dozen beers he considered me his best friend. It was easy to talk him into coming back to my room for more alcohol and war stories.

I closed the window overlooking streets filled with garbage and rats and sat down on the mattress next to my scimitar, its razor-sharp curved blade stained with the private's blood. The bloodlust and black rage that pushed me over the precipice was still inside me, driven by the never-ending parade of young men and women feeding the Middle East machine of conflict.

But perhaps this night would be different. If anyone could end it, it would be him. I called DeShaun at his law office and prayed to gods that ceased giving a shit about me long ago that he was still there.

DeShaun picked up on the second ring. "Hello?" he said. It was funny, hearing his voice. It sounded soft, civilized.

I waited a few seconds, then cleared my throat. "DeShaun, it's me."

There was a pause, then a loud sigh. "Look, I don't know who this is, but—"

"Twenty-seven point two klicks north of Rafah. February 3, 2003. You took two slugs in your gut. I took one in the right bicep just above my skull and crossbones tat identical to the one you have on your left shoulder. The slug went clean through, and I was back out on patrol in a week."

Another pause, then: "Where are you?"

I gave him the address and told him to come alone. He said he would, and I believed him. Even after all these years, I knew DeShaun as well as one man could know another. We had shared too many battles for it to be any other way.

I pulled out three single pieces of carefully folded paper from my shirt pocket. I don't remember if I was ever going to send the letter to DeShaun or not. Sometimes I think I had written it just to put into words the madness that entered my world, to try and give that horrific time meaning and context.

Now I kept it to remind myself of what I was and what I hoped I could be again. Its words were smudged and faded, but they still held tight their dark chakra of that night twenty years ago and 6000 miles away.

*****

Tuesday morning, February 18, 2003

Somewhere north of Rafah

"ENEMY AT THREE O'CLOCK!"

That's how it started, Dee, with some private first class (your replacement, can you believe it?) fresh from the states, screaming his lungs out at four in the morning.

But you know all about the craziness here as much as I do. At least until that night. Because that night, man...that night took the insanity that was our normal up to a whole new level of fucked.

I've tried to write my folks and explain to them about what happened. But unless you've been here and had this 24/7 living hell burrow under your skin until you want to join the Shaikh who dance like madmen in the streets of Riyadh, it's just not possible to understand.

That's why I'm writing you, Dee, even though I don't hold any hope that the fascist army censors will let this letter get through. But I need to tell someone that I'm not crazy.

And if I am, I need someone to understand why it happened.

Anyway, this PFC—name was Jacobson—started screaming like a round of magnesium tracers had hit him. I poked my head out of my tent into the star-lit night, expecting to see a squad or platoon of Iraqis. There was sand, some scattered tamarisk shrubs, and nine tents of our demolition squad nestled in a small ravine.

There were no enemy soldiers.

"Jacobson—calm the fuck down and get over here!" I yelled in my best commander voice.

Private Jacobson—he looked so damn young I bet he didn't even have hair on his balls—who was 10 meters away on the near edge of our perimeter, looked at me with wide eyes that were full of fear, then dropped in a dead faint.

By that time, Andrews, Martinez, Matthews, Zitek, Kaufman, Daven, Sung, and Johnson—all of the old team that had gone out with me for another Recon mission looking for the mythical Iraqi weapons of mass destruction (you'd think with our billion-dollar satellites we wouldn't need to send men into harm's way before the 'real' war starts and we turn Iraq into one big sand dune, but hey, what the hell do I know?) came out of their tents, ready for a fight. They had AK's in their hands (yeah, I know the brass wants us to use M-16's, but we both know what an unreliable piece of firepower the 16 is here; hell, if yours hadn't jammed up you'd probably still be here, and I'd be minus one potential medal of honor) and were led by Andrews, who gave a war cry and ran full out into the night while his AK sang a 150-decibel song.

I know you're thinking: 'where's the L-T's usual standard military protocol?' My only answer is that I was getting tired, Dee. Fucking exhausted. Weary of going out for weeks at a time to blow up shit Saddam had hidden and buried so deep in the fucking desert that he couldn't find it. Of watching fellow warriors get shot and exploded into chunks of lifeless flesh. Of seeing you, my best friend, get almost killed.

It was wearing on me, Dee. I didn't tell you, but I was going to ask for a transfer once my tour was over. Get me a nice little desk job in Germany or Korea, find some blonde Fraulein or little Mama-san to screw day and night, and spend the rest of my time collecting government paychecks until I was old and fat and retired.

Funny how some things don't work out.

So, I didn't do a damn thing as the rest of the boys followed Andrew's lead and started running and shooting and having a grand old time. Just pulled back into the tent, put on my flak jacket, and waited for them to run out of ammunition so I could go see just what was going on without getting shot to hell.

But then it got quiet. So quiet I swear I could hear the thick layer of cordite from my boy's guns fall onto the dry, parched earth. So fucking quiet that I could hear my heart pounding like Alex Van Halen on his drums five seconds before I realized how scared I was.

Besides the unreal muteness, I could smell something over the gunpowder, over the omnipresent heat of the land, over all the death and hate and bullshit that infected the entire Middle East. It smelled like something rotted, infected, old—no, not old, *ancient*. It scared me down to my cynical soul and all I wanted to do was lay there in my own sour sweat and pray to Jesus to come take me back to Detroit.

But these were my men—my *family*—and I just couldn't lie there. I took two deep breaths to clear my head, grabbed a M-60, loaded it, threw a couple belts of shells over my shoulder, and moved slowly out of the tent.

The camp was nearly deserted. One second my boys had been filling the air with thunder and lead, and the next second they were gone. It was totally empty except for Jacobson, who was still lying on the ground next to our encirclement of Razor wire.

There were no bodies. Absolutely nothing! I tried to think—gas, some exotic Iraqi bio-weapon, but nothing clicked. Almost all of the men had disappeared into the blackness of the night.

I think I would have lost it if it wasn't for Jacobson, who finally came to and started wailing like a six-month-old baby for his momma's tit. I walked over toward him and finally saw what had turned his brain into curdled mush.

You have to believe me, I was straight that night, as straight as anyone can be and still function in such an insane place. This thing wasn't a hallucination, no bad DT's, no after-effect from some bad uppers. It was real, Dee. And more terrible than any sane man can imagine.

It was eight klicks outside the camp at three o'clock. The thing was hunched over then stood up, at least 15 meters tall. Its skin was a sickly, decaying yellow, like sand that had been pissed on by fifty men.

Patches of festering sores oozed congealed puke-green seepage off its scarred torso. And its face was straight out of some cheap-ass horror flick: Sickly red eyes, smashed in nose, and a mouth filled with more sharp teeth then in that huge shark we caught off the coast of Ra al Khafji. This fucking monster looked at Jacobson, looked at me, then walked toward us like a drunken giant on legs as big as tree trunks.

My finger squeezed down on the trigger of the M-60 with no thought involved. I hit the freak square on. I know I did. I saw a line of gaping holes appear in its chest, and thick, black fluid pour from those holes. I must have hit it at least at least a hundred times.

My arms ached from the recoil, my ears sang from the bullet reports, and that bastard kept walking without missing a step. He got to the razor wire, reached down, and picked up the Jacobson, who was still squealing like a pissed-off baby.

What could I do? I had just put over a hundred rounds of death into the ugly fucker and he didn't flinch. Like some giant garbage disposal, his shark mouth opened wide and he stuffed the private into his mouth. A few pops, a few chews, and one Alan Jacobson, PFC, gone. Two more steps and the freak was standing over me. He reached down with hands as big as a Jeep and I dropped to my knees, grabbed the crucifix at my chest (you remember, don't you, as they were taking you away in the Cobra, you pulled the chain you had the cross hanging from around your bloody neck and made me swear to wear it), and waited to become another midnight snack.

I must have been kneeling all night. The next thing I remember was the sound of choppers in the morning that carried me away to Jubbah. A week later I asked about getting a report on that night and was ordered to keep my eyes shut and my mouth shut even tighter.

Yeah, right. Like I'm any good at following orders from assholes.

I learned from a Sufi holy man that the area we were in that night was sacred ground for them. Sacred might not be the right word though; more like an epicenter of their culture, a place where the first Mesopotamian was formed out of the warm sand and where the last will be buried at the end of time. The Sufi told me that ghuls, a type of monstrous djinn, were placed there to keep watch and ensure the land wasn't desecrated.

I don't know, Dee. A year ago, I would have laughed the whole fucking story away, but now, who am I to say what is and isn't anymore? I only know I've been in this damn psycho-ward in Saudi Arabia for two months now and if I didn't tell someone, I really will go insane.

I hope by the time you get this letter you are able to read it, and I hope by the time I get home (seven more weeks if I can believe my doctors) we can get together.

Maybe then you can help me figure out what happened. Help me understand why I'm the only bastard out of the mission still alive.

*****

The knock on the door was solid and loud. "Come in," I said.

DeShaun pushed the door open; the hissing florescent light in the room silhouetting his tall frame. The ebony skin of his face held wrinkles and lines, and his kinky thick Afro of youth was now graying and sparse. He carried a large-caliber semi-automatic pistol in one meaty hand and I smiled to myself. He hadn't lost all of his edge.

I think he recognized the smell of the carnage before he saw the body of the soldier. Dee walked in two more steps and slammed the door shut with his foot.

"I never believed all the stories I heard." He motioned with the barrel of the gun at the dead young man on the floor. "At least not until now."

He pointed the gun at my chest, then continued. "What happened to you, man? You used to be the guy who would do anything for his comrades, and now you're killing our brothers!"

He paused again, probably waiting for some type of explanation.

I said nothing.

"I tried for so long to get in touch with you," he said, "even after you disappeared when you got stateside. Then a year later, the boys from the brass started to show up and told me that you massacred all the men in our unit. They asked me a million questions and showed me pictures of things they said you did. I never believed them. Then in '05 things went quiet until '11, when they showed up at my door and said you were again on a killing spree. But in all of these years I never believed them. You were the best L-T we ever had, the best *friend* I ever had. There's no fucking way you could be a stone-cold killer."

Dee glared at me, and I could see in his light green eyes the betrayal I knew he felt. With his free hand, he pulled a cell phone out of his pocket. I heard three beeps as he punched in some numbers. I assumed 9-1-1. He put the phone to his ear and said the name, address, and room number of the hotel.

I took hold of the scimitar and stepped toward him as I felt the deep, ravenous swelling grow inside the smoldering pit of my soul. Dee pulled back the hammer of the gun in one smooth motion.

"Pull the trigger," I said, trying with all my might to hold down the beast. "Dee, pull the damned trigger before it comes out!"

"What the fuck are you talking about?" He stepped back until he was against the closed door. "Stay where you are, man, or I swear I'll—"

"He let me go so he could send some part of himself over here," I said, my voice becoming garbled as I felt my mouth stretch and widen and my will to die shrivel away. "He wanted to come to America. To where all the men and women who desecrated his home lived. He's killed them all, Dee. Every soldier from our unit, or any unit, that walked over that area. All except you and me."

Dee dropped the phone and gripped the gun with both hands as I smiled. A very wide, very hungry, razor-sharp smile. Dee fired the gun three times. The black, vicious fluid that poured out of the bullet holes in my chest quickly congealed and dropped off my healed skin like bloated leaches.

Before he could get the fourth shot off, I severed him completely through the waist.

Dee's upper torso rolled over next to the body of the soldier. I carefully stepped around the wide pool of blood and guts on the cheap Linoleum floor and moved over to my dying friend. He looked up at me with confused eyes as his frantic heart quickly beat away the last remaining seconds of his life.

I unhooked the chain holding the crucifix from around my neck and carefully placed it around Dee's neck. As his eyes glazed over in the universal sign of death that I knew all too well, I felt the dark, vengeful side of the beast become silent in the dark crevices of my soul.

The hallway of the hotel was empty and quiet. A large gray rat moved close as its keen nose picked up the scent of a possible meal in the room. I kicked at it and it scurried away. In the distance I heard the sounds of sirens.

"Maybe now the djinn will consider dues paid," I said out loud to whatever gods were listening. "Maybe now he'll let me rest."

The rat reappeared and leered up at me. I went to strike it with the scimitar when the first police officer burst into the room and leveled her gun.

"Drop your weapon!" she yelled. Even before I had taken the first step toward her, I realized with maddening certainty that the demon had tasted too much American blood for him to ever rest again.

HUNGER

by J Benjamin Sanders Jr

Tobias woke to pain. His head and chest throbbed, and his left leg had no feeling until he tried to move. Then the stabbing pain wrenched a scream from his bruised mouth. Twisting his body brought the rushing river into view, no more than a dozen paces away, the icy crust shattered. There was no sign of the horses and mule, nor of any of their stores. Hitching himself into a sitting position against a shattered trunk, he took a quick inventory. Holster empty, hat gone, leg busted, and maybe an arm. Tobias still had his skinning knife, but no food and no way to get any.

Scanning the river bank Tobias spotted Hans about twenty feet away. The boy lay waist-deep in the river, head first, face down, and unmoving. In his condition, twenty feet might as well have been twenty miles, but there wasn't much choice. Falling onto his belly, Tobias began to crawl, digging his fingers into the smooth river gravel, and pushing with his good leg, over and over. Inching his way forward, drawing closer until a stretched hand could finally touch the boy's leg, the dead flesh as cold as the river water. Panting heavily, the icy air burning his lungs, Tobias gave up and collapsed.

*****

Tobias gripped the reins with his right hand and

leaned against his saddle horn to ease the growing stiffness in his spine. He was leading his little train through the snow-crusted mountains, paralleling the frozen river on his right, fifty feet below. Gripping the brim, he pulled his hat low against the wind, with his thick woolen scarf tucked into his coat, it wrapped his head up to his eyes. Kicking his horse to urge it forward to force a path through the deep snow. His young companion, Hans, followed, leading the pack mule heavily loaded with their winter take of prime beaver and fox pelts. Above them, towering pines covered the mountain slopes, their boughs heavy with snow, and occasionally a sharp crack echoed when the weight became too much and a limb would give way.

Both kept their heads down, riding quietly because it was too cold to talk with the sun hidden behind thick threatening clouds hanging heavy and gray above their heads. Tobias heard a slow rumble coming from the mountain slope above him and jerked on his reins to stop his horse, spinning in the saddle. The ground shook and he stared upslope through the trees, spotting a roiling surge of white between the picket of boles. The towering pines wavered and bowed as the ice struck, and shed their snowy crowns in an eruption of white.

"Avalanche," Tobias yelled, and whipped his horse with a fury born of fear and raked its side with his spurs, trying to urge more speed from the animal. It drove forward, screaming in pain, but only floundered in the deep snow, now flecked with blood.

A hoary surge rose and threw a veil of

obscurity over the world. The rumble grew louder, like an iron-horse plunging down the side of the mountain, mingled with the crack and snap of broken trees.

*****

Tobias woke with a gasp as the memory of the events faded and the reality of his situation set in. He couldn't have said how long he lay there but must have passed out for a bit because when his eyes opened the invisible sun had faded behind the mountain tops. Tobias needed to get somewhere out of the weather, or else he wouldn't be able to survive without shelter or food.

Tobias used his knife to cut off Hans's belt and tucked it into his ragged coat. Then scanned his surroundings. There was plenty of wood strewn about, carried down by the avalanche, and more washed up by the surging river. Tobias also spotted an undercut in the riverbank, only a couple of feet deep, but it should provide him some protection from the weather.

Tobias crawled forward, dragging several pieces of wood along until he had collected a nice pile in front of the undercut. Then used his knife to shave off several long strips of curling wood and made a pile, then with shaking fingers struck the back of his steel blade against a stone until it sparked. Tobias worked slowly to try and coax a flame, then fed it with curls of dried wood until he managed to get a decent blaze going. The heat washed out and drove the chill from his fingers and thawed his face. Exhausted, he fell back into the undercut that caught and trapped the heat, keeping him warm while he slept, then came the memories.

*****

"Tob?" Hans screamed, his horse spinning in terror.

"Get down." Tobias swung out of his saddle and jerked the reins, forcing his steed's head down. Then the horse went to its knees before flopping onto its side. The trapper hoped it would provide a break between him and the snow slide. Hans sat frozen in his saddle, staring gap jawed at the onrushing wall of ice.

Tobias could do nothing to save the boy, so he hunkered down behind his horse to try and save himself. Then the surge of snow hit. A womanish scream rose, and Tobias couldn't tell if it came from the horse, the boy, or both. The force of the cascade rolled his horse, and it drove them both down the slope and over the edge into the void until a slamming jolt thrust him into darkness.

*****

The pain in his broken leg worried Tobias from his nightmare-haunted sleep and he woke to a world of white. It took a moment for him to realize snow had begun to fall, fat flakes drifted from the gray heavens, and covered the world with a pale shroud. It covered the spot where his fire had been, now just a dark lump in the dirt Groaning in frustration, he scooted over and desperately scooped the snow to uncover a mound of ash. Digging deeper until he exposed a bed of glowing embers, then fed them feverishly with small sticks and twigs until a pitiful fire flared up.

Determined not to let it die, Tobias forced himself to stay alert and feed the flames while the thick snow fell around him. Tobias heard death whispering in his ear and knew it was only a matter of time unless he could find some food. His meager stores had vanished beneath the rushing river along with his horses and mule. In no condition to hunt, that left scavenging. Only there was nothing to scavenge.

Tobias found himself drawn to Hans's snow-covered legs still protruding from the river, his upper body now encased in ice. Tobias tried to ignore his body begging for sustenance as his belly cramped, his limbs trembled, and a fever ravaged his body.

Pawing through his collection of broken branches and brush, he pulled out the straightest limb and lashed it to his broken leg with his and Hans' belts. Jerking them tight, Tobias screamed when bone grated against bone and passed out. In his fevered dreams, the boy Hans stared at him with haunted eyes.

"Why didn't you save me?"

"I tried." Tears leaked and flowed freely.

"You promised my mama you would take care of me."

"I know. I'm sorry, Hans. I did all I could."

"You failed me, Tob. You let me die."

Day after day, Tobias lay there and grew weaker while the weather grew worse. At night Hans would still visit, staring silently with accusing eyes until Tobias screamed for him to leave him alone. Then came the eerie howling of the wolves, their eyes glowing from the reflected firelight as they surrounded him. He desperately prayed some rider would come by and spot his smoke, but no one did.

Hunger drove him to despair; he even attempted to gnaw on the bark of the fallen trees but ended up with belly cramps until he shat himself. Tobias began to cast his eyes on Hans' remains, even as he fell into a fitful sleep.

*****

Tobias came to his senses, and found himself halfway across the gravel-covered bank, clutching his skinning knife in his fist. Eyes locked on the cracked leather of the boy's boot sole as he dug in and pulled himself closer. His belly twisted and he had to pause to catch his breath and gather his strength. Shivering feverishly, his body numb from the cold, Tobias reached Hans and let his head fall against his calf while sobbing.

"I need food."

"If you do this, Tob. There's no going back. Remember those injun tales of men who broke that taboo? They became monsters."

"I don't care. I can't take any more. God forgive me."

The wolves had been at the body during the night, stripping one leg of most of its meat. Holding the blade in his shaking hand, Tobias cut away the boy's boot from his remaining leg, and slit his trousers to expose the blue marbled flesh. Tears stinging his eyes, Tobias raised his knife, then chopped down and began singing as loud as he could in his raw coarse voice. Perhaps hoping the song would drown out the sounds of his sin and avert the eyes of God. Timing the lyrics with each blow, aiming for the joint behind the knee. "Mine eyes have seen the glory, uh, of the coming of the Lord; uh, he is trampling out the vintage, uh, where the grapes of wrath are stored; uh, he hath loosed the fateful lightning, uh, of His terrible swift sword; uh, His truth is marching on. Uh, Glory! Glory! Uh, Hallelujah! Uh, Glory! Glory! Uh, Hallelujah! Uh, Glory! Glory! Uh, Hallelujah! Uh, His truth is marching on. Uh."

Tobias repeated the song, his voice growing weaker, until the joint finally gave away, and with his head spinning. Tobias clutched the cold dead meat to his breast while crawling back to the undercut. Leaving Hans's leg close to the fire, Tobias worked his way to the rear of his shelter and collapsed. Lying on the cold ground, shivering and feverish, delirium came. Hans called to him, then crawled out of the river until he sat on the bank and stared at him. The boy leaned forward and rubbed the knee where Tobias had severed it, before flopping on his belly and crawling forward, flashing a ghastly smile and gnashing his broken teeth.

"Get away," Tobias moaned, tossing back and forth. His dead friend towered over him and reached out with gnarled hands, nails broken and jagged. Tobias snatched up a flaming brand and drove it into Hans' face when the boy reached for his missing leg and screamed. "No. It's mine. Mine."

Wailing, Tobias jerked up, his eyes darting to the frozen river. Hans still lay there, half in and half out. Then his eyes jerked down to the leg, no longer blue. Whimpering, he rolled closer to the fire and tossed on more of his meager supply of wood. Taking his knife, Tobias used it to slice off strips of flesh and wrapped them around a small limb with shaking hands, before thrusting it into the flames. The air quickly filled with the aroma of searing meat, so strong and tempting it made his stomach knot. Pulling the smoldering stick away from the fire, Tobias savagely gnawed on the half-cooked and charred meat. It burned his mouth and tongue as he gorged to fill the emptiness in his gut, washing it down with handfuls of dirty snow. Even then Tobias cried and begged Hans to forgive him.

Tobias stayed there on the riverbank, next to the frozen water, feeding on what remained of his young partner, until he began to regain his strength. Soon there was no more wood to be scavenged for his fire, nor more of his partner's flesh to be salvaged. Hans didn't talk to him anymore, not since Tobias had committed the ultimate sin. Nor could the old trapper say how much time had passed, weeks, months, or more. Tobias only knew he couldn't stay there any longer, not if he wanted to survive.

With his knife in hand, and his broken leg tightly bound, Tobias crawled up the slope until he reached what remained of the trail. Then began to work his way down the mountain, praying someone would come along and save him.

*****

The storm had been blowing for three days when a hard knock echoed off Mary Strothmeir's door, followed by a loud voice. "Mary, it's Jacob McKinney."

Mary dropped her sewing and set it aside, then hurried over to open the door. Jacob stood there, clutching what appeared to be a bundle of rags in his arms. She stepped aside to let him pass, and shut the door in the face of the growing storm, barring it behind him. "Jacob. What are you doing out in weather like this? It ain't fittin' for man or bear."

Jacob stopped by the fire and let the bundle fall. Then dropped to his knees and slowly peeled back the stiff rags. "I was on my way home after running my traps up by Beaver River when I found this. I figured the boy wasn't fit enough to make it to my place, and you were the closest."

A face that looked to be carved from ice peeked out, all sharp angles and hollows beneath a ragged beard. His cracked and scabby lips pulled back in a tooth-baring grimace. "He was passed out in the middle of the trail and I near missed him, except Jenny shied when that danged mule almost stepped on him. The damned fool has got himself a busted leg and the rest of him is in pretty rough shape."

Mary threw more wood on the fire, then grabbed the lamp and brought it closer. "Jesus wept. What has this poor man been through? Well, Jacob. Get him out of those rags and toss them outside, there's no saving them. I'll grab a couple of bearskins and we can make him up a pallet here by the fire."

Mary put a kettle to heat water to wash his wounds, then fetched several thick pelts and spread them on the floor, with another to bundle him up and keep him warm. After stripping him down, Jacob helped wrestle him onto the pallet and then the two managed to scrub most of the filth from his bruised flesh. Nearly clean, the man looked to be a sorrier sight than he had been before. All the bruises and scrapes stood out and the poor man looked to be little more than skin and bones.

"Don't know about that leg, Mary. It's busted up pretty bad. We might not be able to save it. If we do, he might not ever walk again."

"We'll do what we can, and the Lord will handle the rest," Mary said. "I'll cook up a pot of soup. He'll need it if he's going to get his strength back."

"I hate to leave you like this since you're alone and all, but I need to get back to my family with the storm blowing the way it is. I promise to get back within the week and see how the two of you are getting on."

Mary wiped her hand on her apron after setting the pot over the flames to heat water for the soup. "You go on your way, Jacob, and don't worry about us. I'll be fine until Hiram gets back, which shouldn't be more than a day or two. The Good Lord willing."

Jacob left and Mary managed to get a bowl of thinned soup down the stranger, but she was more worried about his fever. Sitting in her hand-hewn rocker, Mary watched while the nameless man tossed and turned upon the pallet, softly muttered words and phrases of nonsense slipped from his delirium. Begging forgiveness from someone called Hans.

After things quieted her weariness descended upon her like a tattered shawl, slumping her shoulders and etching her face. The fire in the hearth, filled with the slowly burning oak timbers, shed a dim light across the room. Yet it was enough to fill the corners with ghoulish shadows that twisted and danced mockingly in the crook of her eye.

"Hot, hot. Burning," the unnamed man moaned in his delirium, as the fever ravaged his body. The internal fire seemed to tickle his nerves and sear their frayed ends.

Lashing out with his good foot, the delirious man kicked the covers aside. Dirty and broken-nailed fingers scraped across his chest, dragging through the matted hair as sweat beaded and pooled in dimpled places on his lean, pallid flesh. Nails raking the festering wounds brought forth a hoarse cry of pain.

A low animal-sounding groan rattled deep in his raw throat. Mary rose and moved forward; her cool hand stretches out to touch his burning brow. Murmuring softly, she dipped a cloth into a pan of water and wiped down his face. She hoped the coolness was enough to suck the fever from his flesh.

Done, Mary pulled his cover high and tucked it around him. Soon, the man was lulled back into that fevered world haunted by his dark dreams.

With her patient now resting easily, she returned to her rocker and lay her head back. The heat of the fire, the closed confines of the single-room cabin, and the sheer exhaustion from the nonstop tending to the man, all worked to send her drifting into that twilight world between wake and sleep, where reality entwines with dreams. In that eerie half-world, a beastly shadow seemed to overlay the stranger, a spare creature of knotted muscles and lean hunger. Mary sat frozen, joints locked, eyes open, and watched the battle between the two, one seeking freedom, the other to maintain its control of the hunger-driven creature. The shadow beast seemed to gain strength as her patient grew weaker, till they merged with a silent scream. The conjoined creature rolled off the pallet and flowed across the floor to tower over her, his shadow, a dark stain cast against the wall. An elongated hand tipped with gnarled and twisted fingers stretched out and wrapped itself searingly about her wrist. With a squeeze, it jerked her from the twilight of her sleep. Terrified, she stared into the blank face of the naked stranger, his shadow-smudged eyes burned emptily and his lips pulled back from his yellow teeth in a grimace of hunger. The terrifying sight ripped a scream from her raw throat.

Some residue of humanity must have reared up and clawed back his animalistic urges, and forced them down into that deep well of consciousness. With a sob, the crazed soul released her and staggered to the door, grabbed the bar, and ripped it from its brackets to let it fall. The force of the wind blew the door back and he staggered out into the swirling snow until swallowed by the raging storm of howling winds and driven ice.

Fearing for his safety, Mary grabbed her coat and plunged out into the storm. Shading her face and leaning into the winter squall. Pulling her coat tight, she spun around in a circle trying to spot the man, calling out for him to come back, only to have her words shredded by the howling wind.

*****

Free of the walled enclosure and the searing heat, the beast dropped to all fours and ran, reaching the edge of the forest the lean creature scampered beneath the welcoming canopy where the smells were clean and enticing. Unlike the odious stench of the cabin.

Pausing to raise his head, the beast crowed. *"Cold, so deliciously cold. Free. Free to hunt. Free to feed."*

The pain in his leg was a dim memory, he faced

the whipping wind and crouched on his haunches to gaze back across the ice-covered slope. The wind wove its way through the trees with a low moaning keen as it scoops up crystals of ice and tosses them against his ruffled silver pelt. Hunger gnawed at his belly like a wolverine in the carcass of a deer as it lets loose with a silent howl of demand. But he ignored the hunger and waited patiently, his gnarled hand clutched a twisted limb, naked but for a sheath of black ice, which cracked and popped as it sways in the harsh wind. Like a dark naked bone whose rough texture and smooth cover barely crept into his awareness as he focused on the lone figure who fought to drive through the drifting layers of felled ice.

The beast lifted his snout to the wind so as savor the approaching creature's scent and a feral grin spread across his face.

The beast hungered. "*Warm meat, hot blood.*"

The beast anticipated gorging on her bloody flesh and savoring the crunch of marrow-filled bones. He could taste the creature's fear, the tantalizing seasoning that can only make the meat so much sweeter. The creature snuffled harder to rip the aroma from the wind's greedy clutches. Patient as the prey stumbled weakly, trying to escape the determined clutches of the ever-growing drifts. Her moist breath panted and blinded her to the world with its spreading fog. A hunched shadow hunkers down, waiting for the weakening creature to blunder ever closer. Saliva churns between his clenched jaws and oozes across his chin.

His prey reached the forest edge, a wall of naked limbs that clacked on the wind like the long-abandoned bones left on a hanging tree. It came straight for him, blind to his stillness, the wind, the cold, and its own weariness. Her scent slapped him in the face, a teasing and cloying tang that reached out to his roiling hunger.

"Patience, patience."

The prey coming closer and closer, gasping for more of the lung-biting air, feet scuffing against the powdery ice, ice that clung to her coat in an elfin web spun from water and air. His hunger once more clawed for attention, only to be driven back through sheer force of will. He must not strike too soon, or else chance losing his prey. Crouched loosely atop the icy mound, his talon-tipped feet sunk deep to get a purchase against the frozen ground. The prey stopped and tossed back her hood, eyes searching, face etched with strain.

*****

Following the man's trail, as it cut through the deepening snow, Mary soon found him huddled beneath a bare limbed tree; his arms wrapped around the crenelated trunk while making little mewling sounds deep in his throat. Crouching, she reached out and touched his shoulder and his head whipped up, eyes burning with an inner madness.

Mary jerked her hand back and cried, "Oh, dear God."

His jaw dropped to expose blunt yellow teeth and diseased gums. The beast lunged and Mary screamed a scream that turned into a liquid gurgle as she fell to the blood-splattered ground.

End

BOG BOOTS

by Derek Des Anges

Oliver had gone to the moor with Neighbour Kevin and Mr. Salim Yusuf, because they were doing Mummy a favour. It was one of those autumn days where everything was different shades of brown and grey, not the bright orange and red in picture books, and rain seemed to hang in the air everywhere and not actually fall, so that you bumped into it while you were walking and there was no point in an umbrella, and the inside of your raincoat got as wet as the outside because it wasn't even really cold.

But Oliver tried to make the best of it, because he liked Neighbour Kevin and Mr Salim Yusuf, and in the summer the moor had been very nice and full of ponies he wasn't allowed to pet, and sheep he didn't want to pet, but also an ice cream van. There wasn't an ice cream van now, but he was sure if they waited long enough there would be one, and if he knew one thing about Mr Salim Yusuf it was that he liked ice cream almost as much as Oliver did, and a lot more than Mummy.

At the edge of the moor there was a forest. That wasn't red and orange either, just a sort of manky dark green-grey that looked like a big shadow squatting on the hill. Neighbour Kevin said it was a plantation, for making paper. They made paper out of trees, he said, but only a specific type of tree.

Inside the forest the hanging rain didn't hang as much but it was very dark and there were flies everywhere, so it was also worse.

They came to a bit of the forest that was all stumps. Oliver didn't like it: the hanging rain came back here, and all the stumps looked like open mouths all white against the dirty ground, and the whole place seemed sad. Next to the dirt road there was a rut and, in the rut, there were pools.

Oliver was wearing wellies, so he got down in the rut and sloshed through the dirty water until he was away from the dirt road and the open mouth tree stumps, and he sloshed past a wall made of stones with gaps between them.

"Don't go too far," said Neighbour Kevin, "it's gloomy and I won't be able to see you."

"And what, the Beast will eat him?" asked Mr Salim Yusuf, laughing. "Let the little boy wander. It's what they do."

"Yeah, but there's mineshafts all over the place out here," Neighbour Kevin said, pinching Mr Salim Yusuf in the arm. "Do you want to be the guy who let a little boy fall down a mine?"

Oliver waded past the wall.

On the other side the trees were different, like trees in picture books instead of trees on Christmas cards, all twisted up and covered in patches of yellow and green on their branches. The rut went into a dip, and the water started to smell of farts.

"Yuck," Oliver said, so they'd know it wasn't him. "This water smells of farts."

"That's methane," said Neighbour Kevin, who liked explaining things. "Microbes make it when they're decomposing leaves. It gets trapped under the water."

"The earth is farting," said Mr Salim Yusuf, who preferred joking about things. "It ate too many beans."

Oliver waded a bit further and stopped.

He stopped because there was a little flame, like a candle, dancing on the surface of the water ahead just beyond a fallen tree, and he'd never seen anything like it before in his life.

The little flame carried on burning even with the hanging rain in the air and the water directly underneath it. Dirty brown grass ran up the banks but none of it touched the little flame.

"What's that?" he asked, completely awestruck.

"It's methane," said Neighbour Kevin. "It's burning in the air. It's not touching the water, so it doesn't go out. Some kinds of fire don't go out when water goes on them."

"It's a fairy light," said Mr Salim Yusuf. "Be careful not to touch it."

"Because fairies will take me?" asked Oliver, still transfixed.

"No, because you'll burn yourself," said Neighbour Kevin, and Oliver knew he must have given Mr Salim Yusuf a little pinch, because he did that sometimes. "And it will hurt."

"Can I stay here?" Oliver asked, as the rain hung around him and up ahead the little flame did its little dance, not quite touching anything. It looked like someone quite happy, wearing all orange. It was the only orange thing in the landscape except for Mr Salim Yusuf's jumper.

"No, of course not," said Mr Salim Yusuf.

"But you can wade as far as that tree," said Neighbour Kevin. "Don't go any further, you have to be able to reach both of the banks at the same time, and the stream gets wider there."

"Why can't I go further?" Oliver asked, still looking at the little dancing flame.

"Hell, I don't know," said Neighbour Kevin, a bit impatient. "Because you don't know how deep it gets or what's down there. I can't swim and Salim is wearing his best jumper, do you want us to drown getting you out of a pond?"

Oliver shook his head.

He waded along the stream as far as the fallen tree. It was black and slimy and had tiny little mushrooms growing on the underside, and bright green moss on the top. It looked like a sort of bridge, and it dipped into the water at one end and climbed up onto the bank at the other.

"That's far enough," said Neighbour Kevin. "Time to climb out."

Oliver lifted up one leg—he wasn't sure about left and right legs yet, but this one was definitely one of his legs—and stretched up to put it on the stream bank.

But when he tried to pull up his other leg, it just wobbled around in the bottom of the stream and made a sticky *glop* sound.

The mud was so thick it was like a hand holding his boot in place.

"Um," said Oliver, trying to pull his foot up again. The hanging rain had got in his hair.

"Come on," said Neighbour Kevin, holding his hand out behind him and waggling it to encourage Oliver up the bank. "It's raining."

"Kevin, it's been raining all day," Mr Salim Yusuf snorted. "Why does that suddenly matter now?"

"It's also getting dark," Neighbour Kevin said, "and I promised your Mum I'd be back in time for your dinner."

Oliver thought that wasn't strictly true, because he'd heard the conversation: Neighbour Kevin said,

"I'll have him back for his tea," and Oliver's Mummy had said, "I suppose you must."

But his foot was still stuck, so he didn't mention that. He held up his arm like he was in class and said, "Um, my boot won't come out."

"Oh dear," said Neighbour Kevin. "Do you want me to help you out?"

"Yes, please," said Oliver, trying to pull his foot out again.

He only wobbled a bit more and waved his free foot around. He was worried if he wobbled any further, he'd fall over. The water smelled very, very much of farts.

Neighbour Kevin reached down and grabbed both of Oliver's hands with his big, warm, dark brown hands. He gave a little tug.

Oliver's boot stayed stuck.

"Salim?" Neighbour Kevin said.

Mr Salim Yusuf rolled up the sleeves of his orange jumper and gave Oliver one of his silly little smiles, the kind that always made him feel like they were both in on a joke, even though Oliver never knew what the joke was.

"Other side," Neighbour Kevin said, "or we're just going to end up pulling Oliver over into the stream."

Oliver didn't want that at all. Neighbour Kevin held him very firmly by the hands, reassuring him he wouldn't let go.

Mr Salim Yusuf hopped over the steam and walked down the bank to where Oliver was stuck, nodded to him, and grabbed him by the waist.

"Up we go, Oliver," he instructed, and with a big heave and a dry slither, Oliver came out of the stream.

His boot did not.

"Rats," said Mr Salim Yusuf, looking at Oliver's dinosaur sock as it dangled off the end of his foot. "You've abandoned your frog boot to the bog."

Neighbour Kevin pulled Oliver onto his side of the stream and held him up to pull off his other boot.

When he'd finished, he put Oliver on his shoulders, which was almost worth losing his boot for.

From this high up the plantation looked even bigger than before. He could see all the way down the stream too, but he wasn't sure he wanted to look at it anymore.

Neighbour Kevin and Mr Salim Yusuf both looked down at the dark water with its farty smell and the little dancing candle flame and strange white shadow under the surface and the uncomfortable sheen on the top.

"Yeah, I'm not sticking my hand in there," said Neighbour Kevin, patting Oliver on the foot. He held onto Oliver's other boot. "Tell your mum we'll buy you a new pair."

Oliver wasn't very sure Mummy would be happy with him claiming that. She would probably call him a liar unless Neighbour Kevin said something first. But he didn't say that: he just looked down into the water again from above.

There was something white down there. It was probably just a plastic bag. People threw them away all the time, even though Miss Adewunmi at school said that was killing the environment.

Oliver looked at the sky instead, which was full of grey nothingness, and less worrying.

He held onto Neighbour Kevin's hood as they left the stream and went back the way they'd come.

They walked back through the plantation with the big thick dark branches that hid the grey sky and made it feel like night; they walked back through the open place with the chopped off tree stumps that looked like pale open shouting mouths or eyes against the black soil; and they walked back out of the gate on the far side of the plantation, where the fence was on top of another wall, and there was Neighbour Kevin and Mr Salim Yusuf's big jeep sitting there by itself. There still wasn't an ice-cream van, but Oliver didn't mind that anymore.

Neighbour Kevin pointed his key beeper at the jeep and said to Mr Salim Yusuf, "If you keep writing things like that, they'll kick you out."

Mr Salim Yusuf shrugged and wiped hanging rain off his face. "I'm not wrong," he said, very calm, "things only have power when you believe in them. There's no point in trying to lie to a population that inherently distrusts you already."

"Things only have power when you believe in them?" Neighbour Kevin repeated, and he held onto Oliver's leg to keep him steady on his shoulders as he reached for the door. "Oh, now that's heresy."

"Have it your way," said Mr Salim Yusuf, opening the door on the other side of the jeep. "But you tell *me* that's not what the placebo effect is."

Oliver liked going out with Neighbour Kevin and Mr Salim Yusuf, even if there was no ice cream, he thought, as Neighbour Kevin put him down on the huge jeep seat and buckled him in. Even when they disagreed, like now, they didn't yell at each other. They didn't say horrible things.

"Are you okay there, little man?" said Neighbour Kevin, putting his one lonely boot down on the floor of the jeep. "Not too wet from that bog?"

"I'm alright," said Oliver, because adults liked it when you said that. "My boot looks lonely though."

"It'll be fine," said Neighbour Kevin, getting into the passenger seat. "Your boot can retire when we get you some new ones. Don't forget to tell your Mum."

Oliver wasn't quite so sure it would be fine, somehow.

*****

When he got home and Neighbour Kevin and Mr Salim Yusuf had parked their car and gone into their own house, Oliver told his Mummy about the bog boot.

Mummy said: "This is absolutely typical of you, Oliver. You will *not* take responsibility for your things! How am I supposed to budget for anything in this house if you keep forcing me to spend more money picking up after your consistent laziness and do you think I don't want to be doing something else? Something that isn't going around bloody shoe shops with you? I have places to be, Oliver."

"It's your own fault," said Daddy, from the sofa. He was still wearing his work suit. "You can't expect those [a word Oliver had been told never to use outside of the house] to care what happens to his belongings, it's not like they believe in family lives. But, of course, you don't care what happens to our son, you just *plonk* him into the hands of some ignorant perverts."

"I have to have time to myself, Timothy!" Mummy shouted, as Oliver slipped past her to the kitchen. "You wouldn't understand because you're not at home all day with him driving you bloody mad!

You're out, all the time, at all hours. Who else am I supposed to get in? You *screwed* the last baby-sitter I tried to…"

Oliver got a packet of crisps out of the kitchen cupboard.

"Maybe if you bothered to do your share of the childcare."

Daddy was also shouting, in a not-quite-shouting voice, the way he did sometimes—by putting his head back and saying things in a very loud voice to the ceiling and pretending he wasn't talking to Mummy at all.

"Oh, I wonder whose money is paying for your nice lifestyle, *Violet*? I wonder how we *get that money* other than me working every *god-damned hour* instead of having that precious 'time to myself'? When was the last time *you* brought a single penny into this household?"

Oliver took off his coat and tried to hang it up. He still couldn't reach the coat-hooks, and if he left it on the floor Mummy would be even more cross with him.

He gave up and went upstairs to his room with the crisps just as the shouting really started.

*****

At bedtime, Daddy said he was too tired to read Oliver a story and Mummy said that since Oliver only cared whether Daddy read to him and not her—which wasn't true—she would just leave him to go to sleep by himself, thank you. She also called him "emotionally manipulative", which Oliver still didn't really understand the meaning of, and walked out again with a glass of wine as she turned the light off.

He could hear the shouting through the floor.

When the shouting had finished, Oliver took the covers off his head and looked at the ceiling. Ibrahim at school said when he'd moved into his new bedroom there had been little glow-in-the-dark stars stuck to the ceiling, and as the glue peeled off them, they'd fallen down on him over the first few nights. There were no stars on his ceiling. He'd asked, but Mummy said it would damage the resale value of the house. He wasn't sure what that meant, either.

He looked at the end of his bed. By the wall, where the toy box was, there was a loose toy.

There weren't normally loose toys. Mummy said if he left things out, she would assume he didn't want them, so he put them back very carefully every day. Miss Adewunmi at school had commented on how tidy he was, even.

But there was a loose toy, and he squinted in the dark at it, because he didn't really recognise it.

It was quite big, about the size of Across-The-Road's orange cat Bobbit, who was friendly unless Oliver was with his Daddy, and then Bobbit usually hid under a car and wouldn't come out. But it wasn't orange, like Bobbit. It was a washed-out sort of white, like a plastic bag under water, and it looked a bit like a My Little Pony, maybe that had been left in the sun and gone pale, not one that had been white in the first place.

Oliver stared at it. He was very sure he didn't have anything like that. Daddy was very firm on boys' toys and girls' toys.

The washed-out white pony toy was dirty at the edges. It looked old. The room smelled sort of funny, a little bit like he had brought some of the horrible farty water back from the moor, and a little bit like when leaves went rotten in the late autumn, and turned from nice crispy orange and brown things into horrible slimy black and brown things that you slipped over on.

The white pony from the bog said, "You left your boot in my bog."

Oliver thought it must have been the pony, because he didn't remember thinking the words, but he didn't think he'd heard them either. The words just sort of appeared in his memory like someone had said them, without speaking, and without a voice.

He couldn't have said if the white pony had a high voice or a low voice, if it sounded like a boy or a girl, or a horse or a person. It just stayed where it was on the floor and looked at him.

"You left your boot in my bog," the pony repeated, inside Oliver's head.

"I'm sorry," said Oliver, into his blankets.

"Please come and get it," said the pony toy. It turned its head very slowly to look at Oliver.

He couldn't see a join in his neck like in a normal toy, and he didn't like the way its neck bulged when it turned.

"Littering is bad," said the pony toy.

Oliver took a deep breath and put his blankets all the way over his head. He thought about Neighbour Kevin up on the moor with his reassuring coat on, saying in his reassuring voice that the water is full of methane from things rotting at the bottom of it, and that's why there is a little fire. Methane catches fire in the air.

He thought about it and thought about it until the room stopped smelling of dead leaves.

When he came out from under the covers the white pony toy had gone.

*****

Oliver ate his breakfast. Oliver went to school.

At school, they said what they did at the weekend. Oliver said he went to the moor with Neighbour Kevin and Mr Salim Yusuf, They did Maths, and even though Oliver's Support Teacher explained The Maths, Oliver still got most of it wrong.

Then Oliver went home, and Mummy listened to the radio in the car. They were talking about Climate Change, and Mummy said, "Because of that, you're probably going to drown before you're fifteen anyway. At least I won't have to worry about my pension," and turned the radio off.

When they got home it was raining quite hard, and Oliver had to play indoors.

Daddy had come home from work earlier than usual. He said, "Well, look happy. I'm here wasting time with you instead of working on the Blackwood merger. Can't you even look like you want to see me? I thought not," while Mummy was hanging up her coat and Oliver's coat.

Mummy said, "The world's overheating and we're all going to die, do give me five minutes to put on a bullshit face for your personal gratification, *Timothy*."

Oliver went into the living room and sat down on the floor. The television was on, but Daddy had turned the sound off, so all he could see were numbers on a blue background in a rectangle, and a woman with very big stiff blonde hair talking with an angry face.

He looked out of the window instead.

"Oh, come *on*, Violet," Daddy said, with the special laugh that went along with the smell of the drink he had left on the table next to the sofa, "you know that's a nonsense conspiracy. Absolute poppycock dreamed up by liberals. It's only going to bother a couple of nose-bone savages in the Pacific and we're going to make a killing accessing the Arctic oil."

"Of course, this has absolutely nothing to do with you not wanting to sort the recycling," Mummy said in a very nasty voice. "Anything that interferes with you lounging around the house."

"Oh, you're a fine one to talk," said Daddy, slapping the wall with his hand. "When all you do is spend all day on the internet getting twisted up by too much Twitter and pretending what you do here is difficult! Hanging around with your blasted friends drinking wine and complaining! *Some* of us have jobs to do!"

Next door he could see the little lights around the inside of the window that Neighbour Kevin put up. Daddy called them "poof lanterns"; Neighbour Kevin said they were called "fairy lights" and that he liked them because they made the inside of the house feel sunny even when it wasn't outside.

He tried to see further into the window to see if they were home. Maybe they were watching television. Sometimes when Mummy was seeing her Groups, he had dinner with Mr Salim Yusuf and they watched videos about whatever Oliver wanted to watch, like mountain goats or how to make very fancy cakes. Mr Salim Yusuf always said that he had "exquisite" taste in cakes.

Daddy followed Mummy into the kitchen, both of them still shouting. Oliver couldn't see anything except the little lights.

*****

The argument was one of the bad ones and went on until it got dark, and Daddy broke his favourite mug and then shouted at Mummy for making him do it, so by the time he went to bed Oliver had completely forgotten about the toy pony in his room. He didn't think to check for it.

It wasn't until he lay down to go to sleep, and Mummy said that Daddy didn't want to read to him and that she'd Had Enough For One Day of Tolerating Men's Whims, that Oliver remembered it had been there at all.

But Mummy had already turned off the light, so Oliver lay in the dark looking at the orange rectangles where the streetlights shone through his curtains and thought about how nice it would be to go to sleep without anything weird happening.

He looked at the end of his bed.

On the floor this time there was another pony. It was almost exactly the same as the last pony, and he would have thought that it was the same washed-out white plastic toy if it wasn't so much *bigger* than the pony last night—the size of a medium dog, instead of a cat.

"Oh no," said Oliver out loud. Secretly he hoped it was loud enough to make Mummy come back, but she didn't like coming back in once she'd turned out the light.

You left your boot in my bog, the same voice said inside his head. *Please come and get it.*

"No," said Oliver, burrowing down in the bed as the white pony toy moved very slowly across the carpet. He wasn't sure how it was doing it, because he couldn't see the legs moving. It left dirty marks on the floor.

Throwing things away is making the planet die, the pony's voice said inside his head. *I deserve to be left in peace. I deserve a peaceful sleep.*

"So do I," Oliver said, and he put his head under the covers, and thought very hard about Mr Salim Yusuf and the fairy lights, and he thought very hard about Mr Salim Yusuf saying *things only have power if you believe in them.*

He stayed under the covers until his face got too hot, and when he came out there was nothing on the floor except the dirty marks.

*****

Oliver ate his breakfast. Oliver went to school.

At school, he asked Miss Adewunmi about whether believing in things made them real.

Miss Adewunmi said, "That's a very good question, Oliver," which was what she said when she didn't want to answer something. She talked about the Water Cycle instead.

When Mummy collected him from school, she wasn't paying attention and nearly drove into the back of someone's car. Then she got out of the car and shouted at the other mum for a long time while Oliver slid down his seat and stared out of the window at an old lady across the street, who had a big grey dog.

When Mummy got back into the car, she told him not to tell Daddy about it.

"It'll only upset him," she said, glaring at him in the mirror. "He's under a lot of stress recently."

Then when they got to the house she asked where his PE kit was, and Oliver couldn't remember.

"You are useless," Mummy said, slamming the car door. "First your bloody wellies, now this! We're not made of money! You can't just leave things all over the place and expect people to pick up after you! You're not a baby!"

Oliver sat down on the doorstep.

"You had better not be thinking about crying," Mummy snapped, stepping over him to unlock the door. "You know I won't have that kind of emotional manipulation. It's not as if you care about *my* feelings, after all."

When she'd gone inside, Oliver emptied out his school bag and found his PE kit at the bottom.

While he was putting it back into his bag again so that he could show her it was still there, Neighbour Kevin and Mr Salim Yusuf came out of their house. They were talking and laughing about something, and Neighbour Kevin patted Mr Salim Yusuf on the arm as he opened the car.

Mr Salim Yusuf spotted him watching and waved; Neighbour Kevin turned around and waved as well.

"We're buying you new boots tomorrow!" Mr Salim Yusuf called.

Normally it made Oliver feel much better when his neighbours waved and smiled at him, but today it just made him feel worse.

*****

When Oliver lay down to sleep that night, Daddy came in and looked at his books and said they were garbage for brainwashing children into believing lies and went out again without reading any. He smelled of wine, so Oliver wasn't as sorry as he should have been that Daddy didn't want to read to him.

Mummy didn't come in at all.

Oliver rolled over onto his side and looked at his window. It faced the wrong way to look at Neighbour Kevin's and Mr Salim Yusuf's house, so he couldn't see if the fairy lights were shiny. Instead, he could just see the orange light through the slit in the curtains. Behind the curtains was the garden and the fence, then the road, and then a long way behind that there was the moor, which he mostly couldn't even see in the day anyway because of the rain.

He lay on his side and thought about how sometimes he'd rather live absolutely anywhere but in the house where lived.

Then he rolled over to look at the ceiling in case any glow-in-the-dark stars had grown there despite what his parents wanted, but they hadn't.

Then he looked at the floor at the end of his bed and there was a full-sized horse.

Oliver shoved his hand over his mouth to cover up the little yelp of surprise that came out of him.

It was really the size of the ponies he sometimes saw up on the moor, but instead of being a dirty dark brown it was a washed out kind of white, like a plastic bag trapped under water, and it still looked a bit like a My Little Pony toy, but also a bit like the long wet bog grass for its hair, and a bit like the slimy fungus growing on the fallen black tree he'd seen, and its feet were dirty, and it smelled like farts.

You know your mother wouldn't be angry with you if you just kept a better eye on your things, the pony toy said inside his head.

Oliver didn't feel he could really argue with that. He let his hand fall off his mouth.

And your father wouldn't be angry with her anymore if she wasn't angry about your missing boot, said the pony toy, inside his head.

Oliver was less sure about that. Daddy was often angry about all kinds of things. It was because of his job, Mummy said; Oliver had asked him once if he would like to do a job that didn't make him angry all the time and Daddy had sneered at him and said *would you like to live in a bin or a council flat, Oliver? Because that's what happens to poor people who don't work in jobs like mine, and that's what's going to happen to you and that bitch when I finally leave.*

He looked at the way the light from the slice between the curtains fell over the back of the pony. It looked wet, not like it had been out in the rain but like it had been underwater.

Come and get your boot back, said the pony toy's voice, inside his head. The pony toy looked at him with flat eyes like painted on discs and its hair wobbled a bit. *Come and get your boot and your mother and father will be happy again.*

Oliver hesitated, and he lifted the corner of the covers.

Don't be selfish, the pony toy voice in his head said. *Think about how they must feel putting up with you losing things all the time.*

He got out of bed. The floor felt like a very long way down and the bedroom wasn't very warm when he was only wearing his dinosaur pyjamas.

The pony knelt down.

Oliver struggled onto its back. He'd never been on a pony before, so he wasn't very sure if they were meant to feel cold and slightly slippery. It seemed rude to ask.

He wondered how they were going to get out of the house without disturbing Mummy and Daddy— who would *not* like the marks the pony was leaving on the carpet— but before he'd even thought it, they were outside on the lawn.

It was very cold and damp outside. If he craned his head now, he could just about see Neighbour Kevin's house and the tiny arch of fairy lights around each of the windows, like shining eyes on a smiling face…

None of that, the pony said. It started to move.

The dirty cold pony with hair like wet grass went so fast that the neighbourhood slithered away like rain off a window. Oliver was scared at first that he would fall off, but no matter how much he moved around, he seemed to stay stuck to the spot.

It didn't really make him feel better. It was very cold, and even with the big full moon it was very dark, and now that they were on the moor again. So fast. It was quiet and strange and scary.

"I want to go home," he said.

Without your boots? the pony asked. *Have fun walking home.*

Oliver said nothing.

They went through the dark of the plantation. Even the moon was invisible, except for the place with the cut down trees: there it reflected off the pale wood and made the stumps look like eyes staring at him in the night.

Something went *eek week* in the dark.

Oliver shivered and tried to hold onto the pony for comfort, but it just made his hands wet.

They passed the stone wall.

The moon touched the water. The tiny flame was still dancing on the surface of the pond beyond the fallen slimy tree.

It's at the bottom, said the pony, splashing into the farty-smelling water. *You'll have to swim.*

Oliver clung to the pony. "I don't know how to swim."

The water was up to his feet. He didn't remember it being so deep that it would swallow half a pony. Maybe it was all the rain.

Oliver raised up his feet, but the pony went even deeper.

That's okay, said the pony. *You only have to go down. It's easy. Get your boot.*

Oliver noticed they'd passed under the tree. The water crept up to where his knees had been.

He stood up on the pony's back.

"My boot was further back," he said, turning around on the slippery fur in his bare feet. "I'm not allowed to go this far."

You only have to go down, the pony repeated. It went deeper into the water, until only its head was sticking out of the bog, and the freezing cold water touched Oliver's feet.

"It's very cold," said Oliver, shivering in his dinosaur pyjamas.

Then you should be quick, said the pony, without turning around. *Down you go.*

Oliver squatted down slowly into the cold, cold, water. It was like getting into the sea, he told himself. You just did it slowly a bit at a time, until you were used to it.

Mummy was probably going to be very angry with him for getting his pyjamas wet, but maybe she'd be happy when he came back with his missing boot.

The white light from the moon had turned the top of the water to silver. He could still see the little light dancing on the water, but it was almost invisible with all the moonlight around it.

The pony's head cast a sharp black shadow.

The water was up to Oliver's shoulders now. He took a deep breath and put his face slowly into the horrible, fart-smelling black water, and the cold seemed to tug him downwards.

He climbed slowly down off the pony's back.

And he went down.

And he went down.

And he went down deeper than he thought any bog could go.

On top of the silvery surface of the undisturbed waters of the moorland bog, a second flame of marsh gas ignited under the full moon, and there was silence.

THE INTELLECTUAL THEFT

by Ziaul Moid Khan

Abdul never stole a penny as far as it came to monetary gains; but when Balraj, his nephew, told him that Aapa-Bi had an iron box filled to its capacity with Urdu novels and magazines, he immediately asked Balraj to steal a couple of books only to return them later to their box, after, of course, a thorough reading. For he knew Aapa-Bi would never lend them a single piece out of her collection.

Though Aapa-Bi was an honest woman, a widow for years; yet try to borrow a book from her, and prompt would come her reply: "Abi Allah Mara, I don't have any!"

What Balraj needed the most was a nod from Abdul, and now he'd got it. He at once launched himself into an operation mode. The mission was not impossible. No *Tom Cruise* was needed for this job. The work was easy. And he knew quite well how to dodge the silver haired old woman.

A voracious reader who commanded a refined taste of books, Aapa-Bi lived alone in a palatial mud house. A religious woman. She prayed five times a day. Other times, she'd read Holy Koran, sitting on a wooden *takht* placed in the middle of her three-pillared verandah. Her spare time was spent reading some Urdu romance or mystery, or horror or a mix of all these elements.

But a legend was rife in the village—her house was haunted. Spirits and apparitions roamed around there. In fact, Aapa-Bi was an unflinching lady. They say, one night she was so disturbed by some supernatural presence, she lit her old kerosene lantern, searched all nooks and corners of the haunted homestead thrice, swearing and scolding the invisible spirits. When found none, she climbed up the roof of the dilapidated house and made a thorough investigation there, too.

Next day she said to her neighbor Jamila, "Abi Allah Mara, the *boys* did not let me sleep last night." The message flared up in the village like a forest fire. Talk was: even phantoms were afraid of Aapa-Bi.

Thus, the house seemed to fit in the Gothic Victorian setting: weird, scary, ancient and with no electricity supply. Friends and relatives avoided visiting it after sundown. But Aapa-Bi perhaps had a way with ghosts. She would scold them, if needed, as mentioned above. Lived like a queen, though alone, yet happy with herself. A singular woman of her kind.

*****

As the mosque loudspeaker came to resurrection, and Hafiz Ji began to *azan* for the evening prayer, Balraj wore his shoes before he was off to accomplish his assigned task. Aapa-Bi's place was not far away. He had to take only four turns of the narrow village lanes to reach the (haunted) mud place. It actually belonged to *Bhaiya,* Aapa-Bi's only brother who worked and lived in Delhi, the national capital. Thus, the house was now under Aapa-Bi's patronage.

Shrouded under the evening shadows, the palatial place had an eerie feel. The spacious courtyard had sizeable plants of pomegranate, mahogany, thorny black roses and white lilies. Balraj tiptoed to the front yard. Aapa-Bi as expected was occupied in the evening prayer, sitting on the wooden *takht,* her back to Balraj as he crossed the yard and entered her study, the first room from right.

Finding the iron box was not a big deal. It was of a man's size lengthwise, and around four feet, widthwise. He withdrew from his trousers' right pocket a pencil torch and snapped it on. Its yellow glow was the shape of a fish. The box was ancient and rusty, fortunately not locked. He pulled up the lid and didn't require much force to open it. In a couple of seconds, he had the view of his life—a sea collection of wonderful titles: Mirza Ghalib, Mir Taki Mir, the Biographies of Genghis Khan, Timur, Napoleon and Alexander of Macedonia.

Balraj was mesmerized by the great collection of hundreds of books in neat piles side by side. But Aapa-Bi might finish the *Namaz* any moment and return. He had to make it fast. Abdul's suggestion was to fetch only fiction, and no non-fiction, at all. Therefore, ignoring a great number of wonderful memoires and chronologies, he picked up some random paperback Urdu titles: *Khoya Hua Jazeera,*

Manasgan, Foladi Shikanja, Maut Ka Panja, Hanste Jakham, Purane Kile Ka Bashinda and a few issues of Mashuka—a quarterly Urdu journal published from Saharanpur.

He put them on the room stool that stood beside the iron box, took out a polybag from his left pocket, and quickly stuffed the moth-eaten titles, one by one, into his satchel. As he was giving the final touches to this job, he felt movement of some sort inside the box. *A rodent perhaps*, he thought and quickly put the lid back to its former position.

Having finished his business with precision, he peeped out to see if it was safe to step out the study. To his horror, Aapa-Bi's prayer was over, and now she was folding the pulpit cloth. It was impossible to hoodwink and sneak away from there, unnoticed. A sound from inside the box again, but Balraj paid not much heed to it, for more than anything else now, he was concerned about sneaking away from the room.

Then there was a rescue voice, a woman's, not from inside the iron box but the call was from main entrance at the other end of the courtyard. "AAPA-BI!" The call was promptly attended. This was the only opportunity Balraj could avail. And he didn't miss it. No sooner did he see the old woman going to the other door, he dashed out.

*****

Abdul sat in his study as he went through the pile of books delivered to him. Balraj has his seat across the table as he looked on, seeking appreciation from the old fellow.

"Did anybody see you coming from her house?" said Abdul, turning the old yellow pages of *Toofan se Pahle*, an Urdu bestseller.

"It was difficult, but I managed to come out, inconspicuously."

"Great!"

Balraj wanted to tell Abdul about the weird ruckus from inside the iron box, but then let it go. It was such a trivial thing to discuss with the old man. The purpose was served. He was home with the books he wanted to bring. That was all.

It took them a fortnight to finish each book. Cover to cover. As they'd smelled the refined literature, they wanted more of it, that was their food. And more food was needed now.

*****

The first Sunday evening of the next month, Balraj got ready with the satchel of books to return and a pencil torch tucked into his right pants' pocket. No sooner did Hafiz ji finish his Azan from the loudspeaker of the mosque than Aapa-Bi stood on her pulpit cloth for prayer, Balraj walked confidently to her study crossing the courtyard filled with a night-scented jasmine incense. He took out his torch and pulled open the large box. He was accustomed to it.

Emptying his satchel, he laid the books he'd brought back on the floor, before he could set then inside the box. Still, he could not resist his temptation to have a look at the titles he'd like to pick this time. But his hands stopped midway, for the titles he had seen last time were all gone, replaced by a different set of books. New and glowing. How could it be possible? Aapa-Bi hardly went to the marketplace. Even if she went, she wouldn't buy so many books in one go.

Balraj frowned and piled his books in the left corner of the box. He selected some random new titles: *Arab ka Saudagar, Jal Pariyon ka Ashiq, Gunah Ek Katl Do, Masoom Firangi, Jasoos ka Katl, Murdon ki Basti, Bahu Beti aur Vo,* and *Safed Hatiyon ki Ghati.* He stuffed the titles into the satchel and turned back to shut down the box-lid. Something shook underneath that moved the rows of paperbacks.

For a long moment Balraj kept the lid held in his right hand, but then thought about the old woman outside. Her prayer must be about to conclude. He carefully closed the iron box and left.

Thankfully, she was still in prayer.

*****

"It seems there's something more in the iron box than the books, alone," Balraj said, putting the satchel on the head of the cot a couple of feet away where Abdul sat, smoking a Commander Cigarette.

"Speak plainly, don't cloud your statement," Abdul said, putting aside the hardcopy of *Begum Zubeda aur Heeron ka Haar* by *Mirza Ahmad Baig.*

"Beneath the books in the iron-box, something moves and shakes," said Balraj. "First I thought it to be mice but now I doubt it's more than that."

"Hmm! I see," said Abdul and became thoughtful for a few moments. Then he spoke again, "Can't you check it on your next visit?"

"How can I? There's only this much time I can select and pick some good titles."

"Who's asking you to bring books on the next visit? Just go and check what lies under the piles of books. But be wary, it may turn up some poisonous reptile, too."

*****

Balraj's next visit to Aapa-Bi's house was easier than the previous two visits. The timing of the prayer was perfect. He knew exactly when and how to enter *the chamber of secrets*. Only today he was more prepared than ever before, both mentally and physically.

While Aapa-Bi sat in her usual place to offer her prayers, Balraj opened the enormous Pandora box, some seven by four feet in girth. Though he was less interested in the speculative and romantic titles this time, but more in the *creature* hidden beneath the layered surface of Urdu magazines and novels.

Some fresh titles caught his casual sight: *Himmete Mardan, Kali Nagin ka Intekam, Shikari aur Shikar, Badshah aur Fakir, Tuta hua Pemana, Khatarnak Khel* and *Kabristan.*

Outside rain paltered on the roof. He perceived the overcast sky that brought darkness earlier than usual at dusk.

As Balraj switched on the torch, it spread a dim shaft across the box. Realized he'd have to replace its cells, which didn't have much life left in them. Therefore, the pencil torch did not seem suffice under the circumstances to explore the box. He repented for not bringing some big flashlight today. Life is unpredictable. Sudden things do happen and we have to face them impromptu.

He wanted to make it fast, for Aapa-Bi must've finished Namaz, and then who knew if she stepped into this room for some random errand. It was at this moment that there was ruffling underneath the piles of books. Hair rose on his neck and arms. The sound stopped too. He almost ran out of there, but the ruffling sound kept him rooted. He needed to know what lay beneath the works of authors.

Balraj clutched the torch between his set of teeth and picked up the books and magazines, setting them on the floor beside him. To reach the bottom of truth he needed to reach the bottom of the box.

His hands worked mechanically for the next couple of minutes. The moment he emptied the box, he was awestruck. Transfixed. Stood like an artistic statue.

The bottom of the box was not just the plain surface of rusted iron. It was a mammoth book in itself. Crimson hardcover. Written in jagged Arabic, in night-black ink, the bold raised letters read: TABOOT—which means a coffin. Half of the letters covered the first half of the cover-page, while the other half was covering the remaining width of the page.

The moment Balraj tried to touch the rough surface of the cover, the torch slipped off his teeth and landed on the monster book. The cover page flipped over itself and underneath where the dedication page should have been, came into view the last thing that Blaraj'd anticipated: a body covered in all white, perhaps…a shroud, starch neat. The torch light was still illuminating a slight portion of the interior.

The body stirred and sat up; the high bosom hinted it was a lady. The woman made a rummaging movement with her right hand. Next second her fingers gripped Balraj's torch. These fingers; skeletal thin; knuckles, white as petals of lilies; the nails and cuticles, long enough to have not been trimmed, it seemed for years. A cold shiver ran through his spine. The woman stood ramrod. Her face was a criss-cross of wrinkles from everywhere to everywhere. And silver-grey hair was pushing her to a hundred-year-old threshold. Despite the age, she remained steel strong and sane.

"Stealing is a horrible habit," she whispered and crawled out of the box

Her body parts could be perceived with a little effort. She was slender looking, of average height and her hair, untied, silver white akin to Aapa-Bi's. Her private parts could well be spotted, for she wore nothing else but the shroud.

"May I talk to you, my boy?" she whispered again.

She placed both her skeletal hands on his shoulders. It was a snowy touch, sending shivers again up to his spine. No longer could he keep his eyes open, and he sank to the ground. Heard his own collapse. A faint *thud*. And then he crossed to oblivion.

*****

How much time was passed, Balraj did not know. He felt like he stood in the rain staring at the coal black clouds. Cold drizzling rain-droplets paltering on his eyes and face. Then the moon appeared before him.

He closed his eyes, and when he reopened them, there was no moon and no drizzling rain. It was Aapa-Bi, holding her kerosene lantern in one hand and sprinkling water on his face from a little yellow plastic bucket that stood beside her.

"Abe Allah Mara, Balraj, what the devil were you doing in my study?" said Aapa Bi.

He sat up figuring what story he should cook and serve.

"I… just came over here to… ask you… a few Arabic… no… Persian words. You're a scholar, aren't you?"

Aapa-Bi gazed at him grimly.

He added to convince her, "Didn't find you around, so I thought to have a look at your collection. But… who…who was the woman in… white?"

"You've known today more than anyone ever did," she said and hesitated before making the revelation. "Let me tell you my boy: she was my mother! My words may challenge to your rationale." She locked the iron box with a big rusty latch. "I didn't bury her, rather laid her here in the box. As was *her* will."

"But how the holy shit did her body not contaminate? There seems to be no decay." Balraj barked, narrowing his thick brows.

She put the lantern on the lid of the mysterious iron box. "Do you believe in witchcraft?"

"No!"

"Then you're ignorant to the whole world of dark wizardry. My mother, Aapa, was a clandestine witch. She never told anyone—not even her husband. And through her magic, she made it so her body never decayed." Her potions enabled her body like this."

Balraj did not understand, still he was glued to her as if he was getting somewhere.

"It was her will," Aapa-Bi continued, "her body should be preserved after she is gone. So, I did as I was instructed."

*****

Aapa-Bi now sat on her wooden *Takht* made of Mahogany. Reclining over her pillow, she took out a string of beads, white as pearls. Read some *aayat*—a verse from the Holy Koran.

For a wee while, she remained pensive, then parted her eyes like saucers. Stared for a long while into the vacuum. There was vicious glitter in them as she muttered undertone, "I know… now… I know… who sent you *here*… it's Abdul… wasn't it?"

Balraj was not sure, to respond a yes or a no.

"The curse of my mother will befall on you both," she added.

"WHAT CUR-CURSE?" Blarjaj barked, his feet trembling.

"Your sender will die a madman, and you Balraj… no woman will take interest in you… ever."

"What rubbish…?" said Balraj. "How can you be so callous, Aapa-Bi? Uncle, just sent me here to fetch some books only to return them undamaged. No harm done."

"All sins have their rewards."

"You're just faking. Curses aren't real."

"You will find out soon. Now, away with you," said Aapa-Bi, closing her eyes.

The paltering of the rain had slowed down as Balraj stepped out, musing over the weird curse. It was already night and he had to use the torch to find his way. Baffled to his wits he trudged along the wet street, homeward.

*****

Abdul looked haggard as Balraj sensed something wrong in his manners.

"Uncle, are you okay?" he said.

"Yes, fine," Abdul said. "Just tell me if you found there anything substantial?"

The boy told the old man everything he'd experienced at Aapa-Bi's place.

"Hmm!" Abdul said. "This Budhiya is far more bizarre than our anticipation."

It was still raining. The old man and the young man sat together in the former's verandah and discussed the prospects. Fatima, Abdul's wife served them tea with Parley-G biscuits.

"Aapa Bi has just given a hollow threat," said Balraj, lifting up the cup of tea. "Uncle, better we need not be worried."

"A witch's curse will have to be thwarted with some counter magic," Abdul said, sipping his tea. "Or we're in the soup."

"Maybe she was faking," Balraj said, putting his cup back in the plastic tray beside them and picking up a biscuit.

"She was not," Abdul said, his eyes fixed at a vulture, that had just perched on top of the neem tree in the yard. "See, *gidh* the vulture. A bad omen."

Balraj looked at the big bird that was fluttering its strong feathers. Said nothing. He was not superstitious. But knew well, Abdul could not be wrong in his perceptions.

"I've never practiced Sifli ilm, but it exists," said Abdul, taking another sip of his tea.

"What the devil is Sifli ilm?" Balraj said, his eyes still on the vulture.

"The base form of occult practices," Abdul clarified.

"Come in with me!" He finished his tea and stood up from the cot. Balraj could not say where. He too put down his cup and followed Abdul like an obedient pupil.

They reached Abdul's study. A rectangle shaped room of the ancient mud house.

The old man struck a match and lit a kerosene lamp. Ghastly yellow light spread squarely across the room. Two doors in the left of it opened into the drawing room; while the straight front one led to the last chamber that made a T-shape of the house.

The room had two boxes; the first one was a dowry gift—a king size wooden armoire. The second was an obsidian iron box with a latch but no lock. It contained most of Abdul's books. Hundreds of them. As the old man hinted; Balraj released the latch and lifted the lid of it. It was filled to its ridges. All types of reading material.

Balraj grabbed the top book—the Kamasutra. The cover was of two statues in a compromising position, a wild contortion. It was weird to imagine sex could be done in this way, too.

Abdul snatched it abruptly and put it away on the charpoy positioned just opposite. He handed Balraj the kerosene lamp, withdrew a chair and sat himself in it, its two legs moth ravaged. He started a search.

"A counter-black-spell is necessary under the circumstances," repeated Abdul, putting the book in hand at the edge of the jute-charpoy and picking up some books from the left of the rugged iron box.

Balraj looked on, holding the kerosene fueled lantern in hand. The muscles of his face twitched, in bewilderment, as Abdul withdrew from the box a human skull. Looked at it as if with appreciation. A mannerism to negotiate a talk with it.

"Uncle, where did you get this…skull from?" he muttered, eyes fixed at the human remnant.

"Long story, Ballu," said Abdul, wiping it with a dusting cloth. "But in short, it was a gift from an Aghori Sadhu, who claimed to have once dug an ancient grave to retrieve it from a cemetery. Let's test its power tonight."

Balraj felt uncanny wiping the cold skull. Its grin was giving quivers up to his spine. He wanted to ask more questions but kept a mum as Uncle Abdul was still busy searching in the box, a faint smile on his face. Then he pulled out a black leather-bound book titled *Witches' Blood and Witchcraft*.

*****

The drawing room had two wooden gates connecting it to the master bedroom, and three wooden doors that opened out to the *garhi*—the kuccha Rasta leading to the link road and its bridge over the large village pond.

In the center was a phantom table surrounded by a dozen wooden chairs. The rectangle room had still space enough to accommodate a dozen more people. Two closets of 5x3 were fixed in the opposite mud walls of this chamber. Both of them contained books on various subjects ranging from palmistry to alchemy, history to spiritualism. The cabinets also contained some different size bottles of serums.

The floor looked like pure mud, but strong like marble tiles. At the far end near the third door, Abdul made a circle with a chalk, in the center of which he drew a hexagon shape. Kindled seven tappers and positioned them at the frontier of the circle in a half-moon shape. He sat himself in such a way the eerie hexagon was facing his hands that held the book of dark magic, *Witches' Blood and Wizardry.*

In the middle of the room there was a rectangular wooden table. On both sides there were a set of four chairs. Balraj sat in the second chair on the right of the table. Balraj was the solitary spectator, looking down at Abdul who wore a long black gown on this occasion. Apart from the tappers lined on the circle the other source of the light in the room was the kerosene powered lamp positioned in the middle of the table.

"There, Ballu," said Abdul, hinting toward the almirah to his right. "You'll find a craned shaped bottle. Find and fetch it to me."

Balraj went up to the closet. He gave the wooden doors a little pull and they gave way. A cloud of putrid decay and dust swarmed him, and it was all he could do not to gag. The top two shelves were stuffed with books as big as dictionaries. Most of them moth eaten. Ravaged. The third shelf from above that came to his chest height was a mess with bottles of varying sizes and colors.

He spotted the black, crane-shaped bottle filled with a thick glossy liquid—God knows what it was.

Balraj dared not ask. He grasped it, closed the doors and silently gave it to the old man.

Right beside the hexagon Abdul positioned an *Angithi*, the brazier. He put a few dry billets into it, uncapped the crane shaped bottle, poured the red glossy liquid on the wooden pieces. Finally, he lit the match, and the fire came alive.

Balraj wiped the dust on it with the corner of his checkered shirt. The surface shone crystal clear like the waters of a mountain lake. He saw his reflection. Tongue in cheek. Unlike a common looking glass, it showed things beyond. Balraj felt like watching his own soul.

The hatred inside him for people. The jealousy. The lust in him for young girls. Bad wishes to tear their clothes apart and suck their tits and doing more horrible things with them. Watching them naked and fucking them all. He could not keep on looking for more than four seconds. He'd never realized his head carried such filthy thoughts.

Abdul put the mirror on his right and Balraj positioned the table lamp inside the circle. The old man opened the book of occult practices and read aloud:

"Rabbin Sunni Alla, komal kafrin,
Rabbin sunni alla, komal mursadin,
Rabbin sunni alla Mukid hijran,
Rabbin sunni alla, Aapa-Bi ka fallan…!"

His one hand held the skull and other one kept the book of dark magic open. The old man repeated the weird spell. Twice, thrice, fourth time, fifth time, sixth time, seventh time… hundredth time… and then Balraj lost the counting.

The flames in the *Angithi* leaped up monstrously. Balraj added some more billets to the flamed ones at Abdul's gesture. The old occultist poured more liquid from the crane shaped bottle. More flames lengthened. The tappers were, by now, finishing, giving the last glow of their light.

This time Balraj saw the process more minutely. The glossy liquid was crimson red. A realization dawned upon him: might it be a witch's blood? He shivered at the very thought if it was really… a witch's blood as Abdul repeated *Rabbin sunni alla...*

*****

It was close to midnight. An owl hooted somewhere out. Balraj's eyes were getting heavy with fatigue and sleep. Abdul's chanting was getting rougher and slower than before. Bed never seemed so tempting as it did right then for Balraj.

But then three things happened one after another:

Two enormous black bats came from nowhere and hovered just overhead. All the doors were closed. They seemed to have materialized from the *Angithi* flames.

The second thing was the rattling sound Balraj first thought was that of Abdul's, but it was not. The sound originated from the rattling teeth of the skull. Sleep divorced Balraj as he sat upright. His gaze fixed at the skull that appeared to have been resurrected. Leaving his chair, he stood beside Abdul. Though the young man was still out of the circle.

The third was worse than the first two. As the occultist finally put the ghost skull in fire, the blazing flames rose as high as the ceiling. Followed by a familiar voice: "Stop it, you Lucifer!"

For a moment Balraj could not know the source of the shout. Then he could not believe it. The gothic mirror had produced this sound. The reflection showed a woman. Aapa-Bi's mummified mother. "Stop it now, or burn in hell!"

"—Rabbin Sunni alla Aapa-Bi ka fallan," continued Abdul.

Balraj turned white like a shroud. Two hands protruded out from the ancient mirror. Abdul reclined back, but it was too late by then. They grasped his head, firmly, and pulled it toward the looking glass. Like a trapped animal, the occultist tried to free himself, but in vain. Balraj felt too powerless to help his mate. He stood frozen, like a statue.

The dead hands of the undead old witch proved to be stronger than the physical strength of the living old man. The looking glass shattered with the blasting collision. The shards of the glass pierced into Abdul's skull. Mini streams of blood oozed out from half a dozen places. The bloody witch disappeared with the shattering of the magic mirror. Now it was Abdul's blood, which was emblazing the fire in the brazier.

The bats hovering over their heads had multiplied. Now they were four. Six. Two dozen. Chasing one another without physically touching. Abdul caught hold of his head and screeched hysterically as Balraj looked on. Shocked. His senses numb.

A storm was gathering out, the mad winds pushing the doors. The latches gave way and the middle one was flung open. The fire in the *Angithi* was furious, blazing in all directions.

Abdul forced himself to stand up, struggled, stumbled and tripped over the brazier. His long black gown caught the fire flames. The winds flared it up. He rushed out in the *garhi*. As if from a slumber, Balraj shook his head and ran after the occultist. The old man ran helter-skelter, now his whole body in flames. Balraj behind him.

Finding no option to save his life, the occultist ran toward the main road. He reached there in no time and plunged from the mini-bridge into the old village pond. The fire doused. Balraj halted for a couple of seconds. The pond water under the bridge was pitch dark. He was not sure where Abdul had thrown himself. The night was silent as death. And no stars shone tonight.

He faintly heard the bubbling like the water-sound when someone drowns. Not much time was there to waste. Not even time enough to come out of the clothes. He dived, head forward.

Down there under the bridge—black stale water welcomed him. All the village houses drained in this pond their shit and piss and toilet waste. Balraj fished around, found polyethene, plastic bottles and nameless filthy things.

Then realized, he'd have to go deeper to locate Abdul precisely. Deeper he went. First to his right, then to his left. Forward and backward. The old man seemed to have vanished. Balraj came up to catch some breath and then repeated the pattern. For around five minutes he explored blindly before his fingers touched the toes of Abdul.

Balraj gave his uncle a push upward. Nosed out. Held his hand tightly and dragged the drowning man toward the bank of the pond. He feared the body might go inside again. To avoid that he kept Abdul to the side until he fished him out. Panting and huffing he found the old man's wrist to check his pulse, but the occultist was soulless now.

Balraj cried in the pitch-dark night. The black bats were circling overhead in the open sky. The villagers, with torches and lanterns in their hands, began to gather around the body.

Someone whispered, "What happened?"

Someone answered, "Fatima became a widow tonight."

"Poor woman!" a third villagers said.

"But how did it all happen?" a fourth villager asked.

There was no answer. Just silence persisted.

"End"

THE LITANY THAT WAS ONCE RECITED TO HER

by J.D. Harlock

The cold night had stretched on for longer than anyone in the lone cottage could remember. Windows had been bolted up with whatever the family could get their hands on, and every single hole and crack in the makeshift roof was carefully blocked off with leftover pots and pans. Those who believed it was better to sleep through the whole affair, retired early, hoping rest would ease their minds, but they found little comfort in the straw beds and animal-skin pillows they now had to get accustomed to.

This left Umm Kamila humming old childhood hymns while her granddaughter Nahla fidgeted with a contraption she'd found during the last scavenge with the village children. Neither seemed to have much to say to the other in the hours that had passed in shared solitude, and this is how they would have carried on as the storm raged had Nahla not finally tired of playing with the broken gears that once captivated her. Instead, she walked over to her grandmother seated on a cushion of old clothes by the fire dying in the hearth and, without saying a word, lay down in her lap as she used to when she was younger. Now staring out the window that was facing them, Nahla pondered the world around her…

"Teta," Nahla said, ending the silence that had subdued them that night. "I was wondering."

"Yes, *habibiti*," Umm Kamila replied, ruffling gently through her hair. "What is it you want to ask?"

"If our world is suspended in space…"

Umm Kamila raised an eyebrow. "Yes?"

"… what's to keep it from falling into the abyss?"

"Oh, my," Umm Kamila chuckled, extending her arms out to the heavens. "Why, an angel, of course."

Nahla's eyes widened. "An angel?"

"Yes, an angel that shoulders the world with its magnificent wings." Umm Kamila now spread her arms. "Wings that span the Earth from pole to pole!"

Nahla rose from her grandmother's lap. "But what does this angel stand on?"

"This angel stands on a slab of the finest gemstone," Umm Kamila responded.

"A slab of gemstone?" Nahla wasn't sure what to make of this. "Is there a reason it stands on gemstone, in particular, Teta? Wouldn't steel be sturdier?"

"That's not for me to answer." Umm Kamila smiled. But, for once, it seemed forced, strained even. "Don't you want to know what supports the slab?"

Nahla, who still wanted an answer to her prior question, nodded. "What supports the slab?"

Umm Kamila moved her hand so that the back brushed against her lip, and her fingers seemed to protrude out of her like some strange appendage.

"Kuyutha, of course."

"Ku-yu-tha?" Nahla tried to pronounce the name, but it felt foreign to her tongue — as if it was from another culture she couldn't understand. "Kuyutha." She muttered again, and picking up on her granddaughter's perplexion, Umm Kamila feigned shock.

"You don't know of Kuyutha?!" she exclaimed, then leaned over to tear off a cog from a rusted machine and tossed it into the fire. "Now, where were we? You don't know of Kuyutha!"

"No, Teta." Nahla shook her head with a look of embarrassment. "What is it?"

"My child." A zeal was now palpable in the old woman's voice. "Kuyutha is the cosmic beast with forty thousand horns and forty thousand legs and as many eyes, ears, mouths, and tongues!"

"Forty thousand horns, legs, eyes, ears, mouths, and tongues?" Nahla's voice shook with unease. "How tall is it, Teta?"

Umm Kamila raised her hand as far as she could.

"The Kuyutha's horns are said to reach the Throne of God itself, entangling it like a crown of thorns." She then flailed her arms about, losing herself in the wonder of it all. "Its nose is in our seas, the two nostrils pinned against holes in the slab of gemstone, enabling it to breathe, and when it breathes once a day—the seas rise and ebb!"

Umm Kamila then arched her back, praising God in all His majesty, as the thunder outside suddenly sounded so much louder to Nahla. Strange thoughts coursed through her young mind—so wild was the image she had conjured that she felt shaken by the sheer madness of it all. To think that the world around her could be filled with such marvel.

"Does Kuyutha alone carry us?" she finally dared to ask, her curiosity getting the best of her again.

"No *habibiti*, Kuyutha is carried by the Bahamut," Umm Kamila chuckled again with an eye on the storm outside. "and before you ask, the Bahamut itself is suspended in endless water for its own stability."

"But if Kuyutha is so big, how can the Bahamut carry it?"

Umm Kamila pinched Nahla's nose.

"The seas of the world, placed in one of that fish's nostrils, would be but a heap of sand in the desert. That's how on its back, it can carry a beast, an angel, and the rest of the universe, including six hells, the earth, and the heavens."

Nahla was at a loss for words. "Why would God create all this?"

"Nahla, before this, the earth tossed and turned without rhyme or reason," Umm Kamila avowed, thanking God silently, then gazed down at her granddaughter, who seemed transfixed by whatever was happening outside those windows. "Like all of his creations, these creatures were gifted to us by God to bring us peace."

"Peace?" Nahla glanced up at her grandmother wearily. "How?"

"Not only do they stabilize our world, but when they quench their thirst with our seas, they hinder the rising tide and prevent our world from drowning in its own waters."

"My God!" Nahla whispered to herself, for she could say nothing else.

"God is great." Umm Kamila nodded in affirmation.

"But we aren't," Nahla muttered.

"Nahla…" Umm Kamila held her granddaughter's hand, noticing for the first time how small and coarse it was. "Oh, what's become of the world."

Nahla smiled as best she could. "That can't be all of it, can it, Teta?"

Umm Kamila raised her eyebrow again. "What do you mean, *habibiti*?"

"There's always more," Nahla muttered to herself. "Is there anything underneath the Bahamut?"

"Oh yes, my dear." The old woman forced a mischievous smile. "But do you really want to know?"

Nahla went silent, wondering for the first time in her life if it would be better not to. But her grandmother carried on, hoping to lighten the mood.

"Beneath the Bahamut is the great serpent Falak, residing in the seventh circle of Hell." Umm Kamila playfully moved her hand towards Nahla's face and clasped it before her as a predator's jaw would before its prey. "So great is the Falak that it is said that it could devour our world whole."

"You mean: our world could end?"

Umm Kamila caressed her granddaughter's cheek and smiled.

"Yes, all things must end. But worry not, my child. That will not happen anytime soon, as I assure you the Falak will never be the one to consume us."

The old woman then moved to embrace her granddaughter. Nahla asked her in the faintest of whispers, "How are you sure of that?"

"Why, its fear of God the Almighty, All-Knowing, and Most-Merciful prevents it from doing so, of course."

Nahla took a deep breath, trying to calm herself down before her grandmother added, "And as you know, God will always be with us."

"Teta," Nahla suddenly found it hard to speak. "How do you know all of this?"

"My child, these are the stories that have been passed down to us from the very beginning," Umm Kamila recited the litany that had been recited to her once upon a time, only to pause for a moment and lament: "And these stories will be with us until the very end."

A moment of silence passed, one that felt like an eternity to young Nahla, who now found it hard to breathe.

"But Teta," She finally broke that silence, her eyes widening with fear as she glanced over at the storm raging past her windows, "if the Kuyutha and the Bahamut are nourished with the Earth's water…"

"Yes?"

"What happens now that we have tainted it with our machines?"

Umm Kamila took a deep breath—one she hoped would not end—only to find herself holding on to her granddaughter with all her might.

"Teta?" Nahla asked once more when the fire in the hearth finally died down. "What will happen to us?"

But all she could tell her was: "It's best not to think about it, my love…"

NOTE: Bahamut and Kuyutha are mythological figures described in 'Aja'ib al-Makhluqat wa Ghara'ib al-Mawjudat: عجائب المخلوقات وغرائب الموجودات *(Wonders of the Creation and Unique [phenomena] of Existence), by cosmographer and geographer Zakariya al-Qazwini, born in Qazwin, Iran, in 1203 AD.*

DINNER PARTY

by Samantha Brooke

Martha Shaw drew her car to a halt outside the elegant townhouse and sat for a moment, gazing up at it. A sigh escaped her lips. She had not wanted to come this evening. She had barely been out at all since *it* had happened. But then, earlier that day, her friend Lauren had telephoned her and insisted that she go to the dinner party that Lauren was hosting at her house that evening.

"Oh, no, I don't think so," Martha had protested feebly. "I really don't feel like going out."

"Nonsense," Lauren had replied briskly. "None of your friends have seen you for months now. You've been living like some old hermit ever since you and Charles separated. You can't stay cooped up at home forever." Her voice had turned wheedling then. "Look, it'll only be a small gathering, I promise. And you won't have to make any boring small talk. You can just sit next to me, and I'll tell you all about the new man that I've found for you. He's perfect, honestly. He's a member of my gym. You should see his body, talk about scrumptious! I swear, if I weren't already happily married then I'd be snatching him up for myself!"

Martha's heart had sunk. It seemed that her friend was not going to take no for an answer. "I'm busy this evening," she'd tried.

"Busy with what?" Lauren had responded, quick as a flash. "You haven't been doing anything at all lately. Which is just why you need to come to this dinner party and start getting yourself back out there again."

"Maybe some other time. I didn't want to say anything, but I'm actually feeling a bit under the weather."

"Stop making excuses. You're coming. End of story."

Martha had known then that she was fighting a losing battle. Lauren had always had an extremely forceful personality, so when she decided something was going to happen, it happened. And Martha really did not have the energy to argue with her.

"Okay?"

"Okay."

"Great!" her friend trilled. "I'll see you at seven."

And so now, here she was. She stared up at the house for a few moments longer. She had dithered for so long whilst getting ready that she knew she must be the last one to arrive. The lights in the house were all ablaze, the golden hue spilling out onto the wet pavement below, making it glimmer. She suppressed a groan at the thought of the long, tedious hours which stretched before her. And the questions from well-meaning friends and acquaintances about how she was, what she'd been doing. Questions which she would certainly not be able to answer honestly. She wished that she had resisted Lauren's pushing a bit harder, but it was too late now. She had made it this far, after all. So, she might as well just grit her teeth, go inside, and get this over with.

She unclipped her seatbelt and opened the car door, a rush of cold air assailing her as she did so. The temperature had dropped so low that the water on the ground was turning rapidly to ice. She picked her way carefully over patches of it, her high heels clacking upon the concrete. She shivered and huddled deeper into her coat as she quickly climbed up the steps that led to her friend's house. She was eager to be inside now, if only to get away from the biting cold.

She reached the top and rang the bell. She felt a flutter of nervousness as she waited for the door to open.

"Martha!" Lauren wrenched open the door and greeted her like she was a long-lost family member. "How absolutely wonderful it is to see you." She enveloped her in a hug and ushered her inside before closing the door. "Gosh, what a filthy night it is out there."

"Yes," Martha replied, already shrugging out of her coat. She could hear the sounds of music, laughter, and the general murmur of voices in conversation from deeper inside the house.

"Here, let me take that for you." Lauren took

the coat and hung it up on a peg beside a dozen or so others. Martha's eyes fell upon one in particular. A dark brown, suede one which looked awfully similar to the one that her husband always wore. *Ex-husband*, she reminded herself bitterly. But surely not - surely Lauren would not have done this to her...

"Lauren, is that Charles's coat?"

Lauren put in, seeing where Martha's gaze was. She bit her lip, looking guilty. "Yes, it is."

Martha reached to retrieve her own coat.

"I'm sorry. Really." Lauren hurried on. "I had no idea that he was coming until he turned up ten minutes ago. Patrick invited him, I forgot to tell him that you were coming, and we just got our wires crossed."

"And you didn't think to call and tell me?" Martha demanded. "I never would have come if I'd known that Charles was going to be here. You must have known that."

"Well - you're here now, though," Lauren said defiantly. "And you know, maybe it'll even do you some good. You were always going to have to see him again sometime. Tonight, you can just get it over with once and for all and then move on."

"Yeah - because it's that easy, isn't it?" Martha snapped.

'I'm not saying it's easy.' Lauren's voice became

gentle, the expression on her face sympathetic yet firm. 'But it has been almost a year now.'

Martha opened her mouth to respond, but before she could do so, another figure emerged into the pristine hallway.

"Martha, so glad you could make it!"

"Hello, Patrick."

"Everybody's just having drinks in the living room. Come on through and join us. Sarah was just asking after you, actually."

Feeling sick with apprehension, Martha was left with no choice but to follow him, Lauren trailing closely at her heels. No doubt to ensure that she didn't turn around and try to make a last-minute break for it.

She held her breath as Patrick led her into the living room and then announced to the room at large, "Hey, everyone, look who's here!"

The murmur of conversations died away as faces turned towards her - all of them smiling and welcoming, but nevertheless Martha was cringing inwardly. She felt like she wanted to turn and run out of there like a shy schoolgirl fleeing an assembly. Or for a hole to open up at her feet and swallow her. Anything to get away from all of those eyes that were turned upon her.

"Martha!" Sarah cried, rushing over to hug her. "How wonderful to see you, it feels like it's been absolutely ages. How are you? You're looking well, you look nice and slim, anyway. Have you taken up a new exercise regime?"

Nope, I just have no appetite and can barely manage to force myself to eat these days.

She simply shrugged in an 'oh, you know' kind of a way, and hoped that would be the end of the subject. Thankfully, at that moment Lauren came up to them and pressed a glass of Chardonnay into Martha's hands. She took a sip gratefully, hoping that it would help to fortify her nerves. She glanced around the room, relieved to see that most people had now returned to their previous conversations. Although, now and then, she could see a few of them flashing curious looks over at her. She knew that her absence from all social gatherings for an entire year had caused much speculation amid their social group. Lauren had told her so many times, during the weekly phone calls to Martha which she had insisted on making. Perhaps, Martha reflected now, she had been too harsh on Lauren. As caught up in her own problems as she had been, she hadn't really appreciated her friend's loyalty and concern towards her. She ought to be grateful. It was true that Lauren could be rather insensitive at times, but her heart was always in the right place, and she was only doing what she genuinely believed was best for Martha. Even if Martha herself did not quite agree.

"Dinner will be in about ten minutes," Lauren announced. Martha took another gulp of her wine. Unused to drinking alcohol as she had now become,

she could already feel the effects of it spreading throughout her body. "The caterers have done a lovely job. Of course, they're not at all cheap - but it's really...
"

Martha did not hear any more. She seemed to have become temporarily deaf but for the high-pitched ringing which had started up in her ears. She had spotted him at once as he wandered through the living room door, drink in hand, and made a beeline for where Patrick stood beside the mantlepiece. Martha felt her stomach plummet as though she were on an impossibly high roller coaster that had just reached the top and was now hurtling back towards the ground at a thousand miles an hour. Nausea rose up within her and for a moment she really thought she was going to be sick - especially when she saw with a jolt that he was not on his own. There was a woman beside him - a beautiful woman, obviously younger than Martha was, with stunning golden hair and curves in all the right places. As Charles came to a halt to speak to Patrick, the woman clutched at his arm possessively and pressed her body close to his.

Martha choked. "Who is that?"

Lauren glanced over her shoulder to see who it was that Martha was referring to. She gave a very awkward little laugh. She and Sarah exchanged a look before she replied, "That's just Anna. She's a friend of Charles's."

"A friend?" Martha breathed. "Funny. It looks like more than that to me." Her eyes were still fixed unblinkingly upon the woman. A hot, bubbling rage was searing through her chest now, every muscle in her body becoming tightly clenched.

Stop, a voice in her head said warningly. *This is too dangerous. You need to get out of here. Get out of here before you lose control of yourself.*

But these words were completely drowned out, obliterated by the roar of jealousy that pulsed through her blood, blinding and deafening her to everything else.

"How long has he been seeing her?"

A heavy, uncomfortable silence met her words.

"HOW LONG?!"

A ringing silence followed. Once again, she was acutely aware of the fact that all heads were turning in her direction. Only this time, she didn't care. Let them look! In a moment, they would all have something to look *at*.

"Martha!" Through the haze of fury, she heard Charles's voice ringing out. He stepped towards her and she saw his face clearly amidst the blur that now surrounded her. She registered the look of surprise upon his face. "I wasn't expecting to see you. I mean, it's good to see you. How have you been?"

Before she could even try to formulate a response, another voice piped up.

"Charles, darling, aren't you going to introduce

me?" Anna's voice simpered, the sound was like nails on a chalkboard to Martha, her lips drew back into an angry snarl, and she knew then that it was already too late to try and prevent what was about to happen.

"AAHH!"

Screams filled the air as she transformed - her body growing stronger, more muscular, covered in coarse hair. Her teeth grew deadly sharp, her face lengthening into a snout. Growls rumbled from deep within her chest as she saw people scramble towards the doorway in flight. But she was much too quick for them. One leap and she had blocked the only exit. The window was too high to jump from. She had them all had her mercy now In an instant, she had her gaze narrowed in on Anna and had reached out and grabbed the awful woman before she had a chance to move.

The woman let out an ear-splitting scream as Martha's claws dug into her flesh while she dragged her victim closer. Her movements were swift, unhesitant as she bared her teeth and plunged them into the woman's throat - ignoring the cacophony of panicked shouts and screams that were rising anew as she did so. The stench of the woman's perfume was replaced by the sweet scent of blood - filling Martha's senses as she bit down, again and again, as hard as she could. *Why* had she been denying herself this for so long? It felt good. *She* felt good. Strong and powerful. Invincible. Nobody could get in her way. Nobody could stop her.

She dropped Anna's limp body onto the floor,

the head almost completely severed from the body. Terror was palpable in the air as the people all around began pushing at each other - some still trying to run, others grabbing whatever makeshift weapons they could find to try and use against her. She swiped at them at random, feeling her claws tear through flesh, blood spurting as she slashed. Screams filled the air, bodies dropping to the ground. Patrick lunged at her, poker held aloft in his hand. She casually reached out, struck him hard across the face, and then sank her teeth deep into his throat. His yells became mere gurgles as he choked pathetically on his own blood. She heard Lauren's sobs, the sound was immensely loud and irritating to her - so she turned to her next, blood dripping from her mouth as she opened it and prepared to strike again...

*****

Her eyes fluttered open and she looked around, her gaze bleary and bloodshot. She was slumped in a sitting position against the wall, her legs drawn up tight to her chest, and the room around her in utter carnage. They were dead. All of them. Dead. She had killed them. Just one moment, one instant of letting her emotions get the better of her, and this was the result. Bitter tears of grief and remorse fell from her eyes. Her vision seemed to burn red, as though she were crying tears of blood. Maybe she was. She was certainly covered in the stuff - as was everything else in the vicinity.

She took a shuddering breath and staggered upright, her hand pressed against the wall for support,

151

trying not to look at the mauled bodies of her victims which lay scattered all around. Poor Lauren. And Charles. Oh, God - Charles. The man that she had loved so very deeply. Deeply enough for her to end their marriage once she became - what she was. She had not wanted to risk hurting anyone at all - but especially not him. She had known that she would never be able to live with the guilt. Now, she had gone and done it anyway. She had destroyed everything, everyone. Including the one person that she had been so desperate to protect.

Sobs wracked her body, her chest heaving until she almost vomited. Her heart beat violently in her chest. As she felt it, she realized what an abomination she truly was. She should end it now, stop that heart from beating once and for all. She should -

"M - Martha?"

She froze as she heard Charles's voice from somewhere behind her, sounding tentative but relieved? *It couldn't be*. She was losing her mind. Charles was dead. She had killed him. She had killed everyone.

"Martha, are you alright?"

She turned around slowly and there he was. His face was pale and shocked, but he appeared to be unharmed. Her sore eyes trailed over him, from head to foot.

"I didn't– mean to, " she croaked. "You're not..."

"Dead?" He shook his head gravely. "No."

She was shaking badly, finding it difficult to catch her breath.

"I'm sorry," she said, as fresh tears spilled from her eyes. She knew how utterly inadequate it was, but it was all that she could think to say. "I'm so sorry! I didn't mean to. I never, " She gulped. "I can't control it."

He nodded. "This is why you left me, isn't it? And why you've been avoiding everybody for so long. It all makes sense now. I should have realized that something was terribly wrong."

"No! It isn't your fault," she put in quickly. "Not at all!"

"Why didn't you tell me when it happened?"

"I didn't want to risk doing you any harm. I thought that you'd be safer away from me. As far away as possible. And now, you see," She gestured around the room, her voice rising hysterically. "Now you see that I was right! I could easily have killed you and I have killed everyone else!"

"It's not your fault," He stepped towards her, his arms outstretched as though to embrace her, but she backed away immediately, shaking her head in horror. "you said yourself, you can't control it."

"That's not an excuse!" Her eyes burned and she tried to blink away the tears as Charles's face swam before her. "If there's a dangerous animal on the loose, then what happens to it? It gets put down. And that's what should happen to me! I would have already done it by now, if only I wasn't such a coward."

"Don't say that!" Charles retorted harshly.

"How can you try to defend me?" She waved an arm again. "Look around you! How many innocent people have just lost their lives tonight? Including your girlfriend." Even now, she could feel the jealousy burning deep within her and had to fight to suppress it.

"She wasn't really my girlfriend," he said. There was a deep frown on his face. "We hadn't even known each other that long."

"It doesn't matter. Either way, she still didn't deserve to die, Charles."

"No. She didn't."

"None of them did! And now look at what I've done," More of her sobs filled the air, but now they were being drowned out by another sound. Sirens. Blaring loudly. Growing louder by the second as they drew nearer. Martha's eyes widened a little. The police were coming. They would arrest her and lock her up for good. And rightly so. But what would happen to her once they found out what she was?

"The neighbours must have heard the commotion and called the police," Charles's face was tense, his voice filled with alarm. He rushed forward and grabbed her arm. "You need to leave!"

"What?"

"Now, just go. Run!"

"But I…"

"There's no time." He dragged her through the house, to where the back door and shoved her out onto the concrete steps beyond. "Please, Martha. You have to, there's no choice." He paused. They could hear the screeching of tires now, as the cars sped onto the lane at the front of the house. The expression on his face almost broke her heart. 'Do it for me.' Hardly knowing what she was doing, she gave a brief nod and then set off across the shadowy ground, breaking out into a run and not daring to look back.

*****

Charles closed the back door quickly, locked it and then sank down onto the kitchen floor. He could hear the rumble of many footsteps rushing up the front steps, voices shouting, and frantic knocking upon the door. It would only be a few seconds until they broke down the door. He would not say a word about Martha and there were no other witnesses left to do so. The police wouldn't suspect him of trying to cover anything up, he was sure. They would just see him as another one of the unfortunate victims of an attack. Especially with the bloodied wound that was on his arm, from where Martha had bitten him...

The front door crashed open.

End

<u>5 YEARS</u>

by Sadie Cardenas

The moment I clear the front door, I run.

I run even though it feels as though my lungs are being compressed with a vice of steel. I run even though I am out of breath. I run even though I know it is hopeless.

I run because, even after five years of preparation, I don't want to die this way.

The hellhound snaps at my heels, a beast of pure shadow and malice dreamed up by the dolorous minds of old poets who knew there was something darker at bay. It needs no air to keep going, no pumping blood - this beast has only one goal in its terrible mind: to end my life in this world.

"Aaron!" Edgar shouts from behind. "Come back!"

His voice slices at my heart, and for a moment I am tempted to turn back, but because I know I will only hurt him more, because he cannot see what I see, I press on deeper and plunge into the forest ahead.

I breeze past staggeringly tall redwoods that I barely register before they vanish as blurs. I hear the howling wind like a widow's wail and the sound of footsteps both human and demonic on the dead leaves, crunching like tiny bones. I feel the patter of rain begin to quicken and grow stronger, signaling a downpour.

The hellhound growls once more, and Edgar calls my name, and I think of a night five years ago, a night just like this one, when I sealed my fate for good.

*****

The night of Christmas Eve, my car lurched to a stop on gravel-covered ground. Yanking the key out of the ignition, I stumbled out into the night.

The air was a harsh biting cold, yet strangely active though there was nothing alive for miles save for me. Four roads lead to the barren crossroads; even the solitary saloon on the far right looked to have been abandoned for decades. The only color that brought light into the stark scene derived from the yellow shrubs that grew in clumps at each corner of the crossroads: yarrow flowers, the witch's herb, used to attract demons.

I always found myself to be a logical person- the tactician in a world full of dreamers. Everyone in both mine and Edgar's family seemed to agree, including Edgar himself. "He's going to need someone like you to keep his head out of the clouds," his grandmother Ruth always joked. I humored her every time, not knowing just how true it was.

Even when I was little, I was never one to believe in fairy tales. I knew that the monster in my closet was my raincoat casting its shadow, and that the boogeyman was a creature my parents concocted to get me to behave. I would look over my shoulder and flinch only for a moment at the fleeting shape I glimpsed, but I dismissed it just as quickly. I was simply too smart to fall for anyone's tricks, to believe that there really was something beyond any reasonable explanation lurking in the darkness.

I should have trusted my instincts. I should have let myself believe.

And yet, no matter what I chose to believe, I would have always ended up in the center of the crossroads.

When it happened, no one else knew what to do. Holiday dinner with Edgar's family, a rich, opulent feast in the living room warmed by the fireplace, a holiday greeting card for the ages. Everything had flashed by so fast: Edgar choking on his wine, one hand clawing at his chest, the glass slipping free from his grasp and shattering on the ground alongside him, the perfect moment thrown into disarray. Everyone was screaming and flailing about as cousins Raveena and Aria sat Edgar up against the foot of the couch, hands shaking and voices quavering as they tried to keep him from leaving us. Edgar's mother called the ambulance, which showed up in minutes, taking the love of my life away on a stretcher.

Only Ruth had remained calm throughout the entire debacle. She sat in her wheelchair like a goddess on her throne as she beckoned me closer. "My grandson is dying," she told me. "Those men in the hospital cannot help him. Only you can. Are you willing?"

"Yes," I breathed desperately. "I'll do anything."

And so, she told me of the witchcraft she had learned in her past, of hell's spirits that made the shadowy imps of my childhood sound like playthings. She told me of the demons that were tethered to crossroads worldwide, obligated to make deals to hopeless souls.

"The night is fading, Aaron," Ruth rasped. "Hurry. Save him."

I left without saying a word to anyone, just got in my car and drove miles away from home, thinking only of Edgar's cold body lying alone in a hospital room, the weight of his life on my shoulders. I didn't stop driving until all civilization was behind me, and the only thing I could see were the endless wheat fields and the circle of crushed stones up ahead.

The things we do for love, I thought, and stopped the car.

Step after tentative step, I wondered just how many others walked the same path as I, until I found myself in the center of the crossroads. Kneeling down, I fumbled with the glasses case in my pocket. Inside were bits of the essentials that Ruth had given to me: graveyard dirt and a bone from a black cat. I slipped my driver's license out of my wallet and stared back at my likeness- close cropped brown hair, umber brown eyes framed by thin glasses, pale skin that no days of sun could touch. Dropping the card inside of the case, I snapped it shut and dug a hole in the gravel with my bare hands like a dog in the dirt. Once the box was covered, I rose to my feet and waited for the demon to arrive.

For a brief, insufferable minute, nothing happened. I felt like a fool, driving all this way on an elderly woman's superstition, leaving Edgar all by himself. I turned to leave, thankful that my keys were still in my pocket when a gust of wind blew on my back, cool as a kiss, sending chills down my spine.

I spun around. Perhaps I should have expected it. But when I saw Lucifer's messenger standing before me, I knew that I could not run from this.

He was not what I had expected at all.

He was an angel of death set in a Southern gothic crossroads. He donned a black pinstripe suit that clung to his slim figure in all the right places. His skin was the unnaturally pale pallor of milk, almost glittering under the moonlight. His hair was ink-black, greased up with a product that withstood the sharp winds. His face was long and delicate in shape, with a defined jaw and wide, graceful mouth, a cupid's bow peaked perfectly in the middle.

Under normal circumstances, I might have watched him pass by on the street. I might have remarked to Edgar that men like *that* made me believe in God. But it was his eyes that ruined the image.

Those eyes, bloodred, without pupil or iris, gazing with amusement into my soul; the eyes that would haunt my nightmares five years later.

I stared, unable to fathom a proper sentence. "Holy…"

"Holy?" The crossroads demon smiled, revealing a flawless set of ivory-white teeth. "Are you so sure, Aaron Masters?"

"How did you-"

"Word down in the pit travels fast. I take my time in getting to know my clients." His voice was a South-singed drawl, lilted with natural mirth.

It took a few seconds to realize that his newest 'client' was me. Quickly, I regained my composure. "Then you know why I'm here."

"To save your fiancé from his little heart murmur, I know, I know. I've been summoned for less."

How flippant, I thought, with a twinge of annoyance. "If you care so little, then why did you come?"

"It's not about whether I *care.*" The demon loftily flicked his wrist. "It's my job, baby. You ask, I oblige, and that's that. It's just a little cash grab for Mr. Antichrist downstairs."

The Devil. I resisted the urge to shudder.

The crossroad demon noticed, and his lazy smile sharpened into a grin. "Ah, don't be so uptight. You do know what I want in return, right?"

I knew. Of course I knew. I had been thinking about it the whole drive over. Ruth had made it one of the last things she told me before I left.

"To save Edgar, you will have to give up your soul."

My soul. Such a trivial thing when put into words. You would think that I would have had second thoughts there and then, if my freedom was really worth Edgar's life. You would think that my heart would skip a beat at the mention, that my breath would catch, that I would feel *something*.

And yet.

It had taken less than an hour to come to the conclusion.

I had gone over the facts. For two years, I had been working in the New York Times gossip column. I made my living by giving middle-aged women something to buzz about over coffee, by turning someone's secret into the next big scoop that the world got to enjoy- until something new came along, at least. I wouldn't be missed, not by my coworkers, who I never considered my friends, and not by society, who probably wished I would pack my bags and get up off the planet anyways. I was just a buzzing little bee, snooping around for pollen, reporting back to the queen. No one would mourn when I was squashed;

there would already be another drone ready to take my place in the hive.

Edgar, on the other hand, had a far bigger role in the world than me. As a cardiac surgeon, he was an essential piece in the puzzle. He actually did something to save lives, unlike me. He was needed, I wasn't.

Then there was my family to think about: my parents, Esther and Michael Masters, college sweethearts who gave birth to me. I was the one who stayed as far away from the spotlight as possible-Agatha was always the star. She dabbled in all sorts of art forms- local plays, performance poetry, even glassblowing -before settling on painting abstracts, and it worked well for her. Our family showered her with praise, and she basked in our affection. If I left the picture, it would leave a gap. They would cry for me, and ache and wallow and wonder what they could have done, but they would move on.

That wasn't the story with Edgar. The only boy in a family of one mother, one father, and three other girls, the spotlight shone upon him before he had much of a say in the matter. He lived under the watchful eye of his parents, tearing through heavy medical books as light reads and developing dark circles under his eyes that became practically permanent. He was looked upon as the savior of his familysavior, the guardian angel who would grow strong and protect them. He would be mourned forever, pictures of him decorating the house without ever collecting dust. It was the one thing I could not let happen.

I was just one tiny speck in the world- no one would even notice I was gone.

Except Edgar.

I pushed that one crucial detail out of my mind as I faced the demon. "I know what I have to do."

"And you're sure about this? Because there's no take backs."

"I'm sure." I made my voice clear and steady. "In exchange for Edgar's life, I will give you my soul."

The grandeur of my proclamation washed away fast. My voice didn't even echo. Another gale of wind flowed past, kicking up a tumbleweed in its wake.

The demon's smirk did little to embolden my hopes. "How sweet. You humans, so ready to give up *everything* for the ones you love."

"Take it," I spat, standing my ground. I refused to let that monster see me falter.

"Already done. Tell you what, since I'm feeling particularly generous, I'll give you five years of bliss with your hubby. Better not waste it."

As the words left his mouth, I felt something leave me- a sense of exhilaration, a charge of adrenaline through every nerve ending in my body, gone in an instant, leaving me finally numb.

Five years. Five years to rue and suffer and dread as they passed by.

I released a breath. "Well, isn't there a way to confirm this? Don't we shake hands, or-"

"Oh, Aaron," the demon cackled. "Did you really think it was going to be that easy?"

"I just-"

His hands shot to my arms, fingers tight above my elbows, pulling me forward and cutting me off. His lips closed over mine, and I froze.

Of all the tasks that I had to perform that night, it was this one that I feared the most, the one that would stay with me forever along with visions of bloodred eyes. I had cautioned myself about it the whole drive over, and yet nothing could have prepared me for the real thing.

His hands on my arms feel like a corpse's steel grip, refusing to let me go. His mouth tasted of the turning seasons, from winter to spring to summer to fall to overwhelming decay. Suddenly, it was so foul I had to think of Edgar to keep from pulling away and-

Edgar. There I stood, kissing the Devil's servant under the moonlight so that he could live instead of me, and it felt like a betrayal to everything we had promised.

The crossroads demon drew back, and I gasped for clean air to fill my lungs. When my eyes fluttered open he was gone, and I wondered vaguely if I had dreamed up the entire exchange.

A cold pinprick on the top of my head brought me back. A drop on my shoulder, on my shoe, on the gravel-laden earth.

And then it began to pour. Not even the beginning drizzle, but sheets of cold, heavy rain down from the clouds, salty as the tears I would have cried if I had anything left to feel.

Thunder boomed powerfully from a heaven I would never reach. A bolt of silver lighting struck the pebbles on the road ahead of me, as if Lucifer himself had declared my sentence. And it was at that moment that I knew that everything that had just happened was very, very real.

*****

I flash back to reality and discover that my body has moved without my mind.

I have been set on autopilot, tearing through the forest, trying to evade the pursuits of my cruel reaper, who still follows close behind. Ragged breathing reaches my ears, and I realize with a start that the hellhound isn't the only one on my trail.

"Aaron," Edgar pants. "Baby, please, come home."

You're hurting him, I curse myself. *The exact thing you promised to never do.* I of all people know that his heart can't take it, the pain I am causing him, but I also know that he cannot see the hellhound that is chasing me. It is after me and me alone. If he gets any closer, he could be hurt even worse. And that is one thing I will not let happen.

If it's the last thing I do, I vow. *I will not let this darkness touch you.* I leap over a fallen tree and forage ahead.

Right as I reach a clearing, horror stabs me in the chest. A fence blocking a construction site sweeps enforcingly into view.

I freeze for a second- just a second, bones locked up with fear. But as I do, a shadow launches over my head, holding the shape of a rottweiler that's magnified to the size of a direwolf. I pick up my pace just in time to narrowly escape the ferocious, gnashing jaws of the hellhound, who howls angrily and snaps at my heels.

Think, think, I berate myself as I come closer and closer to the gate. At the very last minute, I surge for the fence. I feel a sense of relief as my fingers lock around the box-shaped links on the fence and my toes find footholds, and I scramble up the fence like a squirrel up a tree. Vaulting over the fence, I waste no time launching into a sprint through the construction zone.

Behind me, my pursuer, rather than jumping the fence, chooses to bust it down completely. Releasing a vociferous howl, it wastes no time in bounding after me.

Cursing, I race through the site, avoiding the planks of wood, skipping over potholes, kicking aside clumps of hard earth as I run farther and farther away.

"Aaron," Edgar calls hoarsely. "Aaron, please."

I barely begin to look over my shoulder when I see what lies ahead.

A half-built bridge cut off in the middle, constructed over the ravine that cuts an ugly gash through the face of the terrain. Edgar had promised to take me once it was finished. I almost laugh at the coincidence.

It's like all the energy is leached from me in a single breath. My footsteps slow as I reach the beginning of the bridge, and I am fully aware of the toll that this chase has taken on me, the small cuts on my face that running through branches have given me. I feel the throbbing in my sore legs that have taken me so far. I feel my own thudding heartbeat in my chest, sending breath after weary breath out of my mouth.

For the first time in five years, I feel completely at peace.

Three steps onto the bridge, I hear them catch up with me.

My hellhound arrives first, hot breath searing my legs. It does not attack me, does not move at all. Instead, it stays grounded behind me, watching me. Waiting for me.

Edgar arrives second, his footfalls heavy and tired. He takes in breath after deep breath, and it feels like an eternity before he speaks again. "Aaron," he wheezes, like it's killing him. "What are you doing?"

I take a single step closer to the edge and turn around to gaze at my husband one last time.

His black hair is wild and windblown, his chest pushing against his Claymation Rudolph sweater with every breath he inhales. His cinnamon-colored skin shimmers in the moonlight, at least to my delirious mind. His puppy-like chocolate brown eyes are wide with anguish. "Where are you going?"

Far away from here, I think, feeling as though I'm about to cry, but the tears don't come. Because I knew this was coming. Hanging on to every word Ruth told me, driving to that crossroads, running out of the log cabin we had rented specially for tonight, I knew it was going to end this way, and I still gave myself away.

I did it for you, I want to say, but I perish the thought, filled with rage so sudden and fiery that it shocks me. I didn't give up my soul for Edgar, he didn't ask me to, and he certainly wouldn't have wanted me to. It would destroy all the plans we had made in the years we would spend together. We were supposed to love so much longer, live our lives in this world to the fullest and leave it together.

And I still did it. Not for Edgar, but for me.

Because, in the end, I couldn't bear to live without him.

"'Till death do us part,'" I mutter, laughing a little. "Wasn't that always a funny line?"

Edgar doesn't understand. Years from now, he never will. "What do you mean?"

This isn't how it's supposed to happen. This isn't how I am supposed to say my goodbyes. This is supposed to go with a too-tight hug from my mother and father, a kiss to Agatha's forehead, a caress to Edgar's face. But this was the ending that I chose.

In my still-closed fist, I drop the silver wedding ring into the violent ravine at my back, the source of strength that I have been holding on to all this time.

"I love you," I whisper, and let myself fall.

The hellhound lunges after me, and Edgar yells my name; I'm falling down, down, down into the abyss, until the last sound I hear is the rushing water, and I am nothing at all, and everything turns white.

*****

When I open my eyes, I am back on the edge of the bridge where I fell.

Disbelief comes first, before anything else. Didn't I just fall? Convince myself that I was doing the right thing? Leave all this behind? This couldn't be- this was my life flashing before my eyes, a final vision. It couldn't possibly be real.

And yet everything I have dreaded, right in front of me, the exact thing I wanted to avoid: the aftermath. The hellhound has vanished, but Edgar has remained at the foot of the bridge. He has sunk to his knees, his back is rounded in agony. His hands cover his face in a wrangled mask, and his shoulders tremble with his sobs.

Oh, Ed, I think as I step forward on instinct, thoughtlessly reaching forward. *I'm sorry-*

Pain blooms in my chest, excruciating pain, impossible pain, pain that I shouldn't feel because I am dead. And yet it laces through my veins and reawakens every nerve ending in my body until everything is burning worse than any pain I have ever felt.

My eyes flick down to my chest. A harpoon protrudes from where my heart should be, forming a grotesque red flower of a wound. I open my mouth to scream but can't. A crow's squawk escapes my lips instead, and I feel my heart slamming against my ribcage, fighting to get out. *How can this be?*

I don't even have time to wonder when the harpoon is jerked backward, and I am yanked off my feet and falling again, this time faster and harder than before, because it is against my will. The wind feels like falling through plate after plate of glass, and the river- I crash into it. It feels like liquid steel, crushing me back into a fetal position, forcing itself down my throat and replacing the air in my lungs, making me feel lucidly, terrifyingly alive in a way that I have never felt before. And suddenly I'm free falling through nothingness that only lasts a second before I hit the ground.

I cough out blood and suck in clouds of dirt that cling to the inside of my throat like parasites. The harpoon is gone, leaving a bloody crater in my chest. Everything hurts, everything is broken, yet I still find the strength to stand.

I am in the forest again, except the cabin that Edgar and I were staying in isn't there. Countless redwoods fill every inch of my vision, and beyond the white noise that fills my ears,

I hear it.

Hellhounds. Angry, howling hellhounds in all directions.

"Aaron!" Edgar's voice yells, faint as a twittering bird, but I hear it. "Aaron!"

It isn't real, and yet it is: my immortal nightmare, my new reality.

The hellhounds get louder, and the growling behind me is enough to get me going. I start off hobbling, then I jog, and the howling turns into an all-consuming roar.

I am alone. I am quivering as I run. I am calling for my friends, my parents, my sister, my love, because even though I know it is futile, I have never felt so afraid.

"Edgar!"

"Edgar!"

THE END.

EVIL IN THE WOODS:

The Legend of No-Face Charlie

by James R. Coffey

Folks say it was the worst blizzard in Western Pennsylvania history. There was a wind-chill of 65 below zero, five feet of snow lay hard on the ground, and the forecast called for at least twelve more inches by morning. The date was December 10, 1971. A date I will never forget.

We'd been holed up in Bango's mother's basement for the past two days and somehow got the bright idea that we better take a cruise before the worst of the weather hit. The brilliance of that idea no doubt came from boredom and the two bottles of Schnapps we'd bottomed between us. So, the three of us piled into Bango's '60 Regal-green Buick Electra and for some inglorious reason, let Buddy drive. I seem to remember that he claimed to be the most sober and we chose to believe him.

I don't recall discussing where we were heading, only that we were suddenly flying up Old Nine-Mile Road about ten miles out of town, wheels barely touching the ground. That old country road hadn't been plowed or even salted yet that year but was traveled often enough to keep it flat. Ice kept it slick. And on either side of this narrow, snow-battered gravel road, two great claustrophobic walls of snow and ice had risen, making it impossible to see anything beyond it.

At each bend in the road the entire right or left side of the car would careen up at a forty-five-degree angle--then skate back onto the flat on the straight-aways. And since Buddy never drove slower than sixty, it was every bit a waxed-blade sled-ride down a Wild-Cat roller-coaster track.

It was after we'd taken a dozen or so of these gut-wrenching, insanely dangerous turns that Bango looked back at me and said, "We're never gonna make it past the next curve." And there was something in the way he said it that made me believe him. Bango was kinda witchy that way. I leaned back against the seat and braced myself for the inevitable.

Just as we hit the next bend, a hard left, Buddy lost control of the car. First, the front wheels pulled us straight up the bank then before we knew what hit us, the rear tire chains grabbed hold and threw us up and over the top—sending us airborne. Ripping free-fall through a stand of snow-heavy oaks and tangle of frozen brier, we set down, wheels-first, in a frozen backwash about thirty yards beyond the road.

Freezing water rushed in through rust holes in the floorboards forcing us to jump out into the icy swamp. And feeling no pain when we left Bango's that night, not one of us thought to bring a coat. At least I had on a heavy sweater.

Between moaning and chattering teeth we

made our way up to the road, Bango bitching at Buddy for driving like such an asshole. We watched as the Buick sank into the slush until the icy water bubbled up and over the plush velvet seats. "Mother fucker," Bango ranted. "So now we're not just stuck in the middle of fuckin' nowhere, we're gonna need a fuckin' tow-truck to get my car out of the fuckin' swamp. Good job, fuck head."

As we stood there in the biting cold, rubbing our arms and stamping our feet to keep from freezing to death, we looked up and down the road trying to figure our next move. The moon was almost full but black clouds kept hiding it as if they needed the light to keep warm. Painfully sober now I suddenly realized where we were.

"*Fuuuuck*! Does this look familiar? Do you know where we are?"

"What? Where?" said Buddy, lighting up a cigarette, moaning under his breath as he incessantly did.

"No Face Charlie lives out that way."

"Fuck! He's right," said Bango, his nervous breath forming clouds around his cherry-red face. "We need to get the fuck out of here."

Though none of us had ever seen No-Face ourselves, or even knew anyone who had, even little kids around the Valley knew the legend and knew better than wander anywhere near his old house in the woods. When my dad was a boy, two brothers disappeared from these very woods and everyone believed No-Face Charlie took them.

A few people said they caught a glimpse of him from far off, creeping through the woods, and that he was just like people said: he had no face. Just big, black and blue flapping lips like an old Negro man—but no other facial features to speak of. Slits for eyes and a hole where his nose should be—like a skeleton's skull. And he had enormous gray ears that looked like they were made of clay or rubber that stuck straight out like bat wings. And what little skin was left on his face and head was scarred and burnt and looked rotted. At least, that's what they said. But most folks just said he was the most hideous thing you could ever meet in your nightmares.

No one knows for certain how No-Face got the way he was, but some said he got electrocuted when he picked up a powerline that fell on the road during a storm. Some say his father tanned hides and No-Face accidentally fell into a vat of acid and it ate off all his skin. Some say he was born ugly and insane because his mother and father were actually brother and sister.

Bango's older brother Woody said No Face still does tanning up there in his daddy's old barn and made human-skin raincoats out of those two kids that disappeared and stew out of their meat. But no matter what the truth was, all that mattered to us was getting as far away from there as possible before No-Face knew we were there.

*****

We'd all grown up in that part of Beaver Valley and knew it was a good ten miles to the old Falcon truck-stop down at Four-Corners, and there was no possible way we were going to make it there on foot. We'd freeze death before we'd even gone two miles. And we also knew that only idiots like us would be out on this of all nights.

We hadn't gone more than a thousand yards when one of us said, *What the fuck is that?* Even through the blizzard that now tore into us we could see a dim, yellow light twinkling through the distant trees. "Yeah, what the fuck is that?" Buddy said.

"That's gotta be the old cemetery," I said. "As far as I know there's nothing else out here."

"Well, what the fuck is somebody doing in the cemetery *now*," Bango said, stopping in his tracks to get a better look. "That's pretty fuckin' weird."

"You think that's weird? This whole fuckin' thing's weird if you ask me," Buddy said, hurrying ahead. "I mean, who the fuck thought this was a good idea anyway?

As Bango and I double-timed to catch up, the tiny yellow light grew more intense and Buddy was running directly into it. I began to doubt the light was coming from the cemetery at all. But if not the cemetery, then what?

Buddy was now far ahead, seemingly flying. And as I became more and more convinced that it wasn't a light from the cemetery, the more hopeful I became that it was someone who could help us. Someone lost or broke down, maybe a camper or a hunter? If that was a fire burning, at least we could get warm.

But as Buddy disappeared into the light and a large shadowy shape appeared behind it, I realized we'd made a horrible mistake. The light was coming from a house. And the only house out there was No-Face Charlie's! We were running in the wrong direction.

"Buddy, stop," I screamed. "*Stop*! We're going the wrong way! We gotta turn around!"

"Huh? Are you fuckin' kiddin' me?!" Bango panted.

"I wish I was, but I'm positive that's No-Face's house. And if he doesn't know already, he's gonna know we're here."

"But, what about Buddy? We can't just leave 'im."

"Bango, listen, if we go up there to get him we might never get out. I hate to say it but we have to think of ourselves."

Suddenly there was a loud bang from just ahead.

"What the fuck was that?" Bango said.

"A fuckin' gunshot?! Come on. Let's get the fuck out of here! *Hurry*!"

Slipping and sliding we fell on our asses, trying to run faster than the ice would allow. I've never been so terrified. Somehow, freezing to death seemed preferable to being shot, skinned, and eaten, I knew the gunshot we'd heard was for Buddy and that he was dead. Further, I knew that when No-Face caught up with us, he'd kill us too!

Then the snow started coming down ever harder. I couldn't see my hand in front of my face and in just seconds completely lost sight of Bango.

No words can describe the terror that seized my senses as I ran—knowing I was running for my life! A moment later I heard a second shot--and knew No-Face had caught up with Bango.

I began to sob uncontrollably, tears freezing on my lips and face as I ran headlong into the blasting snow. My two best friends were dead and I was certainly next. And there was nothing I could do to stop it!

Without intending to, I found myself leaving the road and heading into the thick of the woods, away from the gunshots.

Tripping and falling, I frantically clawed and crawled my way over the ice and snow, through brier and fallen trees. Losing all feeling in my legs, I crawled until I hadn't the strength to go on.

They say freezing to death is one of the more pleasant ways to die. I now know that's true. I died there.

*****

It was three days before I was able to explain to the Sheriff how I came to be laying in the ditch along the frozen highway. Another two before the roads were clear enough for him to make his way out there. But by then, the snow had erased any trace of us—and No-Face Charlie.

Spending half a day searching the countryside, the Sheriff decided it was a waste of manpower. Said by the looks of things, it had been months since Charlie or anyone else had been out there.

It wasn't till spring, when Bango's car finally became visible, that anyone started to believe my account of what we faced that night. And by then it didn't matter.

The doctors had to amputate three fingers, my left foot and my penis to save my life. I still have nightmares about that night and my buddies are always in my thoughts. Becoming part of the No-Face Charlie legend was the last thing I ever expected or intended to do. But I am.

FRIEND OF THE DEVIL

by Tom Larsen

Macará Ecuador—Sometime in the past.

Santiago Flores took the straw hat from his head and wiped the sweat from the interior with a red bandana he always carried with him. He used the bandana to wipe his eyes as well. He had labored in his squash field, hoeing weeds, and loosening the black earth since before dawn. Now the sun was approaching its zenith. Santiago was used to working hard with little rest, but the frustration of it all was enough to make his eyes fill with tears, which mingled with sweat to make his eyes sting.

In normal times he would periodically during the day pause his labors and go to the small stream that ran through his property from the Cenepa River, the border with Perú. The cool water would refresh his spirit as well as his body, and he could return to work with renewed vigor.

These were not normal times. The river ran lower than he had ever seen, below the outlet to the small stream. The stream had run dry more than a month earlier, leaving behind only the smell of rotting vegetation and dead fish.

Santiago had tried frantically with a pick and shovel to lower the point where the stream and the river intersected. But amid these efforts, his wife Valeria contracted a strange stomach disease and died within weeks. By the time he recovered enough to go back to work, the river level had fallen nearly a half-meter lower, rendering his efforts to lower the stream entrance futile. His squash plants were now nothing more than brittle leafless sticks, tangled with the aggressive weeds that found enough water for themselves despite this prolonged drought. Now he worked every day from sunrise to nightfall, not in hopes of salvaging his crop, but from habit and the lack of anything better to do with his days.

Santiago and Valeria had not been blessed with children, for reasons known only to *pachamama*, the female deity that controlled all aspects of life in the Andean mountains and the surrounding fertile lowlands in which Macará lay. Santiago had prayed to *pachamama* for a child as fervently as he had prayed for his wife's return to health, and as he had prayed for an end to the drought that was currently destroying the only thing he had left—his three hectares of rich black earth.

His prayers went unanswered, but he never lost faith, nor did he berate the goddess for heaping so much misery upon him. Neighbors and acquaintances spoke of him in terms of respect and affection.

"What a fine man is Santiago Flores," they said. "Always ready to lend us a hand even in his darkest hour. Surely, he will be blessed in the end." Some even prayed for him, but as far as physical aid they had nothing to offer. They were the victims of the same drought as he was.

*****

At noon Santiago returned to his modest home for lunch. The small house was constructed of pine logs and *barracoa*—a mixture of mud and straw bound with vines. His shoulders slumped and his eyes downcast, he was almost to his front door when he saw that the huge guayacan tree that provided shade for three generations of his family had fallen during the day. Just a few months earlier, in the spring, the tree had been abloom with small bright yellow flowers, providing a fragrant aroma along with the shade that made living in the area a pleasure. But weakened by the lack of water, the ancient tree had finally given up the ghost and crashed to the ground, crushing the front half of Santiago's house as it went.

Santiago sat on a big rock at the edge of the small clearing that he had painstakingly created, and wept. His wife was dead, his crops were ruined, and the chickens and one old cow that provided eggs and milk had been slaughtered to provide enough food to keep him alive. Now his home, humble as it might be, was all but destroyed. He slid to the ground and leaned against the rock. It was too painful to look in the direction of his ruined home, so he directed his gaze out toward the surrounding hillside. A black dot far in the distance could have been a rock outcropping or the burnt remnants of a *ceibo* tree, but Santiago surely would have noticed it before. Since Valeria's death, he had spent hours on that very rock gazing out into the distance.

Then the black dot moved, slowly but in a straight line that would lead whatever it was directly to his small *hacienda.* As Santiago stared with his mouth agape, the dot became larger and then it became a coal black horse with its rider dressed all in black. When the horse and rider came nearer, Santiago saw that it was his childhood friend, Carlos Ortega. He had never seen his friend dressed as he was now. He wore ebony silk pants. He wore a long black cape and a wide-brimmed black hat sat rakishly upon his head. In his joy at seeing his old friend, Santiago quickly forgot about his odd manner of dress. Carlos dismounted and they embraced for a long time. Hugging Carlos, Santiago felt something in his friend's back. It felt like a kind of metal rod, but with all the emotion of the moment, he didn't think much of it.

"I heard the news about Valeria," Carlos said, removing his hat and revealing the curly black hair that had always been his pride. *"¡Lo siento mucho!"*

It occurred to Santiago that these few moments with his old friend had been the longest amount of time he had spent without thinking of his late wife. The memories flooded back, and Santiago wept again. Carlos comforted him as best he could.

After the greeting and the catching up, Carlos said that he was going to town and get some workers to move the tree, but first he asked for a favor in return.

"Baaah! It wasn't for friendship that you came to see me," Santiago said in the manner that the pair had employed when speaking to one another since they were five years old. "You are not the friend that I know, you're all about money now." The smile on his face felt strange but good, nonetheless. "I'm joking," he said. "You know that I'll help you with whatever you need."

"Good, thank you," said Carlos as if a great weight had been lifted from his shoulders. "There is some merchandise coming from the East that I must pick up tonight. I need you to come with me because no one knows the hills like you. Without you I would go wandering in the mountains for weeks," he said.

"Of course, my friend," said Santiago with a sigh of relief. "Knowing you, I thought that you were going to ask me something difficult. What type of merchandise is coming from the mountains?"

"Just things that I need for my business. Nothing important. Did I tell you that I have begun a new business?"

"What kind of business?"

"The funeral business."

"Funeral business? Is that why you're wearing all this black clothing?" Carlos' cape, Santiago noticed, extended nearly to the ground, and seemed to be alive. It rustled and flared even though there was no breeze.

"Yes," said Carlos. "It turns out that very few people want to dedicate themselves to this type of a business." He shrugged. "Maybe they're afraid being around death. But not me!"

When Carlos smiled, Santiago noticed that his teeth were smaller, and each one came to a sharp point. His tongue was a darker red than he remembered and constantly in motion. *Had they always been that way?*

Carlos shook his hand in preparation for leaving. At his old friend's touch Santiago's mood improved and all questions went out of his head.

"Okay, Carlos," he said with a smile. "Just don't tell me that we're going into the mountains to pick up a load of coffins."

"How did you know?" Carlos responded with a look that was both suspicious and curious. "Maria bought these in Eastern Ecuador, close to the Colombian Border. They're made of teak wood by a real craftsman. They'll sell here for a nice profit."

Maria! Santiago tensed at the mention of her name, but Carlos didn't notice. In his heart Santiago had always blamed the woman for taking his childhood friend from him. She filled his head with visions of great wealth. He followed her to faraway places in search of business opportunities and the expected riches that would be sure to follow. Carlos came home less frequently, and Maria never came with him. Nor had the anticipated bounty ever come to fruition. Santiago, being the kind soul that he was, had never mentioned his animosity toward Carlos' wife and he wasn't about to start now.

"Excellent." Taking Santiago's silence for a tacit agreement, Carlos clapped his hands together making a sound like a thunderclap. "I'll go now and send some workers to clear away that tree. We'll meet at seven tonight." He mounted his black horse and rode away, his cape flowing behind him.

Santiago felt a chill run through him. Here less than two hundred kilometers south of the equator, it would be full-on dark by seven. Though he had roamed these woods at all hours of the night since he was a child, the prospect of accompanying a load of coffins through the darkness was unsettling, to say the least.

Hopefully, there are no bodies inside, he thought to himself. A nervous chuckle escaped his lips. Looking back, he saw Carlos stop his horse and glance in his direction, before trotting away and disappearing into the woods. Though the sun was near its highest point he shivered and hugged himself for warmth. All thoughts of lunch were driven from his mind, and he headed back to his squash field to continue his fruitless labors. *What else could he do?*

He dedicated himself to his work, but he couldn't keep his mind from wandering. It had been far too long since he had seen his old friend, and that made him happy—as happy as a man in his current situation could be. But Carlos was different now, and not in a good way. They had always been different types of men. Santiago remembered how horrified he had been when Carlos stole a bag of sweets from the local *tienda.* He had refused to take any of them when his friend offered. Carlos just shrugged, and Santiago went back to the store and paid the old lady for the stolen candy, without telling his friend. All through their teen years Santiago had gone behind when one of Carlos' schemes went awry and made things right.

Then Carlos met Maria, and within a month he was gone, returning to their hometown only every couple of years. It was rumored that Maria was the daughter of a powerful *bruja*—a witch—and Santiago embraced that rumor wholeheartedly. From the beginning they had a mutual dislike for one another that bordered on hatred. Santiago of course had never mentioned this to Carlos. It appeared that Maria hadn't either because Carlos remained blissfully ignorant of the friction between his wife and his best friend.

*****

Night falls quickly in the plains of southern Ecuador. One minute the sun hangs just above the distant hillside, and the next minute it is gone. The temperature drops just as precipitously, and Santiago put on a heavy woolen sweater against the sudden chill. The memory of Valeria laboring for days at the foot-powered loom to create this colorful garment for him counteracted any warmth that it might have offered. Santiago set off at a rapid pace up the mountain, and the strenuous climb soon warmed him.

When he arrived at the meeting place Carlos was already there. Carlos sat upon his black horse, which seemed larger than he remembered. A Sorrell mare with a blanket for a saddle stood nearby. Santiago climbed onto the mare's back, and they rode off. As Carlos urged his mount forward, Santiago thought he saw a slit open about halfway down the long black cape that his friend wore. He would swear that a tail in the shape of an arrowhead protruded from the cape. It was gone in an instant. Unsure if he had really seen it, Santiago said nothing. He spurred his horse to come alongside Carlos.

"Where are we headed, my friend?" Santiago asked. When Carlos turned to face him, Santiago saw that his eyes had turned as black as the shiny volcanic rock that dotted the hillside. Once again, he wasn't sure if his eyes had deceived him. He closed and opened them quickly and his friend's eyes were once again the warm chocolate brown that he remembered.

"Monte Diablo." It was his old friend's voice, but there was something different about it.

"What?" Santiago pulled back on the reins and the mare halted immediately. *"Monte Diablo?* The devil's mountain? His home here on earth. No, Carlos. You're my friend and you always will be, but I'm not setting foot within a hundred meters of that place!"

"But Yago," Carlos said, using the diminutive nickname that Santiago hadn't heard in years. "Remember the favor I did for you today? Are you no longer a man of your word?"

Santiago recoiled as if he had been slapped. The only thing he possessed of any consequence was his word. Hearing that accusation from his oldest friend stung him. But his overwhelming fear prevailed. He dismounted, handed the reins to Carlos, and was headed back down the mountain when he heard his friend's voice. Again, like everything about Carlos since his return, his voice was different somehow. Santiago couldn't put his finger on it, but whatever it was it drew him back.

He remounted the mare and prepared to continue the journey. He would guide his old friend to this accursed place, and then he would go home and hope never to see Carlos again. He glanced in Carlos' direction. He was too frightened to look directly at him, but even in the darkness Carlos' eyes had returned dark as coal color—with one addition. Encircling the irises were streaks of green, like the will-o'-the-wisps that he sometimes saw at night in the swampy lowlands. Rather than dancing playfully, however, the light burned fiercely at him. Santiago dug his heels into the Sorrel's flanks to spur her onward. The sooner this business was over, the better.

*****

When they reached the ridge that topped a narrow canyon. On the other side stood *Monte Diablo*, shrouded in thick fog although the night was otherwise clear. On the other side they saw a pair of mules, each carrying two coffins tied one on each side. Santiago could see that the coffins were very expensive, but he was surprised to see that no one was driving the mules.

They plodded steadily up the side of the mountain as if guided by some unseen force. They stopped near a massive rock outcropping and stood motionless, not even lowering their heads to graze.

"What is going on, Carlos?" Santiago could hardly speak. "Where is Maria? I thought we would meet her here." He swiveled his head in all directions looking for his friend's wife.

"I am meeting her up ahead," said Carlos without looking back. "You can go now, my friend. Thank you for bringing ne here. I would never have found it by myself, and Maria and I would never be together again."

"That makes no sense," Santiago complained. Please Carlos, if you were ever my friend tell me what is happening here, or I will go mad!"

Carlos turned, a thin smile on his face. His eyes had returned to the warm chocolate brown that. "I'm not the friend you remember, Yago," he said in his old voice. I have done things to make money. Lots of money! Things that you would not approve of." He shrugged. "But I have made my peace with it."

"What, though?" Santiago pleaded with his old friend. "What have you done that is so bad? I can forgive you anything, Carlos. Just tell me."

Carlos smiled again and shook his head slowly from side to side. "Not this, Yago," he said softly. "Maria and I sold our souls to the devil years ago so that we could have all the riches that we desired. We always knew that He would come for our souls eventually, and now He has."

"What does all this have to do with the mules and the coffins? Why are we here? And where is Maria?"

As if responding to Santiago's words, the enormous rock on the side of *Monte Diablo* split open to reveal a dark cave. Maria stood in the opening in a long black dress, her arms spread wide as if in welcome. Behind her the interior of the cave was black as night, but electrical charges, like lightning bolts, flew from the tips of her fingers. Flocks of bats, too many to count, swirled from the opening and flew off into the night. The two mules moved of their own accord, entered the cave, and soon were swallowed up by the darkness.

Maria gestured in their direction and Santiago saw a thin stream of light extend from her hand, encircling Carlos like a lasso. Carlos turned and addressed him in a gentle faraway voice. "Those coffins contain the bodies of four men whom we killed on His orders. By doing so we have fulfilled our obligation, and we can now go and dwell in His house for all eternity."

"His orders?" Santiago spluttered. "The Devil?"

Santiago could see the sadness on his friend's face as he replied. "We were always different, you and me. You're a good man. Everyone says so. And me?

From the time I was born, I knew I was different. My parents even told me so." His face hardened, and his eyes turned dark again. "But I didn't care. I lived my life as I wanted, and I've ended up where I always knew I would." Santiago tried to open his mouth, but no words came out.

"You should go now," Carlos said. He dug his heels into the black stallion's side, and it leaped forward as if shot from a cannon. Sparks flew from its hooves, and in an instant the horse and rider were at the entrance to the cave. Carlos leaned down and helped Maria onto the back of the big horse. The flocks of bats had returned, and they made eerie screeching sounds as they fought to re-enter the cage. Neither Carlos nor Maria looked back. Once they were inside, the rocks closed back up and a bright white phosphorescence illuminated the mountain for a few seconds.

As Santiago turned the horse back toward his home it began to rain. A gentle rain, the kind that tends to last for a while, filling the streams and rivers, and nourishing the crops in the fields.

*****

Santiagos' crop was saved that year, and his yield increased every year for the rest of his life. Each year he would add a few square meters to his fields. He never became wealthy, but he lived comfortably. He was able to rebuild the front of his house, and he planted another Guayacan tree—one that grew faster than he or his neighbors had ever witnessed.

Even with all that good fortune, Santiago remained a sad shell of his former self. He never remarried and lived alone in the small house, continuing to work his fields from daylight to dark every day.

The neighbors attributed his continued melancholy to the loss of his wife so many years ago. "Santiago truly loved Valeria," they said. "He still mourns her passing even after all these years."

The loss of his one true love wasn't the true reason for his perpetual sadness. Growing up in the plains of southern Ecuador, he respected *pachamama* and the other minor deities that guided them through life. But Ecuador is a primarily Catholic country: the devil, they taught, was an angel that had fallen out of God's graces. Humans lived amid a perpetual battle between the forces of good and evil. By guiding his friend to the slopes of *Monte Diablo* Santiago, he had given aid to the forces of evil. The continued abundance from his fields and the corresponding comfortable life came not from God, nor from *pachamama*. It came from the devil.

Santiago Flores lived his life in constant fear, anticipating the day when the devil would summon him.

Author's Note: I was fortunate enough to live for six years in Cuenca, which is known as Ecuador's Capital of Culture. In 2016 the Municipality of Cuenca commissioned an outstanding cultural preservation project—to record oral stories, myths, and tall tales from the nineteen small towns that surrounded the city. This tale was inspired by an eerie tale from the town of Chiquintad. For the purposes of my story, I moved the location a few hundred kilometers south to a small town near the border with Perú.

LIQUID MEMORIES
by C. J. Carter-Stephenson

Antonne took a bite of his hot dog as he left the convenience store and walked back along the road towards his house. Coleslaw leaked out of the roll onto his chin. He was supposed to be eating the cornbread and pinto beans his mom had left out for him, but he hadn't been able to face them. Food just wasn't the same reheated in the microwave. Why did she have to keep working late anyway?

A pair of sagging metal gates came into view ahead—the entrance to the Lake Shawnee abandoned amusement park. He paused, thinking of the stories his dad had told him about the place—how it was the site of a bloody conflict in the 18th century; how when it opened as an amusement park, visitors had started dying there; how it was supposed to be haunted by the ghosts of these visitors.

Antonne shuddered as he thought of it and then felt the usual sadness as he thought of his dad. The stories about the amusement park were just a few of the many he had liked to tell. There were stories about places he had visited in his truck as well and stories about Gambia passed down to him by his own dad. They'd bored Antonne at the time, but five years ago when his dad had died in a traffic accident, they'd become very important.

He stopped abruptly. Someone was rattling the gates. He turned and saw a girl standing on the bottom rail. She was about his own age with wavy blonde hair.

She was dressed in a pink dress and knee-length white socks. She waved at him. "Hey."

Antonne had never seen her before, so he guessed she was a tourist. People were always sneaking into the park to look around. He waved back. "Hey."

"Are you busy?" she asked.

He held up his hot dog. "Just eating my supper. You shouldn't be in there, you know? There'll be a peck of trouble if anyone catches you."

She shrugged her shoulders. "Maybe, but I like it here. Why don't you come in for a spell and I'll show you around?"

Antonne was tempted. Although he'd lived near the park his whole life, he'd never been in. What if he ended up being arrested, though, or there really were ghosts inside?

The girl poked his arm. "What's the matter— are you chicken?"

He puffed up his chest. "Of course not." He gulped down the last of the hot dog and clambered over the gate.

The girl led him along a track. They turned a corner and Antonne saw an old Ferris wheel rising from a cluster of trees. It was rusty and draped in vines. The girl threaded her way through the foliage to reach it. "The Ferris wheel," she announced, sitting down on one of the gondolas.

She rocked the gondola back and forwards and then took him onwards through the park to a swing ride. Again, this was badly decaying. Antonne gave a little shudder and pulled his coat tighter around him. If ghosts did exist this was just the kind of place you'd expect to see one. "It's creepy, isn't it?"

"Not to me," the girl replied. "I'll tell you what is, though." She took his hand, leading him to the shore of Shawnee lake.

Antonne was puzzled. "What's creepy about this?"

"Nothing at the moment," she said, "but at night, when the moon shines on it, it shows you things... bad things."

"Garbage!" Antonne said.

The girl stuck her tongue out. "Meet me here tonight and you'll see for yourself."

Antonne looked at the crumbing rides, the looming trees. The thought of being here in the dark did not appeal to him. He shook his head. "I don't think so."

"You <u>are</u> scared," she said.

"I am not," he snapped. "Of course I'll meet you. What time?"

"Midnight."

*****

Antonne shone his torch on the gates as he approached the park. It was almost midnight, but the girl was nowhere to be seen. Then again, she hadn't actually said this was where they should meet, so she might be waiting for him inside.

He went to the Ferris wheel, but she wasn't there either. He kicked one of the metal supports irritably. He should have known she wouldn't come. The wheel shook and he heard something snap above him. His eyes moved upwards. One of the gondolas had torn from its mountings and was plunging towards him. He threw himself out of the way, and it thudded to the ground behind him.

Was it coincidence the bolts holding it had happened to break just as he was standing below? It seemed unlikely.

He ran for the gate. Then something caught his eye over by the lake—a shimmer of pink in the moonlight. It was the girl—he was sure of it. He turned to look, but there was nothing there. He pictured her hiding in the trees somewhere laughing at him and stopped running abruptly.

"Come out. I know you're here."

No response. He headed for the lake uneasily, remembering what the girl had said about it. It looked perfectly normal, just the reflections of...

His eyes widened as the scene in the water changed. It was day and instead of a few rusty relics, the park was filled with working rides. There were people everywhere, laughing and chatting. A lifeguard in a chair by a swimming pool blew a whistle and the swimmers began to leave, all except one boy. He dived down to the bottom and resurfaced. Then he dived down again, and this time, he did not reappear.

Antonne leaned forward and spotted him below the surface. He was struggling frantically, his arm caught on something, bubbles streaming from his nose and mouth. Then the bubbling stopped, the boy was still. He was dead.

The image in the lake changed again. It was early in the morning now, but already the park was busy. Antonne swallowed hard as he saw the girl in the pink dress in the crowd. She joined the line for the swing ride. The ride stopped, so more people could get on, and then whirled onwards. It stopped again and an attendant waved the girl forward to one of the chairs.

A yellow truck loaded with crates of Coca-Cola backed away from a concession stand as the ride restarted. The driver was squinting, dazzled by the sun in his mirrors. Girl and truck collided and it was a mangled corpse that the ride carried away.

Antonne felt cold all over. A ghost! All that time talking to her and he hadn't realized.

The water shifted and for a moment he thought it had gone back to reflecting reality. Then he saw himself walking towards the Ferris wheel. He saw this other Antonne looking around for the girl, saw the falling gondola, only this time, it didn't miss him.

He shook his head furiously as he stared at his fallen body, neck twisted at an unnatural angle. He found he could move again, turned to look at the Ferris wheel and caught a glimpse of himself through the trees. He was lying under the fallen gondola just as he had seen in the water, yet still he didn't believe it.

He tried to run, but a hand exploded from the lake, gripping his wrist. It was the girl, the ghost. He could see her in the water staring up at him, except it wasn't water anymore, it was blood. Her dress was blood-stained and torn, her eyes like two black holes. He tried to break free, but she was too strong. Slowly, unstoppably, she pulled him down into the lake.

I WILL MAKE YOU CRY!
The Confessions of Rosemary Maruzakose
by Val Chatindo

I will make you cry.

If you're a man, that is.

If you're a man, I swear and I promise on my life that I will make you cry. All of you are going to pay. I may not get each and every one of you, as the Lord knows that there exists within the earth billions of you contaminants. Predators within every corner of the earth just waiting to do your harm. But the ones who I do find. *Ha!* The ones who I do find. The ones unfortunate enough to cross my path after lustful captivations inspired the lure of my contoured flesh and honey-coloured skin, baptised in infusions of lavender and jasmine. Infusions of great osmotic potential wafting from my flesh with the intention to seduce and more potent than the hypnosis induced by my highly concentrated pheromones. *Those men!* Lord, those ones, I will make sure I punish them. Not only for their audacity to leave their mother's wombs but for their mere existence.

For what was done to me.

God did not create a man. A man descended from the pits of hell. A man is a creature from purgatory with the same intention to do harm as his brothers, the demons. He looks normal, he seems kind, he will smile at you and play harmless. Make no mistake. He is like his father, the devil. Evil! I know how you all are. How lustful, disgusting and vile your gender is. Always taking, always entitled, never taking no for an answer. Everything should be yours, right? And just like the saints of the bible, you've twisted their mantra to justify your actions driven by lust. *And the violent take it by force.*

Was I not just an innocent woman going about her life? A human being with hopes and deams and misplaced faith in humanity. Unfortunate enough to hitch a ride from a man I assumed wanted to do good. Later, after he had violated me and left me for dead, I remembered the last thing he said to me in my dying moment.

"You aren't so special now, are you? Whore!"

I died that night. Died a lonely death in that forest. They didn't even find my body till weeks later a man chopping firewood stumbled upon and by then I was a disgusting putrid morsel of decaying flesh. Where once I had been beautiful and the object of many men and women's admiration, they now turned their noses up and looked away in disgust. Me! Reduced to nothing but decayed shit. Discarded like a dog. *Poo!* Unrecognisable and ugly beyond measure. How can I not want to make you all pay?

You will hear people tell you. In fact, mislead you into believing that there is no life after death. That it all ends with this brief sojourn we have on the earth as mortal beings but it's a lie. There is another world that exists simultaneously with the physical realm. There are beings that exist within this world who are capable of manifesting themselves in the world of the so-called living. We are here. We exist. We are not stories nor are we legends, camp around the fire tales meant to excite you and fabricate fear in those minds of yours. Sure, some of us may pass peacefully into the after-life. But there are those like me who cling to the earth. Victims of violence deaths with unresolved issues and scores to settle with the living. Tethered by our pain and bitterness to what the living have done to us. And their arrogance. Their audacity to believe that it all ends after they have buried us. That we will take our screams and their secrets with us. *Hell no!*

Tinashe Masendeke thought he had gotten away with what he did to me. Boy was he wrong. *Haha!*

You see, I couldn't rest even after they had buried me. My spirit could find no peace. For months I roamed about the streets of Mutare, my hometown, walking amongst the living like a stranger. I visited my family, stayed with them for days until I couldn't take it anymore. Until their cries and paid become too overwhelming to bear. If only they could have seen me, if only I could have held them and comforted them, told that I was fine even thought that would have been a lie.

It happened though when I least expected it. The materialisation. I had been standing by the side of the road hoping to get into a stranger's car to take me to the next town when a car pulled up and the driver opened his window.

"Hey beautiful. Where are you going?"

Dumbfounded, I looked around thinking that maybe someone was playing a joke on me.

"Rusape. I'm going to Rusape."

He could see me! Well, I had gotten into his car alright and during that 2-hour drive, felt his eyes on me. Of course, he had asked for sex and since I had nothing to lose. We had fumbled around in his car after we parked by a lay-by. The next morning, he was found by a gravesite, sleeping on a tombstone, his genitals missing. He died a day later and when he asked why I had done it I simply shrugged.

With time I discovered my unique gift. That I could materialise in the evenings but only to men that wanted to have me. And so, like a missionary I took up my cause. Going from town to town, standing by roadsides at midnight, hoping to do justice and God's righteous work. I had a calling. I obviously got Masendeke, and soon my legend grew and men were cautioned to stay clear of me.

But they never listened. Lust always prevails. Even my name doesn't give them cause for concern. Rosemary *Maruzakose*, literally meaning Rosemary You've-Lost-It-All. It couldn't be much clearer.

I am the secret that will not be hidden, a confessor of man, an exposed of truth. I was for such a time as this.

I smile as a car pulls up the window rolls down.

"Zimunya, he asks?"

I nod. I feel his eyes on my legs and hitch my skirt up even higher.

"So beautiful. What's your name?"

I laugh.

"Rosemary Maruzakose."

LA MUELONA

by S J Hide

"There's been another one," said one of Carlos's most trusted lieutenants, tossing a newspaper across the low table.

Carlos picked it up from where it landed amid a jumble of beer cans, half-smoked reefers, shot glasses and a 9mm pistol.

"Yeah, I heard. These sons-of-bitches are gonna pay. What do we know?"

The group of tattooed young men sitting around the table looked nervous. Carlos had a temper. And a gun. No one wanted to give him the bad news. Eventually one spoke up, Pardo, his longest-serving *muchacho*, and the one who feared him least.

"The fact is boss, we don't know. We've checked around, and with our contacts in the police, and with the forensics, and it's a mystery."

Carlos took a deep breath. This was the third murder in three months in this corner of Colombia, his home turf, and he knew nothing. His reputation rested on knowing. You control your territory. Or you go down.

Worse, these weren't any run-of-the-mill murders that happened every day in Colombia; some dude with a debt, or a girlfriend who pissed off the wrong guy. These bodies were foreigners. Gringos. And the *way* they died, with, their faces monstrously mangled. It was bad for business.

"Maybe there's another gang out there, someone going it alone, and messing it up," suggested another of the gang, shifting nervously on the sofa.

"Well, we should know, shouldn't we?" said Carlos, angry now.

"Maybe I should spell it out to you. We drug foreigners and take their stuff. But we don't kill them, that kind of shit brings too much heat. Now if someone is out their killing our marks—and cutting them up like Christmas lunch—then we need to end it. And quick. Some don't come back here until you've got some answers, and the fucker behind these killings is bundled in barbed wire and lying in a lake."

As his lieutenants filed out, Carlos sat back to study the news report. He felt a bit better after the rant, but deep down was anxious. Something was wrong.

His gang was low-level. Drugging and robbing tourists hardly brought in the riches of the cocaine cartels. But he had worked hard to move up, now employing dozens of *chicas* who worked the bars and nightclubs of the small city, and he delegated most of the daily running to his lieutenants. He had respect, even from the big guys.

Carlos was particularly proud of his technical prowess; through years of experimentation, he had perfected a drug cocktail to turn tourists into jelly, ready to be robbed or their bank accounts emptied by his cyber team, or "The Nerds", as he called them, they looked like schoolboys, but could empty an overseas bank account in short time.

Then there were the girls, *las chicas*, mostly Venezuelans, migrants desperate for money and quick to learn the drugging techniques. The advantage for them was drugging wasn't sex work; with Carlos's potent mix, even the largest, sweatiest gringo would be unconscious before he could get his pants down.

All *las chicas* had to do was to dance, smile, flick their hair, and slip the white powder into the target's drink, then walk the wobbly tourist to a waiting taxi, also on Carlos's payroll, to be robbed at leisure. Easy.

But now it was going down the drain.

"Fucking hell," said Carlos out loud, poring over the newspaper. "Tourist Killed and Cut Up" read the headline, with the story describing an American traveler, visiting Colombia for the first time, found dead in the bushland on the east of the city, close to the scrubby hills. Carlos knew the area well; he'd taken food parcels to the homeless folk who camped there over the years. Best to keep in with the eyes and ears of the streets.

The victim was found with "deep lacerations to the face, and died of blood loss," went on the report. This was similar to two other murders since the start of the year, one of a Canadian businessman and a backpacker from France, both male.

"*Que desmadre,*" said Carlos. Not that he cared about a dead gringo or two. The more the merrier. His main concern not being the Colombian police—though they could be a problem—rather the drug cartels that moved merchandise through the city. They wouldn't want the extra attention. And they would deal with Carlos if he couldn't deal with the situation.

Already the newspaper was talking of a "special police task force" that had been formed to track down the killer—or killers. The city police were posting warnings in bars and nightclubs around town. None of it sounded good.

Carlos picked up a phone from a pile by the window and called a number on a scrap of paper.

"Pacho, *que hubo.*" (What's up?)

Pacho replied in a low voice. "Don't call me here. The place is buzzing."

Pacho was a police detective, was one of Carlos's guys on the inside, his most trusted, and the one that got the fattest envelope at the end of the month. But Pacho could only help so far, such as a tip-off to a raid. He couldn't protect against murder. And the heat was on.

"Give me something, Pachito. Anything."

"Look, the shit's hitting the fan. These dead guys were on the Tinder aps, and looking for girls, but they bit off more than they could chew. Or more likely, something chewed them!"

"How so?" said Carlos.

"Forensics have never seen anything like it. Faces cut to shreds, like someone really had it in for them."

"Someone sending a message?"

"Could be. Or a nutter. Best to keep low for a week or two, until we get some answers. The Task Force is here now, and no one is safe."

Pacho ended the call.

Carlos dialed again. It was Pardo. "*Oiga marika*, tell the girls to stand down. No more business until I say. Bring the boys here tonight. And any news."

When they met later that evening, in the same backroom behind a club, a drab one on the backstreets—"best not to draw attention," Carlos had said when he moved in—the team filed in.

The stakes were higher now; for the first night in years there were no girls working the tourist haunts. No one was getting drugged. No one getting robbed. No cashflow. No payoffs to the police.

Worse, Carlos had got a text message from the Cartel chief: "Tell me this problem is going away. Or you'll be going away."

But he kept that to himself. Now was not the best time to panic in front of his crew. There was always some *sicario* waiting to step up.

"*Oiga, carajos*, what's the story?" he started, trying to sound relaxed.

"These guys had all been in the bars, but weren't picked up by our girls, or any others, from what we are hearing. There's nothing on the cameras."

"Any freelancers out there?" said Carlos.

Some *chicas* did their own tricks and kept the profits, and sometime other small gangs moved into the city. When Carlos tracked them down—which he always did, tipped off by his network of bar staff— revenge was swift and final. It wasn't just the fact they were taking his profits. Amateur operators had more chance of overdosing the victims, with an accidental death, which was also bad for business.

The last breakaway *chica* Carlos had killed himself, slowly, in front of his lieutenants, to set a good example. He used a clear plastic bag he favored for the prettier girls, tying her to the chair before placing the bag tight, sealing it with tape, and watching the life ebb from her big brown eyes.

Her death went unnoticed. Unlike the tourists, no one missed the migrants, if they even knew they existed in the first place, and her body was buried far away.

But now his boys had been all over the bars and clubs and the message from the informants was the same; no new gang, girls working freelance, and no one behind the murders.

"What about the *caminantes*?" said Carlos. Some tourists—usually the cheaper one—wandered the parks at night to find a sex worker, also the cheaper ones.

In fact, the last body had turned up on wasteland close to Vargas Park, the city's largest late-night honeypot. In fact, all three tourists were found on the edge of the city, but in different directions.

"Do we have a crazy hooker out there? Or a religious nut? Or some whack job getting revenge because some gangly gringo screwed his missus? Find this maniac. And kill him."

But still, nothing was adding up. These were tight-knit criminal communities where anything on the streets was reported up. But now, nothing. His lieutenants were rattled, Carlos could see it in their eyes.

Carlos was a good manager, keeping his team in line with a judicious mix of pain and pleasure, and he knew how to delegate. But he was also suddenly aware that there were moments when he needed to step up.

He'd spent too long in the backroom, getting high, counting his cash, barking orders by burner phones. Why, he hardly ever cleaned his own gun anymore. He knew what he had to do.

"Fuck it, I'm not sending boys to do a man's job. I'll sort it myself."

He grabbed his Sig Sauer from the tabletop, shoved it in his belt, then grabbed a jacket and a baseball cap from the shelf behind, and strode out. No one followed.

The cool night air hit him, and he felt good. This was long overdue. He needed to take charge.

Walking the streets was risky—in theory there were at least six warrants out for his arrest—but it was dark, and he moved fast, and in the shadows, taking the backstreets.

As he reached the downtown area, the scenery changed, with brighter lights and gaggles of foreigners—mostly men, mostly clutching beers— clogging the streets outside the bars belting out rock music.

He moved quickly, invisibly, and no one gave the Colombian a second glance.

At Vargas Park he stopped. It was a few acres of sparse lawns and bushy trees that backed onto the mountain, with some scrubland in between, where townsfolk strolled at sundown, but most people tended to stay clear once dark shadows claimed the spaces between the sodium lamps.

Along the road edge was the pick-up zone where tourists would hook up with *chicas* wanting to "practice their English", usually in a cheap hotel. But tonight was quiet, except for a few dog walkers, and Carlos passed on into the shadows.

He now realized he'd come all this way without a plan. That was unusual, maybe a mistake. Carlos was always methodical. That's how he survived.

But he also felt liberated, the same buzz from years before when he lived on the streets by his wits— and his gun.

And now he would find this nutter, this serial killer, this monster, whoever was topping tourists, and end it. And everyone would know it was Carlos.

And then he saw her. A young woman, with long hair and an old-style dress, in the path ahead. She turned slowly towards him, and in that second, he saw a face so beautiful he could only stop and stare.

"Buenas noches, señor ¿sería tan amable de acompañarme un rato?" Can you please walk with me for a while? The formality of her request caught him off guard.

"I'm here for information, these killings, it's causing problems, someone has to talk…" his toughness faltered, and his voice trailed off as she stepped closer and tilted towards him, her brown eyes searching his face, then the intoxicating touch of her hands as she held his forearms and pulled him gently closer and towards the shadows.

"Shush, Carlitos, be quiet, we don't need to talk, to be together."

Carlos felt the park and city float away as she walked him backwards into the trees. Strange, she knew his name. But then everyone did. The price of fame, he thought, and smiled. The evening might turn out better than expected.

But now in the darkness he was heavy, not light, and her hands were strong, not delicate. Some part of him liked being held fast. But another part of his brain was yelling "danger". He struggled but couldn't move. He thought about his pistol, but suddenly it seemed so far away.

"I've waited a long time for you, Carlitos. You are not easy to find," said the girl, still gripping him, and bringing her face closer. He could hear his breathing, and his heartbeat, and suddenly felt smaller. Or was the *chica* getting bigger?

Whatever it was, she was rising in the darkness above him, bending over him, pushing him down. He wanted to shout out, but his words couldn't reach his mouth, and his arms felt like useless rags dangling by his side.

Then suddenly he could see against the dark sky the eyes inches from his face, searching inside him, the same brown eyes, the ones in the plastic bags, the eyes he had watched flickering out, and now dissolving into black form that pressed against his face.

No noise came, just a gaping fanged jaw that now gripped his head and pushed it deep into the soil.

"*La Muelona*", he gasped, even as he felt huge teeth cleave the flesh from skull and blood trickle into his throat. Then a searing pain. And nothing.

La Muelona, the Toothed One, stood up, recovering her normal size and neat features, and she smoothed her dress with her delicate hands. She sighed. Her task here was finished. Tomorrow she could move on, to another town or city.

One thing was for certain, in Colombia her work would never be done.

THROUGH THE WINDOW

by Shane Pillay

The long, hot Friday afternoon kills your spirit. Nothing moves as slow as the clock on the wall. It ticks but slyly misses a beat when nobody looks. No sense attacking the keyboard. Office work is abandoned until next Thursday. Only the cleaners break the monotony. They empty the bins. Then they leave.

I was stuck on such a day. My youth was cursed. I must find another job. But I didn't have a college education. Good jobs wouldn't come easily. Depressed, my young mind aged like a rubbish heap. Across the desk, Fred Rapetsoa played solitaire on his computer.

"Tell me a story, Fred," I said.

He smiled and refused.

Fred Rapetsoa worked in this company all his life. He was Xhosa. When he spoke, his tongue clicked sounds and words. Each morning, he took a minibus taxi to the office. In the evening, he returned by minibus taxi.

"Why not?" I asked, "Just a story. Maybe two?"

He refused again. I shook my head and opened a drawer, hoping to amuse myself with the contents. But there were only papers and a few broken pens.

"Come on, Fred," I said, "Must I beg?"

His face lowered - a long, pensive look. I knew he had a story. My legs pushed against the desk and, as Newton predicted, my chair rolled toward him.

"I know some stories," he said, "But I can't remember all."

So, I asked for the ones he remembered. He nodded and mourned two haunting tales.

"In the first a young man journeyed home after a hard day at work. He took the train and alighted at the district station. It was three kilometers to his home. But the distance was not a problem. The young man knew the route, he took the path daily. He would soon be at his door.

"It was evening. The red sun threatened to settle over the nearby hills. Menacing long shadows appeared. The young man pulled his jersey tighter around the waist and trudged forward. He wanted to reach home before dark. Something warm would wait for him on the stove plate.

"Presently, another person joined him on the path. He was silhouetted against the horizon and his face could not be seen. They walked side by side, paces alike. The young man greeted the newcomer and the stranger returned the words. The young man asked if he were going home. The stranger replied with two sharp nods. Thereafter the conversation ceased. The young man thought it odd that a complete stranger walked beside him. He expected the stranger to keep his distance.

"The minutes wore on. The young man, tired and uncomfortable, reached into his pocket for a box of Rothmans' cigarettes and Lion matches. He placed a roll between his lips and returned the box to his pocket. Then the match was lit, his cupped hand a shield against the wind. He brought the flame close and puffed to ignite the tobacco. Out of the corner of his eye, he noticed the stranger. There was a sad expression in his eyes.

"The cigarette was lit. He threw the match. Slowly he drew in and exhaled.

The stranger stare was fixed. The young man smoked until the cigarette was half-finished. Still, the stranger held his gaze. The young man could not take it any longer. He turned to the stranger.

"'What's wrong?'

"'Ah,' the stranger replied, 'That is the smell of cigarette smoke.'

"'And?' asked the young man. 'I'm smoking. You can't tell me not to smoke. Go walk somewhere else if you don't like it.'

"'It is not that,' said the stranger.

"'Then what is it?'

"'That smell of cigarette smoke,' began the stranger, 'I remember it when I was *alive!*'

"The cigarette fell onto his shirt. The young man brushed it away and swore. When he looked up the stranger was gone. He searched wildly but the darkness swallowed all vision. The young man quickened his pace and dared not turn his head. When he reached home. he told the story to his wife. She prayed for him. That night he could not sleep. He stared through the window. The stranger might return.

"The next day he disappeared. People said that they saw him get off the train and walk home. He was never found again."

"Never found again?" I echoed, "Is this true?"

"That is the story," Fred replied.

"Yes," I said, "But is it true?"

Fred did not answer. Instead, he started his second story.

"A family in the township had a daughter. She passed away when she was sixteen. The reasons were unknown. Mournful and consigning the event to God, they buried the child.

"Seven years passed. The family lived with the memory of the dead daughter. Then gossip over fences did rounds in the township. They heard rumors that their daughter had been spotted. She worked as a housemaid. The family listened carefully. It did not make sense. Their daughter had died seven years ago.

"Eventually, a neighbor decided to bring the girl to the house.

"'No,' said the father, 'You cannot bring this girl here. We do not know who she is.'

"'I will bring her,' replied the neighbor, 'You will see.'

"'We don't want to interfere with somebody else,' answered the father, 'It will cause trouble.'

"'But you must see this girl,' insisted the neighbor, 'You must see how she looks.'

"At last, the family agreed and the neighbor brought her home. When the parents saw her, they realized she looked uncannily similar to their daughter. But they buried her seven years ago, and filled the grave. So, this housemaid couldn't be the same person.

"For her part, she recognized neither the house nor the parents. They sat in the lounge and questioned her. She was an orphan and lived with foster parents. As the story of her adoption unfolded, they considered her face closely. She was so much like their daughter. At last, they believed. But the girl denied this. Nothing in this place was familiar.

"'But your face, and how you talk,' said the father, 'It's the same. And you are twenty-three. Our daughter would be your age now.'

"But the girl was firm. 'I must go home.'

"'You must come back tomorrow.'

"'I don't know.'

"'Please.'

"'I have work.'

"They coerced her and eventually, she agreed.

"The next day she returned. They took her to see a sangoma, who is a traditional and spiritual healer. The sangoma could explain everything. He cast his motley collection of sticks and bones on a mat and looked at the girl. She grew scared but they held her firm.

"'She is a zombie,' he announced.

"Her body was captured by her foster parents. They used her as a housemaid. The parents paid money to the sangoma.

"'Cure her,' they said.

"He weaved magic with his muti, which are traditional potions. Muti consists of bones, roots, and twigs. There are other contents too, but much worse. Fred did not talk about that.

"The girl babbled as two people—one as the dead daughter who cried for freedom and the other as the zombie who cursed their meddling.

"After some hours, the girl was cured. Or at least she looked so. They took her home. She lay on a mattress in the lounge, buried underneath an acrylic blanket and head on a soft pillow. Soon she fell asleep. The parents switched off the lights and went to their bedroom. In the middle of the night, the girl woke up and ran away.

"The next morning the family found the empty mattress. They decided to visit the sangoma that weekend. He would advise them.

"But things changed that evening. The mother cleaned the kitchen. There were knocks on the door. She drew the curtains and saw her daughter outside. She begged to be let in and given supper. But the woman was frightened. Instead, she passed a plate of food through the window. The daughter ate it up greedily and left.

"This repeated on the following two nights. The daughter knocked, begged for food and the mother passed some through the window. She ate it up greedily and left.

"The weekend arrived. The family visited the sangoma. They told him the story. He scattered his sticks and bones on a mat and considered the shapes. Then he asked for money. In return, he gave them muti.

"'Put this in the food,' he grunted.

"Acting on his advice, the mother added the muti to the plate of food. She passed it to the daughter. The sangoma assured them this would finally cure the daughter. She would return whole and safe.

"The muti had an immediate effect. They heard the daughter fall and cry. The mother rushed outside and brought the poor girl into the kitchen."

"She never ran away again," Fred concluded

"Is that all?" I asked.

"Yes," said Fred.

"What happened to the people who turned the girl into a zombie?"

"The people weren't caught," Fred shrugged his shoulders. He returned to his game of solitaire.

I stared at him. "This is stupid. So, they didn't do anything to the people who turned the girl into a zombie?"

Fred nodded. "I told you the people weren't caught."

"And everything was fine with the family after that?" I asked.

"The girl never ran away again," Fred explained.

I sighed. Just like the first story, the second was also unbelievable. "You can't say if it is true or not. You can never say if things like these are true or not."

"Go tell that to a sangoma!" replied Fred. His eyes opened as wide, exposing the whitesclera and the black dots of his pupils were piercing. and. Then he laughed and returned to his game of solitaire. I laughed too but it wasn't as bold as the laugh of Fred Rapetsoa.

Determined not to be outdone, I rapped on the table to get Fred's attention.

"I got one," I said, "Listen to this."

"Is it good?" asked Fred.

"It is," I nodded, "And it's true too, I swear."

And so I began.

"My uncle returned home from a visit to relatives. He drove his car along the highway. Next to him was his wife—my aunt. Their young son slept in the backseat.

"The car sped along smoothly. The radio played late-night music—jingly and sparse. My aunt nodded to the barren wails of the guitar. It clothed the loneliness of the dark roads. Then the car slowed.

"'What's happening?' she asked, 'What's wrong with the car?'

"'Look there,' my uncle pointed.

"They traveled down a hill. At the bottom was a Stop sign. Its face was wrecked and painted over by the neighborhood vandals. A woman stood next to the sign. Her hand stretched out and thumbed for a lift. She did not look at the approaching car. My uncle peered closely at her face.

"'Don't stop,' cried my aunt, 'Go!'

"'You're right,' said my uncle, and he drove quickly past.

"When they reached home, my cousin was put to bed. My uncle and aunt went to their room. But my uncle could not sleep. He nudged his wife.

"'What do you think?' he asked, 'That lady wanted a lift, right?'

"'So?' asked my aunt, 'What can we do now? It's time to sleep.'

"'But what if something happens to her?' asked my uncle.

"'Somebody would have given her a lift by now,' mumbled my aunt, 'There is no need to worry.'

"But my uncle was insistent. He got out the bed.

"'Where are you going?' asked my aunt. She got out too.

"'I'm going back. I'll give that lady a lift,' he said. 'We shouldn't have left her alone. What kind of people are we?'

"My aunt screamed. 'It is so late!' she shouted, 'You can't go back! Something will happen!'

"'Nothing will happen,' replied my uncle. He tied his belt around his pants. My aunt grabbed him and pulled him back. 'Let go!' said my uncle.

"'You mustn't go!' screeched my aunt. 'Don't you see? It is evil! She is calling to you! Something is wrong!'

"My cousin awoke. He ran to the room.

"'Look at what you've done!" said my aunt, 'You've woken him up. Come here, baby.'

"My cousin cried and fell into his mother's arms.

"'I didn't wake him up,' said my uncle, 'You woke him up with your screaming!'

"'See, your father wants to give that woman a lift,' my aunt told my cousin. He was the only confidante for her. She held him by the head. 'Did you see that woman, baby?'

"'No,' replied my cousin, 'I didn't see her. What woman?'

"My aunt screamed again. 'You hear!' She told my uncle, 'He didn't see her! There's something wrong with that woman! She's a spirit!'

"'He was sleeping!' said my uncle, 'Of course he didn't see her!'

"Finally, my uncle relented and decided to stay at home. It was a troubled sleep. He dreamt the woman called through the window.

"The next day they read a story in the local newspaper. A woman had been killed at that spot. It was certainly the same woman who had thumbed for a lift."

"So?" asked Fred contemptuously, "You make me laugh. Someone found that woman after your uncle saw her. They killed her."

"You're wrong Fred," I said, "They had killed that woman earlier in the day and dragged her to that spot later in the evening. It was proven in court. My uncle definitely saw an apparition, a ghost, a spirit. What do you think of that?"

"Nothing," replied Fred and shook his head. "It's lies."

"No," I said, "It is true. My aunt said that the woman called my uncle telepathically."

"What's that?"

"That's talking to someone through the mind," I explained, "That woman called my uncle. And if he returned and gave her a lift, she would have harmed him. Maybe possessed him or something."

Fred paused. A thoughtful look blanketed his face. I was glad. He wasn't the only one with ghostly tales.

"And you think that it is true?" asked Fred.

"Yes," I said, "It's true. Like those other stories you told me."

"Yes," laughed Fred, "like those other stories. Cultures have many truths. We must believe them all. If we don't, we don't have culture."

"That's an odd thing to say," I shrugged.

"Maybe," said Fred, "Soon it will time to go home. Good luck."

MALVHINA

by Steve Burford

Ostara (Spring Equinox)

She was so beautiful, he couldn't take his eyes off her.

"Her name's Malvhina," said a voice behind him. Startled, he turned to face the young woman smiling at him.

"What's she doing all the way out here?"

The woman came closer in consideration of the object that had so captivated him. She shrugged. "Guarding the well? Some say she gave Malvern its name."

Before them, set into a natural alcove of the hill, was a sculpture in stone and bronze of a woman. She was dressed in ancient Celtic fashion, had long hair that fell past her shoulders down to her hips, and she held a pitcher from which water, drawn from deep within the hills, gushed. "But Malvern's got loads of wells. None of them has a sculpture like this."

"Perhaps this one's special. Or perhaps the others got stolen or smashed because they weren't so well hidden among the hills." The young woman held out her hand. "I'm Sophie."

He took her hand. It was cool and smooth. "I'm Tom."

They sat on the grass in front of Malvhina and talked and laughed until the evening shadows all but hid the sculpture's face. He was a painter; she was a jeweller. Both had come to Malvern on the border of Worcestershire and Herefordshire searching for inspiration from the spa town's natural beauty, and artistic heritage. As they talked, both began to feel they might now have found it.

Over the weeks that followed, they met often at Malvhina's well.

At the end of the third week, Sophie crept up behind Tom as he stood, gazing into the stone eyes of the sculpture, and covered his own eyes with her hands. "I think you fancy her more than me."

Laughing, Tom pulled her hands away from his face. "I just find her … fascinating."

Sophie mock pouted. "More fascinating than me?" Tom pretended to consider. "Bastard! And I had a present for you." She held out her hand.

Tom blinked. "A ring?"

"I made it for you. It's nothing special. I mean, it's not gold or anything," she added quickly as she saw his uncertainty. "You do like it, don't you?"

Tom took the ring, but he didn't put it on. "Yes. Yes, of course I do. It's just…. Well, it's normally the man who gives the ring isn't it?"

A month later, they moved in together. Using a small inheritance, Sophie rented a workshop off Malvern's high street. Tom used their flat over an Indian restaurant as his studio, painting while she went to work. At least one evening every week, they would walk up into the hills, strike off the paths used by the tourists, and head for Malvhina's well. Sometimes, Tom would go during the day too, while Sophie was at work.

Sophie used the colours and materials of the Malvern landscape to create new jewellery, and slowly, her critical and commercial success grew. Inspired by his muse, Tom painted with passion and energy, but his portraits didn't sell. "Y'know, I'm not sure if they're me or her," Sophie said, looking at the paintings that were beginning to fill every available space in their flat.

"Who?"

"Malvhina."

Tom grunted and carried on painting.

Litha (Summer Solstice)

On Midsummer Eve, Tom insisted they go to the well. There, ignoring Sophie's half-hearted, laughing protests about the possibility of being caught by ramblers, he had taken her clothes off, removed his own, and they had made love at the feet of the statue, their bare skin splashed by the icy water pouring from her pitcher.

Afterwards, lying on the grass, propped up on one elbow, Sophie watched Tom. Still naked, he was standing with his back to her, facing the sculpture. "What are you doing?" she asked sleepily.

"I'm making a wish." He held out his hand and let something drop into the stone basin at Malvhina's feet that collected the water from her pitcher.

Sophie laughed and got up. "Seriously?" She picked her way over to him, wary of stones on her bare feet.

"Wells are sacred places. This place is sacred to us isn't it?"

"So, what did you wish for?"

Tom didn't look round. His eyes remained fixed on Malvhina. "I wished that you and I would be together for ever."

From behind, Sophie slipped her arms round him. Her hands were cool and smooth on his bare chest. She nuzzled his neck. "You shouldn't have told me. Now it won't come true."

When he didn't answer, she stood on tip toe so she could see past him to whatever it was he had dropped into the water. He shifted to block her view; so she let go and stepped round him to see, now really curious. From within the stone basin came the silver glint of moonlight reflected from metal. "It's the ring I gave you. But I thought you liked it."

"I love it. And I love you. That's why it was right to give it to Malvhina. She knows how much it means to me, how much of a… sacrifice it was. So, in return, she'll make sure we're always together."

Sophie searched his face for some sign that he was joking. There was none. She stepped backwards, out of his arms. "Someone will see it there and take it."

Tom shook his head. "Malvhina will keep it safe. It's hers now."

Mabon (Autumn Equinox)

As summer slipped into autumn, Sophie knew that night at the well had been a turning point. They no longer talked and laughed the way they had. She worked hard at her art and her business, but at the end of the day she wanted to put them to one side to spend time with Tom.

But Tom did not. He was at his painting before she got up in the morning and still working when she went to bed at night. His portraits grew bolder and wilder. Images of the same woman multiplied around their flat, teasing, imploring, beckoning, threatening. She had long, red hair, like Sophie's – or perhaps like

Malvhina's if she hadn't been made of stone. Twice, Sophie returned to their flat during the day to find that Tom wasn't there. Briefly, she wondered if he had a mistress, but in her heart, she knew the truth was stranger than that. The third time, when she returned to an empty flat after work, she knew her relationship with Tom was over, and she knew where to go to tell him. He would be with Malvhina.

By the light of a cold Hunter's Moon, she made her way to Malvhina's arbour in the hills, and found Tom kneeling, head bowed in front of the sculpture, a sketch book discarded on the ground at his side. She shivered as she walked over to him. "Tom." He didn't move. She knelt down beside him to bring her face level with his. He remained staring down into the water of the stone basin. Instinctively, her eyes followed the direction of his.

She gasped, then gave a small laugh to cover her embarrassment. It was just a reflection: Malvhina's face in the water, looking up at her. She frowned. She wouldn't have thought it would be so clear, even with the moonlight as bright as it was. She leaned in closer, and for one bizarre moment, the reflection of her face overlaid that of Malvhina, so that the two images merged in the water: her cheeks with Malvhina's chiselled cheeks; her lips with Malvhina's cold lips; her eyes with Malvhina's blank, unblinking stare.

She heard Tom stir next to her, felt his hands on her shoulders, on the back of her head. She knew she should move, but she couldn't, as immobile as the stone statue looking down at her from its alcove, and up at her from within the water.

She couldn't even scream as Tom made his second sacrifice.

Yule (Winter Solstice)

He didn't know when he'd started talking to her. Sometime after that night in autumn he supposed. She hadn't spoken back of course, at least, not in words. But he'd heard her - in the splashing of the water that poured from the pitcher into the stone basin: the endless pattering, swishing, plashing of the icy water. He heard it in the morning and the evening, at the well or at the flat. Not that he was at the flat very much now. Some nights he even slept at Malvhina's well, curled up at the feet of the stone statue, in spite of the freezing weather. And he talked to her.

"Together forever. That's what I wished for." On his knees, rocking backwards and forwards, he said the words over and over, staring up into Malvhina's eyes. The water whispered and laughed as it poured from her pitcher. "Together forever."

And although he had lost all track of time, although he couldn't even remember when he'd last eaten or washed, somehow, he knew when the moon rose again, that it was midwinter, the longest night, the dead time of the year. He was glad because after death came life again. Life was the promise of water.

Behind him he heard the crunch of steps on the brittle, frosted grass. "Together forever," he whispered. "Together forever." The steps grew closer, but he did not look round. His face remained turned upwards, his eyes fixed on Malvhina's.

He felt her hands on his shoulders, circling his throat, pushing his head down. They were cool and smooth as stone, burning with an even fiercer cold where the icy metal of a ring circled one of her fingers. From within the water in the stone basin, Malvhina, Sophie and his own reflection looked back up at him.

Tom smiled. "Together forever."

MOTHERS OF MERCY

by Nicola Lombardi

translated by J. Weintraub

Aguscello, Ferrara (Italy)

The first light of dawn framed the shape of Father Pietro's body as he stood on the threshold, his hands buried deep inside the pockets of a coat a bit too large for his slight figure. A sharp autumn breeze stirred his few remaining tufts of grizzled hair.

Behind him, a step or two away, was another man, taller, in regulation cap and uniform.

"Sorry about the early hour, Anna," began the priest, "but I really have to talk to you. Something terrible has happened."

The woman, who carried her sixty-three years rather poorly, was wearing a nut-colored linen gown, worn and frayed, that a knotted belt barely kept closed over her stout frame. Her gray hair was bunched up into a hastily coiled bun, from which fugitive curls, like wisps of steam, swirled around her squarish face. A pair of bulging, leathery bags, streaked with small purplish veins, outlined deep shadows beneath her eyes. She must have already been up anyway when Father Pietro rung at her door, since from the dimness behind her came the strong and inviting aroma of coffee.

"Martina?" she asked simply, her voice hoarse.

The police officer, standing in the priest's shadow, instinctively stepped in. "How did you know, ma'am?"

Anna pursed her lips to form a thin, weary smile across her face. "Actually, I didn't know. But I felt it."

Before the officer could reply, Father Pietro again spoke up. "Anna, this is Carlo. We're cousins, somewhat distant. He's the Chief Inspector at the Ferrara district station. Carlo, Mrs. Anna P__."

The man came forward and, without removing his black glove, extended a hand. "Inspector Gori. Sorry for the intrusion at such an early hour, ma'am. It's an entirely unofficial visit. Pietro . . . Father Pietro told me that you . . ."

". . . that maybe you can tell him something about the 'Mothers of Mercy'," said the priest, interrupting him somewhat abruptly. The cold air was staining his cheeks with patches of red. "Can we go inside, Anna?"

*****

About ten minutes later, the three were sitting around the kitchen table before three cups of steaming coffee. The place was not very clean, thick with the smell of stale food and garbage. The faint early morning light that peeked through the single window hidden behind a torn curtain was not enough to enable them to see into each other's eyes, so Anna also turned on the fixture hanging from the ceiling, a sort of cumbersome, milky-white shell, housing a good number of dead insects.

Father Pietro began to stir his coffee slowly, even though he had not added any sugar. "They found Martina a few hours ago, in the Pedagogy. Dead."

That was the name commonly used to refer to Aguscello's abandoned orphanage. The Pedagogy. By then, that decrepit and sinister building could be said to be well-known even beyond its district and regional boundaries, thanks to more than one sensationalistic television broadcast.

"How did it happen?" Anna asked, her voice flat, almost as if—rather than to satisfy a genuine curiosity—she felt compelled to ask it.

Gori, gloves and cap lined up in martial order next to his coffee cup, brought a hand to his mouth and coughed. "You understand, ma'am, at this stage we're not yet allowed to divulge any details. Once the investigation is completed . . ." He let the sentence hang, seeing that the woman was nodding wearily. No need to waste any more breath. He then shifted his glance over to his cousin, silently inviting him to take over their little talk.

The two had agreed that their meeting would not have even the faintest hint of official misconduct, something that, if known, could have triggered both an awkward and untimely reaction from judicial authority. The Inspector would only listen without asking questions, or at least not too many, so that this more-or-less impromptu visit would not be mistaken for an interrogation, which, in fact, it was not. Anna P_ was in no way a suspect or even "a person of interest," largely because the unfortunate Martina R__, a woman fifty-eight yeas old, was found to have died of natural causes, attributed solely to her poor state of health.

The first theory proposed by the medical examiner, as soon as he arrived on the scene and in the absence of any external sign linked to a trauma, favored a heart attack or a stroke. The position of the body, in particular, was enough to exclude any external act of violence or an accident. The woman had been found lying rather serenely in the middle of one of the more spacious rooms on the ground floor; and if it had not been for her tilted-back head, the grimace of pain crystallized on her face, and her fingers clawing the soil and the crumbling debris littering the floor' she could have been imagined, as she lay there on her back, to be preparing to go to sleep, regardless of the incongruity of the surroundings. Moreover, there were no traces of scraping or dragging, much less of a struggle, in the immediate vicinity. And so, any more accurate answers would have to be provided by the autopsy.

It had been the roar of a motorbike and the ringing of his doorbell in the middle of the night that had drawn Father Pietro from his bed. Looking out of his bedroom window on the second floor of the rectory, he had seen two persons aboard a scooter, both wearing helmets. The driver had raised his visor and had cried out to him, "There's a dead woman at the Peda!" Then he took off at full speed.

Father Pietro had not recognized them, but he had supposed they were some of those many kids who loved to sneak into the old orphanage at night for the strangest of reasons. Having discovered something unpleasant (in this case, a corpse) and not wanting to risk getting involved by calling the police, they had chosen to sound the alarm in this way, leaving the hot potato in the parish priest's hands, before vanishing into anonymity.

Not even for a minute did Father Pietro think that this could be a joke, but before involving the police, he had phoned a friend, a parishioner who lived near the Pedagogy, asking him for confirmation; and then he had dressed in a flash, straddled his bike, and rushed over to the scene. Once he realized that what his unknown terrified informant had shouted out proved to be true, he then proceeded on his own to call the District Headquarters in Ferrara, finding, by chance, his own cousin there on duty.

The reasons that had prompted him to consider putting the Inspector in touch with Anna implied in no way any responsibility on the woman's part for what had happened. Very simply, the unfortunate Martina belonged to that weird group of women known as "Mothers of Mercy," a group for which Anna was regarded as both founder and mentor. Naturally, the priest was careful to emphasize an important point, namely, not to lend the slightest credence to the beliefs of those he euphemistically characterized as "the poor things." But if there was one person who could have provided an explanation, however unacceptable, for Martina's presence in the middle of the night, alone, in the Pedagogy, that was certainly Anna.

Father Pietro carefully set the empty cup back down onto its saucer. "Excellent," he commented in a low voice; then, staring directly at Anna, "She was one of you?"

The woman, still licking her lips moist from the coffee, folded her hands into her lap. "She would have liked to be."

"I don't wish to appear rude," said Gori, interrupting and looking at both in turn, "but I don't have a lot of time. Could we get to the point?"

Blushing slightly, Father Pietro nodded rapidly. "Yes, of course, Carlo, sorry. Anna, tell the Inspector who the 'Mothers of Mercy' are and what they do in the orphanage. Please, will you?"

As the woman then leaned her heavy shoulders against the back of the chair, it creaked ominously. "You, Inspector, surely you know the story of the Pedagogy. Or, better yet, the stories, seeing as so many of them are told."

"I've heard more than one," Gori confirmed, his tone neutral, noncommittal.

In fact, beyond the many variations on the theme passed down orally, it was also possible to trace on the Net all manner of versions regarding the institute's closure in 1970. That the building was considered one of the most mysterious and ghostly places in Italy—a destination for students of the paranormal and enthusiasts of the occult, of psychics, or of fanatical lunatics who delighted in celebrating unnamable nocturnal rites there. There was no end to stories of ghosts and hauntings, and the beauty of it was that all of them seemed to have their own intrinsic authority, as if it were not possible to reject outright one in favor of another.

In fact, the facility was used before the war as a hospital for the treatment of tuberculosis; in 1940, it was sold to the Red Cross, which managed it through a religious order and transformed it into a psychiatric clinic for children. From there it was a short step to viewing the institute as no different from an orphanage for sick and problematic children rejected by their own families. This activity lasted for exactly thirty years, and then the "Pedagogy" was closed, abandoned and left to drift inevitably down that slope that turned it into a veritable icon for the most perverse of popular fantasies. The ambiguity of what was said to have happened within those walls, along with the scarcity of clear information regarding the 1970 closure, created the elements for which the dark fame of that place still showed no signs of fading away. In Aguscello, reports and folklore were intertwined, fabricating and spreading tales based on inhuman nuns, on children sold to pedophiles, and rumors about torture, suicides, arson, contagions, mass graves, electric shock treatments…. And ghosts, of course.

"Inspector," the woman went on, "since I was a little girl, I've always had a certain sensitivity. And from the time I realized how things stood, various women have come to be guided by me for what we call . . . spiritual adoptions."

Father Pietro, suddenly interested in the inlays on the handle of his spoon, lowered his eyes. Gori, on the other hand, remained unmoved, as was fitting for his position.

"There are souls there, still imprisoned. Souls of little children who can't get away. At least, they can't do it on their own. It's really cursed, that place. A kind of limbo. Have you ever been there, Inspector, before tonight?"

"No, ma'am."

"And didn't you feel a sense of uneasiness, discomfort . . . oppression?"

Gori, wrinkling his brow, shifted slightly in his chair. "Frankly, no."

"Please, Anna, move on," said Father Pietro, intervening after having sensed the nervousness of his cousin, who thanked him silently with a slight nod of his head.

"Sure, of course. In short, I provide a way to free the spirits of those children. There are women who desire a child but have not been able to have one, or others who have had children but have lost them. Women who desire. That's the point. Suffering and desire. And I help them. That's all."

"You help them? In what way?" Gori's curiosity, now aroused, had taken a small step forward.

"I help them by making sure that a child's soul enters inside them."

Father Pietro seemed to have turned to stone. He knew what Anna would say. Nevertheless, relying on his status as priest and his distant family relationship with the Inspector, he had obtained Gori's consent to join him there, with the promise that the meeting would have been able to shed a bit of light on Martina's tragic death or, at least, on the reasons for her being found inside there. Listening to those crazy words, however, from the woman's flat, calm voice raised in him the suspicion that he had played the wrong card. It was all so stupid, so absurd. If the Inspector had stood up at that moment, taking leave from both of them, politely and formally, he would have understood.

Instead, Gori continued to observe Anna without batting an eyelash.

"Those poor souls are prisoners of those walls," continued the woman, "and the only means they have of being able to escape is to be welcomed by the

'Mothers of Mercy,' entering into them and sharing their existence. That is a spiritual adoption. To carry a little one in your mind and your heart, every single moment of your life. To feel a child inside you, to speak with them, to love them. Do you think there's something wrong with that?"

At this question, directed point-blank at him, Gori began to blink his eyes rapidly. "No. I would think not. But tell me, how could such a thing be worked out, in practice?"

"It's rather simple. The volunteer and I go over there at night, and she lies down, usually on a cot. A tranquilizer or a gentle sleeping pill can help. Because she has to fall asleep. She has to become receptive. I, on the other hand, watch over her. I sit beside her, and I recite special prayers. And, eventually, the souls of the children appear, and one of them is 'incorporated,' as we say. One of them enters into the new mother."

"And so, ma'am, your presence, as I understand it, is required."

"Absolutely, Inspector. I represent the filter. I make sure everything's in order. Otherwise," She paused for a brief moment, using it to tuck behind one ear a stringy lock of hair that had slipped across her eye. "so many of them would like to 'incorporate,' but only one at a time is allowed. Each 'Mother of Mercy' can welcome only a single child, and I'm the one who has to make sure that things go the way they're supposed to go."

Gori let his eyes drift over to the pine-cone shaped watch draped over Anna's shoulders.

"And you've done this for a lot of women? I mean these 'Mothers of Mercy.' How many are there?"

Anna brought a finger to her lips, pretending that she needed to think about it.

"Twenty-one," she finally said, after several seconds.

"Twenty-one?" said Gori, echoing her and raising an eyebrow.

"I've been doing it for so many years. Inspector. Up until now, I have freed twenty-one souls, yes. And I have brought happiness to just as many mothers."

"All women from Aguscello?"

Anna shook her head slowly. "No, no. Only five are from the town. Others have come from outside, but from the region."

The Inspector cast a furtive look over to Father Pietro, who, in the meantime, had stopped fiddling with his spoon and had crossed his arms over his chest. Before arriving at Anna's, he had told him a little about these women, although without going into the merits of their imaginary situations, describing them as harmless lunatics who wandered about, often talking to themselves. Gori had, without doubt, recognized the type: persons like that could be found almost everywhere, lost in the derelict solitudes of their minds. The idea that these 'Mothers of Mercy' were actually just poor victims of mental illness stood out as the only plausible interpretation of what Anna was talking about.. And yet, there was in that woman's eyes such strength and determination, that an aura of inexplicable fascination permeated her story, and such was the case with almost all the most frightful tales linked to the Pedagogy.

But it was time to get to the heart of the matter. "And Martina R---? You said before she was not a 'Mother of Mercy'?"

Anna's face darkened. "She would have liked to have become one. But I never agreed."

"Your reason?"

"She drank, and her liver was in bad shape. Her blood pressure was high, and she had other disorders. In short, she was not fit for it. What kind of mother could she have ever been? No, I always told her no."

Gori had to repeat to himself that this was not an interrogation. But it was becoming increasingly difficult for him not to go there. "When was the last time you saw her?"

Anna did not hesitate. "Two nights ago. Here."

"She came to your home?"

"Yes, she wanted to persuade me to turn her into a 'Mother of Mercy'. She was very insistent. But for the reasons I explained to you, I simply could not give her that satisfaction."

Gori placed his elbows on the table, intertwining his fingers. "And so, it was predictable that she eventually would have tried it on her own. To go there, I mean, lie down, fall asleep, and all the rest."

Anna, aware also that the priest was staring at her, looked back into the man's eyes. "I think so. Of course, I could never know when she would do it. She was free to...."

The Inspector interrupted her the very moment he realized that the woman had been put on the defensive. "Naturally, no one holds you responsible, ma'am. It was only to find out if the woman had acted on her own accord."

"Completely on her own account, I assure you. If it had been up to me, I would have stopped her, even on my own, from getting close to that place."

Anna sighed deeply, and in that moment, staring directly at her, Gori had the impression that the pale morning light had playfully discolored her eyes, diluting them from dark brown to an ashen grey. But it was a momentary illusion, since the women began at once to rub them, drying off the moist sheen that had veiled them, and a weary expression settled over her face as she stared at him again. "Any more questions, Inspector?"

Her tone was faint, as if from someone who had almost no more breath left to speak.

Father Pietro, silent and motionless up to that moment, stirred himself up enough to echo her, "Any more questions, Carlo?"

Gori thoughtfully stroked his chin and cheeks where his morning stubble was already appearing. "No, ma'am. Not for now at least." He stood up, collecting his gloves and cap. "Thank you for the coffee and the time you've given me."

Father Pietro also did likewise, hastily muttering in turn his thanks.

"Think nothing of it," replied the woman. "It was a pleasure getting to know you, Inspector. I realize that it's not easy to believe what I've told you, but at least you listened to me without smiling or turning up your nose like so many others do." She avoided making eye contact with the priest, but it was as if she had done so anyway. "I was watching you closely while I was speaking. You're a good man."

"Thank you," Gori replied, keeping back a hint of embarrassment. Certainly, he could not express his true opinion, not on that occasion.

Once immersed again in the milky dimness of the morning light, however, just past the threshold, Gori could not help but turn back toward the woman, who remained posed against the dreamy, shadowy torpor of the interior, staring at her two visitors.

"Ma'am, just out of curiosity, for purely personal reasons, if you don't want to answer me."

"You want to know if I, too…?"

Gori smiled, awkwardly. "Yeah, that's it. I guess that's just what I'd like to ask you."

The woman placed her right hand over her heart.

"Of course." Her eyes instantly filled with tears. Her voice did not quiver but lowered in tone. "He's been in me for nineteen years now. But he's only twelve years old. He will always be twelve years old."

Gori heard the shuffling steps of Father Pietro as he moved a few steps further on, mumbling his incomprehensible words. He had to admit it, there was something surreal about that dialogue. And he could not give any explanation for how asking such a question had ever crossed his mind, a question that collided against any claim of good reason or common sense. Perhaps—no, certainly—he felt sorry for that woman. She was not a lunatic, or at least she did not seem to be at all like one. She openly displayed a sorrowful dignity despite the role into which she had been cast. Father Pietro had told him that she was a widow, and she had lost a son a good many years before. A typical traffic accident. If he was unable to believe her, at least he could understand her. Those poor "Mothers of Mercy" were all united by their desire to drown their painful grief, to find a reason for carrying on. He also could have avoided asking one final question, but it burst forth from him impetuously when he saw how moved the woman was by her reference to her own "spiritual adoption."

"And when you, when one day?" He did not finish the sentence. There was no need to.

Anna avoided meeting the Inspector's eyes, looking away instead all around her. From the windows of some nearby houses, curious faces suddenly vanished behind curtains quickly swept shut.

"That day, he will finally be free. All will be free when their 'Mother of Mercy' passes away."

Gori heard Father Pietro mutter an "amen" just under his breath.

A gust of wind raised a small swirl of dry leaves that then scattered, as if startled, just beyond the entrance to an alleyway. A low whistling, gloomy and prolonged, reverberated along the gutter's drainpipes.

*****

That evening, while the clouds, still low and tinged a bloody red, were laying heavily over the horizon, Anna crossed through the park, dried up by the season, and made her way through the brushwood and the rubble, following an invisible path she would have been able to travel even with her eyes closed. The gray walls, soiled with obscene or sacrilegious scribbling, followed her with the empty sockets of their gutted windows, welcoming her with the fallen arms of their solitude. She was not a stranger there inside; nor was she an intruder. Every single shadow, every nook and cranny, every loose stone, every crack and crevice, everything, everything there in that majestic ruin that had once been a psychiatric hospital for children, always welcomed her with respect. The same respect with which she approached, each time, year after year, that little world suspended between dream and madness. By then she had become used to that sense of anguish that so many claimed to have felt, without knowing how to explain it, whenever they dared to venture between those walls; and even the feeling of deep hatred that she, at first, had developed for that place had faded considerably over the years, because even though that crumbling limbo held in its infected belly the souls of children who had died fifty years before, it put up no resistance to their liberation.

Everything was still there, immobile, unchanged. The rusting carousel, the small, overturned chairs, the cots, the dangling railings, the stairs leading up to nowhere. And ghosts, of things and of people, memories never entirely erased, fears, hopes, suffering, piled up like rubble, untenable scribblings over the torn fabric of its reality. Anna never failed to be moved, whenever she found herself within those violated walls, beneath the patches of sky shedding light through shattered ceilings, surrounded by grassy weeds, dark and drooping yet struggling for life between crawlspaces, doorways, stones.

She reached the spot where she usually ended up when accompanying a new "Mother of Mercy," and there she stopped, lowering her head and eyelids. A trembling ran across the entire surface of her skin, and she had to clench her teeth to contain the throbbing. "Don't be afraid," she whispered, raising a hand to her heart. The child she carried inside did not answer her, nor did he even make her aware of his presence. She was not surprised by that. He always took refuge within the depths of her soul every time she returned to that place. He could not bear the sight of those walls, nor listen to the anguished calling of his former companions. That was understandable. So much would resurface, as always, when she looked for him once she was out of there. For the moment, it was best that he stayed away, safe from any dark memory of his earthly life.

Anna then took a deep breath.

Are you there?

Poor, poor Martina. Why didn't she want to listen to her?

Are you all there, my children?

She did not want to, she could not. Like her lost mind, she was lost.

There you are.

God, how very sorry she was, how very sorry…

Children?

Suddenly she lifted her head, the vertebrae of her neck cracking sharply in the silence. Opening her eyes wide, she fixed them on the leaden void hanging over her

A somber prayer stammered out from of her lips.

Thirteen of them still remained after the last adoption, thirteen still to bring out.

But now, now that all of them were around her, weeping silently over her, caressing her with their pale hands full of anger and regret. She was aware of only ten.

"Three are missing," she gasped, keeping back a rough clot of tears. A violent tremor rippled through her soul.

"Where are you?" she asked out loud. Those three words flew from out of her throat like frightened crows, thrashing their noisy and blundering wings against the walls.

She had been honest about everything that morning with Inspector Gori. About everything except for one thing. She had said that the souls of the children would be free once their new mothers had ceased to live. That is what she had said. But really, she did not know. She had no idea at all. She only clung onto some hopes, but those hopes were balanced against so many doubts, so many fears. . . .

Martina was dead because she was not able to withstand the assault of those desperate little souls, souls who did not ask for anything more than to get out, once and for all, from that place, and to pretend to live a life, any life, just to find relief from that torment. She had opened herself up to them, underestimating the danger. And her body could not bear it.

Three souls. Three souls were missing.

"Where are you now?" she cried out. "Where are you?"

Her legs gave way, and Anna dropped to her knees, unable to prevent all the tears of the world from pouring out of her eyes.

*****

Arcispedale S. Anna, Ferrara

Three days later

In the small funeral home, Inspector Gori had, by then through clenched teeth, repeated the few payers he remembered. Aside from those whispered mutterings of his, the only audible sound in the room was the low hum from the electrical refrigeration conduits coming from inside the walls.

As far as he knew, no one had come to pay final respects to Martina R---, now laid out sedately before him in the coffin atop its small metal catafalque. The woman had, after all, lived alone, and even if she had any friends, none of them had showed up. Gori had supposed that he would be able to encounter there at least some of the "Mothers of Mercy," but perhaps it was fated for that poor corpse to depart in absolute solitude. He stared once more at the emaciated face, the prominent cheekbones, the thin nose, the tight line of her mouth. Despite the tension in her features, there was no further trace of the sudden and excruciating pain that had accompanied her death. On the medical report, under the heading "cause of death," appeared "heart- attack/stroke," two unfortunate conditions occurring simultaneously due to a lethal rise in blood pressure. Apart from the distorted reading due to alcohol consumption, the presence of no other substance capable of provoking the violent disorders that had killed her was found in her system.

Gori felt a deep sorrow in the presence of that unfortunate person. He had not said a word, naturally, to anyone about what Anna P--- had told him; and the reasons for that woman ending up inside the former psychiatric hospital of Aguscello alone, in the middle of the night, remained suspended in the realm of assumptions, all of them irrelevant given the probable lack of clarity documented by the final analytic results.

All that business about the "Mothers of Mercy" had continued to eat away at him those last few days, weaving a sort of a gray tapestry as a backdrop to every single thought. Poor women. Each one shut up in a private internal storage chamber, to inhale solitude, to nurture the illusion of having found the answer to her pain. And the idea that the wretched creature lying in that coffin had died from a desperate attempt to fill an unbearable void, raised a swelling lump in his throat.

"We'll be getting ready, Inspector." The two attendants appearing through a side door approached the catafalque, uncertainty in their steps. "Do you want to wait a little longer, or can we proceed?"

Gori shook himself, backing up a pace. "No. I mean, certainly. Just do your job."

The two then gripped the coffin lid that was propped up against a wall, lifted it, and with practiced movements, carried it into place. It was in that very instant that an invisible, icy finger penetrated beneath Gori's ribcage, and for a few seconds altered the rhythm of his heartbeat.

A gasp must have escaped from his throat, even if he did not realize it, because the funeral-home attendants halted with the coffin lid not yet fully in place and stared at him with anxious expressions.

"Is there something wrong, Inspector. Do you want us to…"

"No, no, I'm sorry. No problem, just go ahead."

Gori retreated another step backwards, to stand next to the main entranceway. He could almost feel the skin at the back of his neck sizzling, It was plausible, even predictable, that gloomy thoughts and fatigue had played an ugly trick on him. It was really not possible that the woman in the coffin, a moment before the lid was put into place, had opened her eyes. And it was not just for the simple fact that Gori had read the autopsy report and knew what conclusive surgical treatments had been applied for that heart and that brain. The idea of a reawakening was simply beyond all belief.

"Inspector, you've turned a bit pale. Are you sure you're all right?"

The sterile light that poured from a dirty neon tube, combined with shifting streaks of shadow, must have generated that fleeting and disturbing impression, casting deceptive reflections across the cadaver's face. Gori could have stopped those men, asked them to take a close look. But what a pathetic figure he would have been! He knew very well, as they did, that the woman was dead, beyond all doubt. He would only make a fool of himself. No, all that he needed to do was to get out of there. He really had to breathe fresh air.

"Thanks, I'm fine," he replied. "Carry on."

Carefully avoiding a glance over at the dark slot between the coffin and its lid, he left the funeral home.

As the door shut behind him with the slow, gasping breath of the closer pump, his tired brain once again began to play tricks on him, transforming that hissing sound into the suffocated cries of children, children closed up somewhere, children who were calling him, children he would never answer because he knew very well that they could not exist.

He quickened his pace, as he walked away into the fading October afternoon, stones and bramble having taken the place of his stomach and heart.

THE ABANDONED CABIN

by Samantha Brooke

Arthur lay in his bunk—unable to sleep both because of the lumpy mattress and the uneasiness which swirled within him. He opened his eyes and turned to look at the bed on his immediate right. The silver glow of moonlight which crept in through the draughty window illuminated the empty bunk—with its covers still mussed and the pillow on the floor from the incident that had taken place about an hour earlier.

"Hah—look at that!" Francis had exclaimed. He was the cool kid with the floppy blond hair and the rich parents, as well as the attitude that he could do whatever he felt like. "Little dopey Ellis has brought his teddy bear with him to camp! What a baby! Absolutely pathetic! Aw—is the first time that you're sleeping away from Mummy, is it?"

All of the other boys had laughed, as Ellis looked around at them uneasily with his wide, murky green eyes. He had looked too scared to utter a word in reply. Even if he hadn't been mute. Arthur had laughed, too, though he had felt sickened with himself for going along with such cruel taunting. What would his mother—gentle and God-fearing as she was—have said if she could see him? He prayed that now the other boy had got his laugh, he would simply give it up. Lay down, and go to sleep. But of course, that's never how these things go.

Malice glimmered in Francis's icy blue eyes as he stepped across the room and wrestled the bear forcefully from Ellis's grip. The smaller boy had struggled and fought, receiving only a smack in the face for his troubles. His flattened pillow fell to the floor along with him as he toppled over. Those around him chortled even more.

"You know, I really think you're too old to be taking a teddy to bed with you," Francis said, mouth quirked into a smirk. "I'm doing you a favour, really. And maybe there's someone else who can use this thing instead, like the girl who died in the abandoned cabin all those years ago."

There fell a collective hush at these words. Ellis gave a muffled whimper. Arthur's heart hammered.

"Yes." Francis nodded slowly. "I think she must be pretty lonely. Let's give her a gift, shall we?"

He darted over to the door and wrenched it open before stepping forth into the dark night beyond. Arthur's mouth grew dry as he watched the figure disappear from sight, being consumed by the blackness.

"No!" Arthur croaked, as Ellis scrambles up off the floor and darts out of the door in pursuit. "Ellis, don't!"

But, too late. Both boys had vanished from sight. The rest of them stayed where they were with the scents of a summer forest drifting in through the open door along with the sound of the night insects, waiting to see what would happen next. It didn't take long.

A few moments later, Francis came rushing back in—his face flushed, and that manic gleam still in his eyes.

"Threw the damn bear into the cursed cabin, didn't I?" he replied. "If that pathetic little baby wants it back, then he'll just have to go in there and get it—"

And it seemed that was exactly what he had done, for he still had not returned to his bed...

As Arthur's unease got the better of him, he forced himself out of bed. The snores of the other boys rolled through the room in one unbroken, endless sound. He crept forth towards the door and slipped through it, out into the night.

The abandoned cabin squatted by the woods like a watchful beast lurking in the darkness. He approached it cautiously, his heart picking up speed. The stories that the other kids told about this place...

Even the counselors avoided it.

But they're just stories, Arthur. Don't be so childish. Someone needs to find out where Ellis is. That place is falling to pieces. He could have fallen and hurt himself...

So, little though he wanted to, he approached the crumbling shack.

He made it to the door and pushed it open. It stuck—rusting hinges protesting loudly. Nevertheless, there was enough of a gap for him to be able to squeeze himself inside. The rotting floorboards groaned as he stepped upon them. The smell of mold, dirt and decay permeated the air, making his nose wrinkle.

"Ellis," he called out, in a carrying whisper. 'Ellis, are you in here? Are you okay?'

A whisper of sound came from within, like somebody moving.

"Ellis?"

No response. He took another step inside, his heart pounding faster than ever. The door slammed closed behind him and he jumped.

Calm down. It's just the wind, that's all. Just find Ellis. The sooner you do that, the sooner you can get out of this horrible place.

"Ellis!" His voice was louder now, edgier. He squinted to see through the darkness—a flash of movement caught his eye.

"Look, it's really not safe to be in here! Why don't you just go back to bed? I'll come back here with you in the morning, and we can look for your teddy then. Yeah? It'll be a lot easier when it's light out. And we won't run the risk of—"

He screamed as a hand fastened tight around his left ankle.

A hand with long, sharp fingernails digging

deep into his skin. Hot blood trickled down his foot, and he screamed again, wrenching himself free with a great effort.

He ran for the door. But this time, it would not open at all. In desperation, he launched himself at the glassless window. The hand grabbed at him once more, trying to tug him back.

With a shriek, he pulled himself clear and toppled out of the window, onto the grass below.

*****

He ran like the wind, his lungs burning. By the time he reached the sanctuary of their sleeping cabin, his face was coated with cold sweat and pain burned in his ankle.

He threw himself inside. Moonlight glimmered brightly. By its silver light, he saw Ellis and his teddy bear both tucked up in bed. The boy was sleeping.

Arthur hobbled over to his own bunk. Inspecting his ankle, he saw thick blood oozing from several puncture wounds. Five in all—deeply gouged into his skin. From one hung a fragment of dirty, rotten fingernail.

End

THE DEVIL'S DOG

by Sarah Das Gupta

A cold east wind was blowing through the graveyard of Holy Trinity Church at Rainscroft that November evening. The old elms were bending before the gale, dark clouds hung low over the fields. The broken crosses on the oldest graves leant at odd angles like bony figure pointing at the bleak countryside.

Inside the vestry, Mark Thompson shivered as he tidied up the papers he had been reading. He was beginning to regret volunteering to look through the drawers of papers and objects which seemed to have been untouched for years. Copies of old parish magazines, going back before the Second World War, lists of graves, receipts for grass cutting, rotas for flower arranging—all mixed up with old vestments, a censer, torn hymn books and sermon notes. Just as he was about to close the dark oak cupboard, he noticed a small drawer at the very back. Leaning into the dark interior of the cupboard, Mark pulled out a wadge of papers. The parchment was thin and yellowing at the edges The writing belonged to a much earlier period. From his work at the local museum, Mark guessed the papers dated from the fifteenth or sixteenth centuries.

Sitting in a shabby leather chair, he started reading the old script. The light in the vestry was dim, the prehistoric oil fire, inadequate. Yet the story told in the manuscript was so disturbing, that Mark ignored the chill in the room and the flickering shadows around him. He began to make notes as he read the faded script.

'It had been St Lucy's Day, 1597, the shortest day of the year, the bleak Winter Solstice. The elite of the Sunday congregation sat in the box pews. The Squire and his family in front. The farm workers and servants crowded at the back. It was just as the vicar climbed into the pulpit that it happened. A gale was raging outside the church, lightning lit up the stained glass windows depicting hideous devils torturing dead sinners with pitchforks and daggers. The heavy oak doors crashed open, as if the entrance to Hell had appeared. A huge black hound, its eyes like burning saucers, leapt onto two petrified peasants, snapping their necks like matchsticks. Then closer to the altar, this devilish brute shrivelled up a hapless man 'like a piece of leather scorched in a hot fire.' Howling fiendishly, the monster of a hound moved on to the next village, leaving scorch marks, the devil's own fingerprints, on the church doors.'

At the end of the account, Mark read: 'All down the church in midst of fire/ the hellish monster flew/ and passing onward to the quire/ he many people slew'. Just as he reached this point, the light went out. The room was pitch dark, except for the red glow of the paraffin fire. Gathering the papers together, Mark turned down the wick of the fire and locked the vestry door. He hurried through the churchyard, a strange red glow hanging over the graves under the dark yews. A bone chilling howl echoed above the sound of the gale as Mark opened the door of his car

*****

Later that evening, Mark returned to the papers he had found in the vestry cupboard. Near the bottom of the pile the paper and writing noticeably changed. The texture and condition of the manuscript suggested it was from a more recent time. The neat copper plate writing was typical of the Victorian era and the incident recorded appeared to be based on a local newspaper report. As he started to read, in the distance the town clock tolled midnight. Yet there was something so compelling about these old papers that made him continue.

'The November of 1855 had been unusually cold and stormy along the east coast. The North Sea tides had been high and destructive for most of the Autumn. Near Cromar, the cliffs had crashed into the sea, leaving abandoned houses hanging on the edge of the remaining coastline as the waves pounded the rocks and debris below, like a frenzied monster awaiting feeding time.

The evening of the 15th the night tide had been higher than usual. Waves washed over the promenade in Skegness. At fishing ports, like Lowestoft and Yarmouth, the life boats had been on alert. At Southwold, a schoolboy had been washed out to sea.

In the lighthouse at Rainscroft, the Light Keeper and his assistant were probably finishing their dinners, washed down with a light ale. The wind was approaching gale force. Along the coast, life guards watched the waves hitting the lighthouse. The spray was so high that it washed over the top. For a second the whole building disappeared in a watery blur.' Mark stopped reading. For a moment he saw the scene clearly. The terrifying power of the sea. The two men trapped in the middle of it all. He had been in the lighthouse once and felt seasick with the waves all around and the sense of imprisonment, of claustrophobia in the tiny round sitting room with its scanty furnishings. He turned back to the beautifully written manuscript.

'Suddenly, the coast guards at Rainscroft saw something extraordinary which they later testified to on oath. On top of the cliffs, appeared a huge black dog. Even above the wind they heard its chilling howl. Enormous, saucer-shaped eyes burnt and glowed through the gathering darkness. The dog leapt off the cliffs. As if riding on the swirling mist, this heart stopping beast was carried to the top storey of the lighthouse. At the same moment, an enormous wave broke over the building. The lighthouse disappeared in a wall of foaming water. When it re-emerged from the misty spray, the spectral hound had vanished.'

Mark felt a chill in the room. He switched on a second lamp. Instinctively he looked out at the black storm clouds, scudding across the sky as he turned back to the account. 'Next morning the storm had vanished. The sea was as calm as a mill pond, not a white horse in sight. The coast guards dragged a boat down the beach, intending to row out to the lighthouse, now gleaming in the pale winter sunshine. Preparing to push the boat into the sea, they suddenly saw a body on the shoreline being gently lifted and lowered by the incoming tide. They recognised the Light Keeper and pulled the water-logged corpse up the beach. As they turned it over, water dribbled from a horribly savaged mouth and face. The right hand and wrist were missing.

The local policeman later accompanied them to the lighthouse. They climbed the stairs in some trepidation, their footsteps echoing in the nervous silence. Only the sound of the waves washing over the dark rocks whispered eerily in the background. Fearful, they slowly opened the door to the small sitting room. The assistant keeper sat bolt upright in a chair, a look of sheer terror on his face. There was no sign of a struggle. He had literally died o fright.'

Mark heard the clock strike again. It was almost 2am. Despite the late hour, he lay awake, listening to the wind moaning and the sound of thunder in the distance.

*****

Two years had passed. Mark, busy with a new job in a land surveyor's office and a part-time university course, had not had the time to research the stories of the Black Dog any further. At least he now understood why the local football team were known as 'The Black Dogs'!

One day in late August, Mark's Sunday afternoon reverie in the sunny back garden was unexpectedly disturbed.

'Hey, Mark! Have you read this in the local rag?'

He woke from dozing to see his girlfriend, Steph, waving a copy of the 'Rainsford Echo' in front of him.

'No, I only buy it for the adverts. Remember, we've been looking for an old weathervane for the cottage?'

'Well, you'll be interested in the re-appearance of the infamous Black Dog. You were obsessed with it a couple of years ago!'

Mark sat up quickly. 'Has there been another sighting of him?'

'Well, only his skeleton, thank goodness. I for one, don't want to face mutilated corpses next time I go swimming!'

'Where's the skeleton. How do they know it's Black Dog? If he's the devil's dog, he can't die.'

'Your mum was saying they've been excavating up at Rainsford Castle. Found it buried inside the bailey.'

Mark was already reading the somewhat dramatic headline, 'Black Dog on the Prowl!'

Next minute he was half-way down the garden, dragging a reluctant Steph behind him.

'We must see this before they fill it in!'

The ruined castle, a popular tourist sight, was just outside the town. The entrance to the inner courtyard had been blocked off but a few curious on lookers were hanging around.

'You see, you can't get in. You've dragged me here for nothing.'

'Can't get in? Just watch me!'

Mark bent down beneath the barrier, ignoring the bored policeman on duty. He went straight to the site where the digging was taking place. Steph followed dubiously behind.

'Hi, I'm Mark Thompson. I'm the guy who found the papers in Trinity Church. Must have been a couple of years ago. I'm still really interested in this whole story. Hope you don't mind us trespassing.'

'That's ok. We're just trying to stop a crowd of sightseers traipsing about.' A grey-haired man wiped his muddy hands down the back of his already clay-stained jeans.

Steph looked curiously round the cobbled yard. She pictured the scene on a misty day, the sound of horses' hoofs on the grey stones, the dogs barking excitedly, elegant ladies leaning from the lead casements. She was brought back to reality by Mark's excited exclamation, 'Look at that skeleton. The beast must have weighed over 90 kilos and measured at least 2 metres, standing on its hindlegs.' Steph felt a cold chill. She shivered, despite the sunlight, as she gazed down at a remarkably well-preserved skeleton. The set of the jaw, the yellow fangs, the long backbone were terrifying, even in death.

'I'm afraid we have to pack up now. We'll be here tomorrow, if you want to know more.'

'Ok, thanks. I'll try and pop up after work.'

As they walked back down a grassy hill, Steph looked back at the darkening ruins and thought about the skeleton in its muddy grave.

*****

The next day, Mark spent his lunch hour working so he could leave early. The skeletal hound intrigued him. He was hoping the archaeologists would use radiocarbon dating and be able to give an accurate date for the strange skeleton. Steph reluctantly agreed to accompany him when Mark 'bribed' her with the promise of early dinner at the Duck and Rat which had recently hired a new chef.

It was beginning to get dark by the time they had climbed the hill up to the castle. A cold east wind and overcast sky gave the fortress a grim, rather than romantic, air. They walked into the cobbled court; there was no sign of anyone, only a pile of spades and trowels stacked against the wall. 'As we've walked this far, we may as well have a look. They may have discovered more evidence.' Mark's voice echoed round the empty yard. The grave had been carefully covered with a muddy tarpaulin, held down by stones at the corners. Mark lifted the stones carefully, then pulled the cover back. Steph had been steeling herself to look at the grotesque remains of the ghostly dog. Both stared silently. Whatever they had expected, it was not the yawning, empty space which faced them. Not even the faintest imprint of the skeleton remained. Only red clay at the bottom of an empty grave.

'Someone has obviously stolen the body, or bones, to be more precise.' Mark sounded disappointed.

Steph, to be honest, was rather relieved. She had not slept well the previous night.

'The quickest way out of here is through that gap in the wall on the right of the grave. Body snatchers would go that way through the, fields.' Mark was already through the gap and halfway down the footpath on the other side. Steph reluctantly followed. She didn't want to be left in the gloomy yard, even if the grave was empty.

They walked in silence along the muddy footpath and climbed over the stile at the into a darkening lane. They could hear lowered voices which seemed to come from a nearby field. 'Why would anyone be here this late on a cold evening?' as she whispered, it had begun to rain.

'Goodness knows. But I bet they're up to no good.'

Mark beckoned Steph to follow him as he crept along in the shadow of a rambling hawthorn hedge. He suddenly signalled to her to stop and crouch down. In front a cattle truck was parked in the lane. Two men with a collie were herding sheep up the straw-covered ramp.

'They're rustlers, bloody sheep thieves, taking advantage of the weather.'

Steph nodded. 'We can't take them on. They're probably armed.'

'Go back up the lane and ring the police. You know where we are? The back of Gray's Farm.'

Mark watched Steph disappear into the dark and rain. As he looked back, he felt something moving near him. At the same time a rush of hot air-brushed past. Two huge, disembodied, bulbous eyes moved in the darkness. The eyes stopped at the entrance to the gate as the frightened sheep ran into the truck. Just as the men hauled up the ramp, a giant, black beast sprang at them with a terrible howl, which echoed and re-echoed through the dark fields. It sprang on one of the men, mauling and biting him. He lay in the road screaming while the great hound held him in its yellow fangs, banging his head on the flint lane as if he were no more than a rag doll. The other man drove off with the black terror bounding after him. The fearful howling filled the valley as if heralding the day of Doom.

Mark heard a loud crash, the truck lurched sideways, bursting into flames. He saw a huge hound, its eyes glaring, disappearing into the mist and driving rain.

*****

For centuries the legend of the 'Black Hound' or 'Old Shuck', from the Anglo-Saxon *scucca,* meaning devil, has persisted in Eastern England, even to this day! Usually, a sighting of the dog means death. Yet occasionally, it has been associated with more positive outcomes.

THE HISTORY TRIP

by Sue Barnard

"Oh, for God's sake, Mum, do stop fussing. For the billionth time, yes, I have got everything. Sandwiches, bottle of water, coat, notebook, pen, phone…"

"I thought you weren't allowed your mobile phones at school," I said, as I turned on the ignition.

"Yeah, well, like, we're not. But Mr Barnes told us yesterday that we've got to bring them with us on the trip. He's got a list of all our numbers in case anyone, like, gets lost."

I chuckled as I eased the car out into the morning traffic. "Is that likely to happen?"

"Yeah, well, there's Nev – that sad geek who always, like, reads all the stuff on the walls and makes billions of notes. He nearly got left behind when we went to the Pompeii exhibition. Mr Barnes had to go back and look for him, and we nearly, like, missed the train."

"Where are you going this time?"

"An old prison. Victorian or something. Sounds a bit dull really."

"Maybe. But you might find something interesting."

"Yeah." Caroline clearly didn't share my optimism.

"And at least you're getting a day out."

"Yeah, well, I dare say. And we get out of double Games." Caroline's face brightened at the prospect of avoiding what had always been her least favourite subject. She had never been what anyone could describe as 'sporty'. A bit like me in that respect, I suppose.

"What time do you think you'll be back?"

"Dunno. Mr Barnes said we should be back for, like, four-ish or so."

"OK. Let me know if it's going to be wildly different from that."

"Yeah, OK. I'll text you."

Another reason why we should be grateful for the mobile phone, I thought, as we approached the school gates. A large coach was already waiting by the entrance to the car park, and Caroline's classmates were lining up on the pavement alongside as a middle-aged man (Mr Barnes, I presumed) was ticking off their names on a list.

"Have fun!" I called, as she climbed out of the car.

"Yeah, thanks. See you later."

*****

As I drove to work, I wondered which particular "old prison" they'd be visiting. There were quite a few in the area – stark, forbidding-looking places which were now (thankfully) all decommissioned. Some of them had been restored and re-opened as museums – grim reminders of a time, not so very long ago, when attitudes were far less enlightened and far more unforgiving. Others had been converted to other uses. A couple of years ago I'd visited one of them, which was now being used as a Family History Research Centre. It had managed to retain some of its original features and a lot of its original atmosphere, but as I recalled it was quite small. I didn't imagine that it would contain nearly enough to hold the attention and interest of a group of unenthusiastic fourteen- and fifteen-year-olds for very long.

I arrived at the estate agents to find a new pile of scribbled papers on my desk. My heart sank as I read through them. They were the surveyors' notes for a new – or rather, a very old – property which had just come on to the market.

"What's up, Jan? You look as though you've got all the cares in the world."

"Sorry, Kate," I sighed. "Sometimes I wonder why on earth I ever took this job."

"What do you mean?"

"Here. Just look at this. How on earth am I supposed to translate this into something which will make someone want to buy the place? There are limits to the number of times one can say *bijou*, or *compact*, or *easily maintained*, or *deceptively spacious*, or *with great potential for further modernisation*. On the face of it, the only truthful thing I can say about this one is *two up and two falling down*."

Kate glanced at the manuscript. "Ah, Miss Miller's place."

"You know about this?"

Kate nodded. "Yes. It's a probate sale. She was a lovely lady. I only knew her very slightly, but I gather she'd lived there since the year dot, and it's still in pretty much the same state as it was when she moved in. No nonsense about central heating or anything like that." She leafed through the notes and whistled under her breath. "Gosh – it's even got a proper kitchen range! You could mention that as an *original feature*."

"Really? Does anyone still go in for that sort of thing these days?"

"Who knows? But even so, it would be an absolute bargain for anyone looking for a place to renovate. And it's in a really nice area. Stress that point. Don't forget, you can always play the *unique opportunity to acquire* card." She grinned.

I sighed again. "I thought that usually means *we're having difficulty in selling this one*. And, renovation project or not, this one definitely looks as though it will be difficult to shift. Honestly, Kate, sometimes I feel as though I'm earning my living by telling barefaced lies."

Kate gave me an encouraging smile as she handed the manuscript back. "You're not telling lies, Jan – barefaced or otherwise."

"Well, being economical with the truth, then." I went back to my desk and powered up the computer. "Oh well, better get to work…"

Here is a unique opportunity to acquire a delightful bijou cottage in a very sought-after residential area. This easily-maintained yet deceptively spacious property retains many of its original features, whilst offering great potential for further modernisation…

*****

It was towards lunchtime when I finally finished writing the property description. I was in the middle of checking it when my phone bleeped.

It was a text message from Caroline. But it didn't make sense. It read simply: *It was all lies.*

I frowned. What was "all lies"? My property description? I'd tried to be as honest as possible in what I'd written, but even so, this was slightly unnerving.

Oh, get a grip, I scolded myself. *It was probably some playground argument. Anyway, whatever it meant, she probably intended it for someone else and sent it to you by mistake. It's just a coincidence that it's arrived at this precise moment.*

I was putting the phone back into my bag when it bleeped again. Another text from Caroline. This one was even more baffling: *I am innocent.*

Oh well, I thought, *if she's able to send texts, they're probably having their lunch at the moment. Which means she might be able to answer a call.*

I dialled her number.

"Hi, this is Caz," chirruped the voice at the other end. *"Sorry I can't talk right now. Leave a message and I'll call you back. Ciao!"*

Getting straight through to the voicemail was perhaps even more alarming than getting the texts. Caroline's phone is always on, even when she's supposed to turn it off.

I drew a deep breath and struggled to keep my voice steady.

"Caroline, it's Mum. Those two texts you just sent me… Are you all right? Can you ring me please?"

I ended the call. During the fifteen seconds it had taken, two more texts had arrived:

I am innocent.

and

I was framed.

By now I was starting to be seriously worried. What on earth was she up to? If this was supposed to be a joke, then I must be suffering from a serious sense of humour failure.

I tried again. And again. And again. But still got no further than the voicemail. It must have been a full ten nail-biting minutes before my phone eventually rang.

"Mum? Just, like, got your message. What are you on about?"

"Caroline? Thank goodness! Are you all right?"

"Yeah, yeah, I'm fine. Look, what's all this about texts? I didn't send you any texts. I couldn't have. The walls here are, like, dead thick, and there's no signal inside."

"But…" I swallowed hard, desperately trying to sound normal. "Where are you now?"

"Outside in the prison yard. Geez, Mum, you were right about this place. It is kind of interesting. And it's well scary. Especially the condemned cell. They reckon it's haunted."

"Really?" Now it wasn't difficult to sound normal. I knew that Caroline was just winding me up. She knew very well that I didn't believe in ghosts.

"Yeah, really. It really, like, freaked everyone out. Even the boys. You know, Mr Barnes just told us the last guy to be hanged here went to the gallows screaming that he was innocent. It was, like, dead creepy. Anyway, got to go now. See you later."

"See you later. Take care, love."

As I pressed the button to end the call, I caught sight of the screen. Another text had come in whilst we'd been talking.

It read, simply:

I did not kill him. I should not hang…

This story is based on the old gaol in Beaumaris, Isle of Anglesey, Wales, UK. It is now a museum, and is said to be haunted by the ghost of Richard Rowlands. He was the last man to be hanged there, in 1862, after being convicted of the murder of his father-in-law. He went to the gallows protesting his innocence to the last.

https://en.wikipedia.org/wiki/Beaumaris_Gaol

BLOOD FAIRY

by K. J. Watson

For several hours, Ithell dozed at the back of the coach. Only when the vehicle halted at the final stop did she reluctantly engage with the world and open her eyes.

"Take the book," someone whispered.

Ithell scanned the coach. No other passenger remained on board. Assuming that drowsiness had caused her to imagine the disembodied voice, she saw an antiquated hardback on the seat beside her. She speculated about whether the book might be worth anything. Then she dismissed the idea and left the coach empty-handed.

Evening had fallen. Standing by the side of the road, she heard the rustle of wind-blown trees and the distant crash of waves. Nodding in appreciation, she knew that in this south-western corner of Scotland, she had found the remoteness she sought.

The coach driver tapped her on the shoulder.

"Yours?" he asked, thrusting the antiquated hardback at her.

"No," Ithell replied, annoyed by the interruption to her thoughts.

"You left it on a seat."

"Not me."

"Yeah, right," the coach driver muttered.

He dropped the unwanted volume and boarded his vehicle. Grinding the gears, he drove away.

Ithell peered at the splayed book as its pages turned in the wind. Monochrome illustrations showed beasts that snarled, jumped, and fought among lines of unintelligible text. Curiosity prompted her to squat down and reach out her hand. The edge of a page brushed past one of her fingers and left a cut across her skin.

Surprised by the pain, she rose. As she did so, the binding of the book disintegrated. Caught by a gust, the loose pages swirled about her legs before the wind carried them over a gate into a field.

The voice from the coach whispered again. This time its tone had a greater urgency: "Pick up the cover and pursue the pages."

"Whoever you are," Ithell replied, looking in vain for the speaker, "don't boss me around. I'll go wherever I like."

"I applaud your spirit," the voice said. "The pages, however, will lead you to me. And I have the power to dispel your earthbound sorrow."

"My sorrow? You need to mind your own business."

"To resist me is foolish. I can help you."

The last phrase made Ithell pause. Nobody ever offered her help.

Perhaps I should listen to an incorporeal voice, even if I'm imagining it, she wondered. *I have nothing to lose.*

She stared at the nearby field. A current of air carried the pages, like a flock of starlings, towards a group of trees. Grabbing the book's cover, she pushed back the gate into the field and labored across the neglected land, briars tugging at her boots. Ahead, tumbling and twisting in the twilight, the pages led her on.

Ithell reached the copse but lost sight of her paper guides. Advancing warily between the close-set trees, she emerged to a view of a lighthouse that overlooked a dark, heaving sea.

She stopped and examined the apex of the towering structure, expecting to see a beacon illuminating the dusk. None appeared. Instead, backlit by the fading sunset, a shadow stirred behind the windows.

Shrugging, she lowered her gaze to a building at the base of the lighthouse. Just as she spotted a door that lay ajar, the pages rose up from the ground and swept through it.

My destination, seemingly, Ithell thought and went after them.

Inside the building, the wick of an oil lamp flared and settled. The flame cast an amber glow over a table on which the pages had come to rest in a stack.

"Are you still there?" Ithell asked, determined not to show concern. "If so, what's next?"

"Make the book whole," the voice replied.

"As long as I'm not cut again," Ithell said, putting the cover on the table.

Cautiously, she picked up the pages and placed them on the right-hand side of the cover's spine. The book softly closed itself.

Seductive, calming laughter filled the room. When it faded, a bolt clunked, and a hitherto unseen door swung open. A woman in a gray dress glided across the threshold. Shadows, similar in shape to the creatures in the book, shifted along the folds of her garment.

"Welcome," the woman said.

Ithell took a deep breath to steady herself and said, "From your voice, I take it you're the person who's led me to this place."

"Of course."

"Shouldn't you introduce yourself?"

The woman drifted to the table and ran a silver fingernail over the book. The action excited the shadows of her dress. They clambered up and down, merging into multi-limbed figures, and splitting again into their original forms.

"Read the title," the woman said.

"Why?"

"It is my name."

Ithell peered at the book's cover.

"'Sithiche Fala'," she said. "I don't understand."

"It translates as 'Blood Fairy'."

Gathering the volume in one hand, the blood fairy receded the way she had entered.

"Come," she encouraged.

"Stop giving me orders."

"Don't you wish to conclude your journey?"

"A conclusion sounds final," Ithell said. "A fresh start would be better."

"And an end to sorrow, as I mentioned previously?"

Without replying, Ithell followed. Sudden darkness enclosed her. The glow of the lamp in the room she'd left ended abruptly at the doorway.

"Ascend," the blood fairy said, the word echoing from above.

Striking her foot on something solid, Ithell lost her balance and sprawled forward. She ran her hands over the damp stonework either side of her and realized she had fallen on the spiral steps of the lighthouse. Pushing herself up, she found a concave wall to her left. Using it to guide her, she climbed.

Her surroundings gradually became brighter. Calves aching, she reached the top of the stairs and saw that the radiance came from the risen moon, shining through the array of windows she had seen earlier.

"Join me," the blood fairy called from the far side of a glazed opening.

Ithell stepped out onto the balcony, parts of which had crumbled and fallen onto the sea-washed rocks below. The blood fairy moved closer.

"You have had a life of turmoil and seek peace," she murmured.

"What are you saying?" Ithell retorted. "Are you going to make me jump?"

"I would prefer that you accept my alternative to extinction," the blood fairy said. "I can liberate you forever from anxieties and torments without self-destruction. The choice is yours."

"I don't understand."

"Become part of my story," the blood fairy replied, holding up *Sithiche Fala*. "Let me transform you into my immortal companion. Simply allow me to taste the liquid flowing in your veins."

Ithell raised her hand, framing it against the full moon. A tear-shaped bead of blood oozed from her cut finger.

"The book caused this deliberately, didn't it?" she said.

The blood fairy smiled. "You do understand. I believed you would. Now make your decision."

"I already have," Ithell answered.

THE NORTHWOODS

by Dana Fulton

Evelyn could continue pushing north, until the interstate launches her rusted Corolla into Lake Superior, but the bright glow of the fuel light is a reality she can't ignore.

Flicking on the turn signal wakes her copilot. Roger, her white bulldog snorts and blinks, struggles to lift his head to peer out the window, barely able to see above the plastic door frame. He turns to her, silently demanding an explanation.

"Food. And probably rest for the night," she assures him, convinced that, in his own way, Roger understands.

Though I'm the only one who needs rest, she thinks, wishing her partner could've taken over, even if only for part of the drive. What Roger lacks in driving ability and thumbs, he more than compensates for with companionship. The thought of facing this new chapter alone sits like lead in her stomach. She pulls into the first gas station off the ramp, the trunk rattling on each bump, and realizes it is now Evelyn and Roger versus the world.

Above them, the sky starts its daily transition from blue to brilliant purple; the golden solar orb creeping toward the horizon. Although the tips of some trees are showing hints of red, the warmth of summer is still in the air. Sweat glistens on her hands while she maneuvers around the fuel pump. Once the car is full, she journeys across the cracked concrete, littered with chipped rocks and cigarette butts, to pay inside.

The door slaps against a bell dangling from the ceiling, announcing her entrance to the leathered man at the counter. His eyes scan her body, assessing her curves and pale skin. She offers a tight smile and nod, a typical Midwest greeting, and her skin crawls when she receives no acknowledgment in return.

In and out, she tells herself as she navigates the cramped aisles. The station resembles little more than a tin shed, with picked-over shelves bearing the scars of the weekend rush awaiting Monday morning's restocking. Floor fans spin lazily in a feeble attempt to combat the building's transformation into a sauna.

Evelyn grabs three waters—Roger will appreciate at least one—and scans the minimal food options, finding both salty and sweet, and nearly all expired. And nothing that aligned with her meticulously monitored lifestyle of the past three years. Calories counted, and the highest quality supplements imported to maintain her perfectly toned shape that Jeremy demanded.

She grabs two frosted honey buns and jerky.

"A sweet tooth today." The man doesn't smile.

"Yes." She keeps her answer short, has learned it is best to be that way with men. She's lost track of the number of times Jeremy accused her friendliness of flirting. It was never worth the fight. "And Pump 4."

The man huffs and peers out the window, as if doubting her ability to read numbers.

"What is that?" he wheezes, and the air seems to turn yellow around him.

Evelyn cautiously leans over the counter, catching the stench of some cheap hoppy beer cracked open near the register.

She glances around the parking lot, the towering trees in the background. The only sign of life is Roger waiting patiently on the middle console. Her heart flutters from his cute face.

"That's Roger," she quickly adds, "he's mine."

A deep frown tugs at the man's rough skin and liver spots. He scrutinizes her once more. "But what is he?"

She crosses her arms across her chest, shielding herself from his eyes. "A bulldog. Just a puppy."

He shakes his head, somehow unsatisfied with her answers, and punches in her total. "Cash or card?"

She's surprised a place like this accepts cards. It looks like it doesn't even have a security system, only this gargoyle sitting behind the counter guarding his territory.

"Cash," she says, her voice firm. Untraceable.

His hand reaches out, each finger with cracked and swollen knuckles, and he pinches the edge of the cash Evelyn extends. He slides the change back across the counter, as though he's afraid to touch her.

She scoffs, unintentionally, and scoops up the change when the man's claw locks onto her wrist, anchoring her in place. "Don't be off into the woods tonight," his warning comes out like a growl.

Fear yanks Evelyn back with enough force that she should be free, but he leans in closer, trapping her. "Especially with that dog," he adds, the heavy scent of beer enveloping her with each word.

Evelyn jerks again. "Let go!"

"These woods hide a creature that could crunch through your bones. And that dog," he gestures his free claw toward the window, "is its favorite little treat. It will find you, and neither of you will be seen again."

She rips herself free and stumbles backward, knocking into a display, sending cards and lighters scattering across the floor. Her heart thunders as she flails for her snacks and sprints back to the car, where Roger, oblivious to the threat, gleefully bounces back to his place in the passenger seat.

Her hands tremble as she peels out onto the highway, the old man fading in her rearview mirror, and his warning echoing in her head.

*****

Her phone sits silent and useless in her pocket. If she could just turn it on, finding a hotel would be a breeze. But no, Evelyn is navigating down the darkening, unfamiliar highway through trial and error. The first 20 miles offer nothing but mocking "No Vacancy" signs, pushing her to continue further east. Truthfully though, in her mind, the more rural, the better.

The surrounding forest blocks most of the dusk sky as she zips down the highway. The trees' eerie shadows are like monsters running to keep pace with her car.

In her mind's eye, she sees a furious creature tearing through the wood and pouncing on her car, its teeth and claws mercilessly slashing into metal. Roger would splatter into the dashboard, and her own body would be devoured.

"No," she whispers, forcefully blocking out the mental monster out loud, and she looks at Roger. "And I would never let anything bad happen to you."

As the final drops of daylight fade away, she pulls into The Green Tail Motel's parking lot. Half of the letter lights in the sign are out, and the weathered wooden exterior hasn't seen a fresh coat of paint since Reagan's first term. In the parking lot, a dragon-like statue, long and green, guards the entrance. Menacing fangs jut from its flat head, and thick spikes run along its spine, warning any curious creature that this is the apex predator.

Evelyn's headlights glow into the statue's red eyes as she backs into a spot on the edge of the lot, the car's trunk snug against the forest.

Roger begins a low, protective growl at the illuminated statue, his new foe.

"Shh. It's just wood," Evelyn coos as she pats the pup's head. But Roger continues to growl, his instincts taking over. She sighs, scoops him up, and makes her way to the motel to see if a room is available for a woman and a tiny bulldog.

As they cross between the car and the statue, she notices a worn plaque beneath the beast's head. It reads "THE HODAG" in bold block letters.

"I won't let it hurt you," she assures Roger with a forced smile.

The interior of the lobby mirrors the worn wooden exterior, with paneling stretching from floor to ceiling and discount taxidermy nailed unevenly to the walls. A rabbit, with mangled fur and a marble eye, watches them approach the desk.

"Name?" a voice pops from the office before a pink-haired woman emerges from behind the desk. She's stout and leathered, much like the man at the gas station. They could be related, but her bright eyes and pink hair suggest her aging is the result of a life well lived rather than one filled with tobacco and brown liquor.

"I don't have a reservation. Just need a night," Evelyn says, looking up at a stuffed pheasant to her right, forever caught mid-flight, trying to escape this wood-lined cage.

Roger follows her gaze and lets out a small, protective bark at the bird.

"Gonna need a deposit for him," the woman nods. Her nametag says 'Mimsy,' and, whether or not that's her name, it fits.

"Sure, whatever the charge is, it's fine." Evelyn reaches into her back pocket for her wallet as the lobby doors slide open.

"You double-lunged it. That blood trail was the easiest I've ever followed," a joyous voice rings above laughter. Three men, dressed in layers of blaze orange and camo, walk into the lobby, their sweat and dirt from the afternoon worn like badges of honor.

"And she was so thick, could've almost told me it was an 8-point whose rack fell off," the storyteller says, raising his hands to pantomime antlers.

"Right place, right time." The youngest hunter shakes his head, glancing toward Evelyn, pink flushing across his cheeks.

"Mimsy, can we steal more towels, my dear?" The storyteller leans on an elbow against the counter, a charming smile stretched on his face as though he still possesses the same charisma he had twenty years ago.

Unperturbed by his smirk, Mimsy keeps a straight face as she hands towels from beside her desk across the counter. "Rinse everything off before you start rubbing yourselves with these."

He gives her a salute and sends a wink in Evelyn's direction. "She keeps us in line."

"I see," Evelyn says, shifting Roger in her arms.

"Is that a bulldog?" The storyteller coos and extends a hand to rub Roger's head. He greedily leans into the affection.

"Yes, four months old yesterday," Evelyn says and glances at the younger hunter, guesses he's in his mid-30s as well. "It's just him and me."

Pink stains the hunter's cheeks again, and Evelyn smiles, her first attempt at flirting in years.

"Well, we'll be a few miles down at Barley's later if you and the little mister need to grab a drink," the storyteller said, patting his belly. "I know I need a few."

"Dogs in a bar are a health code violation, Kent." Mimsy quickly drops her hammer.

"He deserves a pint. Plus, if this ankle-biter is truly a bulldog," he pauses for another head scratch, "then he can't be left alone on a Sunday."

Mimsy doesn't try to argue as the hunting party leaves with their stack of towels, the young one stealing a final glance on their way out the door, the storyteller already diving into another Deer Camp tale.

She sighs. "Most of what Kent says should be ignored, but he's right. You shouldn't leave that dog alone tonight. I'd keep him on a leash, too."

Evelyn frowns, waits.

"These woods are home to a lot of things, rabbits and deer and birds, the stuff you see on the walls, and the one you passed on your way in."

Evelyn thinks of the block-letter sign. "The Hodag."

Mimsy nods. "It hasn't been spotted in decades, mostly because around here, we play by its rules. Celebrate it, even. It's the high school mascot, if you can believe it. I think it keeps the beast content. But you, an outsider? With that little snack?" Mimsy points at Roger, who tilts his head, engaged in the story.

Evelyn chews on her lip and pulls Roger in closer.

"White bulldogs are its favorite treat, but it only eats them on Sundays," Mimsy adds, throwing her hands up in resignation. "I don't make the rules. Just keep the little guy close to you. How are we paying tonight?"

"Cash," Evelyn says, her nerves tingling.

*****

Evelyn sits at the edge of the bed, wrapped in a towel, and shoves the second honey bun into her mouth. As she licks the sticky sweet faux frosting from her fingers, she mulls over the hunter's offer. She could definitely go for more food, and certainly a handful of drinks. And maybe after that, she could stumble back to the motel with the younger hunter. Better yet, skip the trip to the room altogether and opt for some quality time in the back seat of her car, enough to shake its frame. A sly smile creeps across her face at the thought.

But she knows it wouldn't be wise to venture out alone. Right now, she needs to stay focused and alert. Beer isn't an option.

Curious about the night, Evelyn gets up and peaks through the window at the front of the room, pulling the curtain just enough to reveal her eye. The parking lot is quiet for the night, with yellow buzzing lights drawing out only a spray of moths, but the forest beyond the asphalt is alive. Her mind drifts into the woods, into its layered shadows. The darkness feels so deep, that she's sure she could slip in and drown.

A tiny whine pulls Evelyn's attention down to her feet. Roger is pacing near the door, his tiny paws padding across the cheap carpet. She sighs and looks at the clock on the nightstand. The bold red numbers blink back at her, 11:43. She steels herself; it's time.

Evelyn slips into her running shoes. With Roger in hand, she exits the room and enters the inky night.

She keeps her senses open, vigilant, and ready to pivot at any moment. An owl calls from the dense treetops to remind her that she isn't alone, and this brings a small wave of comfort, a sense that the night itself is on her side.

At the car, Evelyn digs behind the driver seat, her fingers fumbling in the dark until they find Roger's leash. She clips him in and lets him prance to the edge of the grass to handle business while she continues to dig. One hand brushes against hard plastic, a headlamp she pulls on her head. With the light's clarity, she grabs her old running watch, the one she never wears anymore because of the tan lines it left on her arm, a minor thing that would send Jeremy over the edge. She illuminates the watch's face, 11:45.

Her pulse quickens as she goes for the final item, opening the middle console and pulling out a lock box. She slowly presses the combination and removes the most important item for tonight: a small handgun. Despite its size, the weight of the weapon is substantial in her hand. She takes a deep breath and slides a holster around her thigh and secures the handgun in place with a satisfying snap.

Roger pads back to her side, relief settled on his tiny face. Evelyn looks down and smiles firmly as she closes the back door. "I won't let anything hurt you."

The door back to their room calls from across the parking lot, but Evelyn ignores it. The safe, easy option would be to return to bed, to shove her problem off to another day. But that's not why they're here. She needs this forest and needs this night.

Leash in one hand, Evelyn unlocks the car's trunk with her other. Inside, terrified and smelling of sweat and urine, Jeremy stares back at her through rounds of tape and rope, fear and panic etched into his face.

It began one year ago, on a wine-fueled night, when Evelyn stumbled upon the *Dark Side of Shadows* podcast. A random episode told the chilling tale of a monster in the Northwoods that could make a person vanish without a trace. She'd listened to that episode a hundred times since, knowing it was the only way to save herself, to ensure Jeremy could never hunt her down.

All she had to do was lure him to buy the bait, convincing him that a pristine white bulldog would be the perfect addition to their so-called "perfect" family.

She steadies herself, settling her nerves, and lifts Jeremy's bound legs out of the trunk, terror fueling his jerky movements to try and flee but exhaustion and the ropes keep him stable. It's a short drop from the trunk lip to the asphalt, just enough to crack open his head and end his fight, but the risk of spilling blood, which could draw attention in the daylight, isn't worth it. With one quick movement, she grabs the rope around his chest and hoists Jeremy from the car, knocking the wind from his lungs as she drops him on the ground with a thud, back first.

The lift sends stars exploding at the edge of her vision. Not now, Evelyn tells herself with a shake of her head. Pain and fatigue can set in later, but only after she and Roger are safe and far away from the monster in front of her.

They start into the forest, leaving behind the yellow lights of the parking lot, entering the deep darkness that swallows them whole.

Her lean muscles strain as Evelyn drags Jeremy step by step over the leafy forest floor, the headlamp giving only a dim path of light to follow which Roger bounds along beside, his innocent curious pulling him out to occasionally sniff tree trunks before falling back into the light.

Evelyn can hear herself breathing when she realizes silence has settled around them, the creatures of the night quiet for the approaching monster. Even Roger has stilled, his attention slowly scans the trees searching for the danger lurking within.

"It's time," Evelyn mumbles, fear and anticipation all coursing through her veins.

A growl rumbles through the trees, causing Jeremy to jerk and toss Evelyn to the ground, her hands landing hard on roots and the mossy earth. Her breath rips through her throat as she looks up, her own monster writhing in ropes.

Evelyn's breath catches in her throat as the beast of the Northwoods crawls toward them. Its scaly, mossy skin bears jagged daggers along its spine and thick tail, its claws dig deep into the forest floor with each heavy step. Sinister eyes gleam in the headlamp's weak light as it peers through the darkness.

Roger whimpers and rushes to her, finding protection at her ankles. Feeling him beside her sends the Hodag lore replaying in Evelyn's mind, and she steals a quick glance at her watch, 11:59. Only one more minute left, then Roger is safe. She places her hand on the holster and matches the stare of the beast, whispering her promise one final time to Roger, "I won't let anything ever harm us ever again."

The Hodag snorts, sending curling streams of steam from its snout. Its glowing eyes moved between her face and Jeremy twisting on the ground, and the Hodag tilts its head to the side. It's a move she knows well, a creature weighing its options. And she wouldn't let someone else take the answer from her.

"There's only one threat here to you." She wraps the leash around her hand again, the loop keeping her stable. The Hodag inches closer, just a few years away as she fills her chest with air, making her intentions clear to all the living beings in the woods. "Only one thing worth sinking your teeth into."

There's a subtle settling in the Hodag's eyes; Evelyn feels it chill her skin. The authority of the forest accepts her offer. Her guard begins to drop as the Hodag lifts its claw and takes another step toward Jeremy, angling away from Evelyn and Roger. She removes her hand from the holster, and lets her arm swing free at her side, when the monster's tail swings and cracks into the side of her skull, plunging Evelyn into darkness.

*****

The night is all-consuming when she blinks her eyes open, unsure if it has been ten minutes or ten days. She fumbles with her watch until the screen flashes, the light causing her headache to pulse. 12:08.

Her hands crawl along the forest floor, crunching over leaves and sticks until she makes contact with the headlamp. One click, two, and finally, and apprehension cuts through her as light cuts through the night. She scans around her with the narrow beam of light, revealing the threaded edge of the leash as though it had been ripped in half.

Tears begin to prick the corners of her eyes when a rustling pulls her attention to the side. She holds her breath until the light reveals her tiny bulldog nested against a tree. Content, safe, alive, and gnawing on a severed finger, the pure white bone at the end glistening in the light.

THE UNDERPASS

by DJ Tyrer

"Not this way," said Jim as he and Mac approached the underpass that crossed beneath Queensway. He winced as a car drove towards them along the dual carriageway, the beams of its headlights turning into a bright, unfocused glow through the drizzle.

Mac looked at him. "What?"

"Not this way. I can't stand going through there during the day, and sure as hell don't want to use it this time of night."

"Seriously?"

"You don't know who's lurking down there. Could be druggies or muggers…"

Mac laughed. "Is that all you're afraid of? There's worse than that down Ratman Passage."

"You what?" Jim asked as he reluctantly joined his friend on the ramp leading down to the tunnel.

"Ratman Passage? What, you didn't know that's what it's called? Really? I thought you were from Southend."

"I am. Lived in Southend-on-Sea all my life. But I haven't a scoobies what you're on about."

"You never heard the story of Ratman Passage?" said Mac, his voice echoing as they entered the empty, orange-tiled tunnel. "It's a local…what do you call them? Urban legend."

Jim shook his head. The underpass was dim and shadowy, and he scanned it for anyone who might be waiting.

Was that someone, hunched low against the wall? No, he didn't think so, just some old rags that had spilt out of a torn carrier bag. Nobody in the underpass, just scattered litter and a few leaves that had blown in. That was a relief. Yet as they walked, his momentary sense of security disappeared as he caught the sound of footsteps following them. He glanced back; there was nobody there.

Just the echo of their own steps, he supposed.

"I remember a story, from when I was a kid," he said, trying to drown out the trailing sound, "about a flat on the estate which had a sort of giant mutant spider in it. I don't recall anything about a ratman."

"You'll love it."

Jim shivered. He doubted it. He could still hear the echo of pursuing footsteps. Still, they were nearly through.

He glanced over his shoulder and felt his heart lurch. For a moment, he was certain he'd seen a group of figures standing in the far entrance to the tunnel. Then, he blinked, and they were gone. He blinked again. He was letting Mac's blather and the reputation of the area get to him; there was nothing to be scared of.

"Now, I must admit, I don't know if Ratman is the official name for this tunnel or not—if the name created the legend or it the legend gave it the nickname, but this is the story as I heard it…"

Jim was hardly listening, still glancing back, making certain the tunnel was empty, wary of druggies and muggers.

"There was this old man, right, a tramp, homeless, and one chilly night he came into the tunnel to shelter from the cold." Mac laughed. "Yeah, I know, it ain't exactly warm down here! Still, it was better than being out in the rain and wind. But there were some of these kids, yobbos, that came along and found him and they thought, 'Hey, let's kick his head in for a laugh.' Just the sort of scumbags you were worried about meeting."

"Right." He wished Mac wouldn't treat it as a joke.

The exited the tunnel and Jim breathed a sigh of relief. They began to ascend the slope back up to street level.

"So, yeah, they gave him a kicking and left him for dead. But that wasn't the end of it."

"What do you mean?"

Mac halted and turned to face him, looking at him with wide-eyed intensity.

"While the poor old guy was laying there, the rats came out from their hiding places—and I mean big-uns—and ate his flesh while he was still alive." He gave a theatrical shudder. "Ate his face right off. Imagine the agony.

"And that is how he died. Horrible. So, he came back as a ghost, seeking revenge, a faceless ghoul."

"And they called him the Ratman because of how he died," concluded Jim.

Mac nodded. "Exactly."

The tension that had been filling Jim's body vanished. It was all quite cliché really, just a silly ghost story. Nothing to be spooked about after all. Probably nothing but fiction, although a tramp getting attacked by teens for a thrill was, sadly, entirely plausible.

"I'll be glad to get out of this drizzle. Come on."

As Mac turned so they could resume their walk up the slope, a voice said, "Spare some change, guv?"

Jim swore. A hunched figure in a shapeless overcoat stood at the top of the ramp ahead of them. He hadn't been there before Mac had stopped for the finale of his tale.

"Nah, mate," said Mac, who never had any time for beggars, denouncing every last one as a fraud. "Clear off."

Although the man didn't look particularly big, Jim would normally have felt nervous. But with Mac's brazen manner, he felt confident they'd be fine. Mac was a big fellow who knew how to handle himself. Jim felt safe with him taking the lead.

The figure didn't move as they approached.

"Shift it," spat Mac, striding ahead of Jim.

Still, the figure just stood, immobile. Then, as Mac grew closer, he raised his head and Jim's friend shrieked.

Jim had never heard his friend cry out like that before. Grunt and curse up a storm, sure, but scream? Not Mac.

His friend stumbled back towards him.

"It's him," Mac managed to gasp, face gone white. He swore, and repeated, "It's him," then turned and was running, back down the ramp towards the tunnel.

"Wait!" cried Jim, one eye still on the figure.

There was a thump, and Jim glanced over his shoulder. Mac had slipped on the wet concrete and slammed into the wall, dropping to his knees. He scrambled into the tunnel, struggling to regain his footing as he tried to run.

In the dim glow of the nearest streetlight, he saw the beggar's face. Rather, the lack of face. All that was left of his human visage was a bloody smear of flesh across the outline of a skull from which two malevolent dark eyes glared out in pain and anger.

Jim stumbled back, a taste of bile in his mouth.

It isn't real. It couldn't be real. It was Mac playing a joke on him.

It was real. As he stared into the thing's eyes, he knew it was real.

He fumbled in his pocket.

It had asked for change.

Maybe… Jim's fingers closed on some loose coins and he tossed them at the thing. He was, he realised, at the bottom of the ramp; he almost slipped and fell as Mac had. But he'd caught himself at the last moment.

A glance to his right told him that his friend was still, slowly, fumbling his way awkwardly through the tunnel, one leg dragging behind him, as if broken. At the far end, Jim could see the cluster of figures, blocking Mac's escape.

Looking to his left, Jim saw the stairs that offered an alternative way up.

Jim darted for them and bounded up the steps as quickly as he could.

On the edge of his vision, he saw the figure crumple in on itself, as if the old overcoat it wore emptied, and rats, dozens of them, maybe even hundreds, with huge, burning red eyes, burst out from within the coat, scampering after Mac.

As Jim reached the top of the stairs and ran past the Unitarian Meeting House, towards Lancaster Gardens, he could hear Mac screaming in a cacophony of terror and pain that echoed up horribly from the underpass.

Eventually, he was far enough away that he could no longer hear Mac screams. Trying not to think of what that might mean, he halted and pulled out his phone. He'd call the police, let them go look. Not that he was quite sure what he could say.

Somehow, he doubted they'd find a body. Would they care? Would they blame him?

He swore and hit the first nine. He couldn't do nothing.

Hands seized him, and he slammed back-first against the pavement. His phone slipped out of his hand, cracking hard against several feet from him. He was being dragged by impossibly strong arms, back towards Ratman Passage.

He struggled, kicking and trying to pull free, but he couldn't, the grip was too strong and he couldn't find any way to brace his flailing limbs against the slick surface of the pavement. He looked at his attacker, immediately recognizing him.

"Mac? Mac, is that you?"

There was no reply as he was dragged into the tunnel.

"Mac, let me go!"

There was no light, but in the darkness, he could hear the scampering and squealing of rats. Something heavy jumped onto his chest. Whiskers brushed his face.

Jim screamed. Sharp incisors bit easily into the flesh of his cheek, scissoring away flesh. The pain was excruciating as he felt them tug at his ears and nose. In moments, there were dozens more upon him, biting, tearing, shearing, stripping away his flesh layer by layer.

The tunnel echoed with his cries, a chorus of agony rising like a tide, as if a thousand tortured voices wailed through him, pressing against his skull until it felt like it would split open.

The pain. The sound. Unrelenting.

He was trapped.

Alone in the dark.

Screaming.

GWYLLGI

by Maureen Bowden

"The Black Dog hath a baleful stare

and ghastly death trails in his wake.

Look upon him if you dare.

Look, and then all hope forsake."

My nightmares began when I was seven, after I saw Ryan Slade murder six-year-old Tommy Edwards. Ryan was the school bully, ten years old and big for his age. I was kicking a ball around the Antelope Hotel's car park on the when I saw their two figures on the Menai bridge that crosses from the mainland to the island of Anglesey. Tommy screamed. I dropped out of sight and peeped over the car park wall. Ryan punched and kicked him, again and again, in the head and stomach. Tommy flopped to the ground like a broken toy. Ryan heaved him onto the parapet and pushed him into the Menai Straits.

I sat behind the wall, sobbing and shivering until Ryan ran off and then I made myself stop crying and hurried home. I was terrified that if I told anyone he would come after me and kill me too.

Tommy's body was washed up next day on Beaumaris beach. His broken-hearted parents and the residents of his home village, Llanmarged, believed his death was the result of a tragic accident. It wasn't the first time a child had fallen off the bridge so no crime was suspected and the police asked no questions. Tommy was buried in the village churchyard.

After Ryan left school he embarked upon a life of crime. The last news our neighbourhood had of him was he'd been arrested for assault and battery of some poor soul. I didn't see him again until the night of the Gwyllgi.

*****

Eighteen years later, on our first wedding anniversary, my husband, Jake said, "Well, we made it through a whole year, Lucy. What shall we do to celebrate?"

"Let's camp out under the stars, like we did when we first met," I said.

He hugged me. "Great, we'll do some Googling and find somewhere we've never been."

Our search revealed Llandegla Forest in the Denbighshire hills. The camping guide showed us images of woodland clearings close to the edge of the forest, perfect for pitching a tent.

On a brisk but sunny September morning, when autumn's russet raiment was transforming the countryside, we packed the camping necessities onto the back of our Harley Davidson and headed for Denbighshire. Nearing the village of Llandegla we rode through the Nant y Garth pass and a chill ran down my spine. My sense of unease was heightened when we reached the village pub where we intended to have a meal before pitching the tent in the forest. The pub sign read 'The Black Dog Inn.' Beneath the name it portrayed a snarling mastiff with staring red eyes and fangs dripping with blood. Jake said, "I bet that makes the tourists feel welcome."

The pub's interior was dark and oak-beamed. Framed paintings by local artists of varying quality hung on the walls. They depicted craggy mountains and thunderous skies. We sat at a table close to the window so we could keep an eye on the bike.

The landlord approached us. "Alright, folks, what's occurrin'? You comes by yur on holiday, like?"

Jake said, "Yes, we're camping in the forest."

We ordered our meal and he turned to walk away.

I said, "Before you go, can I ask you something? What's the story behind your sign?"

He pulled up another chair and sat down at our table. "The Black Dog haunts many lands. In these parts he's known as the Gwyllgi. If you knows your Welsh you'll know it means the wild one. His breath has the stench of an open crypt and his eyes glow like the fires of Hell. Any fool, who looks into those eyes dies a terrible death, isn't it."

Jake said, "What happens to them? Does he attack them?"

"Now here's a strange thing, look you. They is found with not a mark on them, but an expression of terror on their face."

I said, "Who do people think he is?"

"Some says he's a Hell hound who hunts down evil souls who are the devil's own. Or maybe he's Dormarch, canine companion of Gwynn ap Nudd, King of the Otherworld, and he leads The Wild Hunt at the winter solstice."

Jake was smiling. "He gets around, then?"

"He does that, but I won't lie to you, boy, he always comes back by yur, to the Nant y Garth pass, where he belongs."

I remembered the chill I'd felt when we rode through the pass, and I shivered. Jake had stopped smiling. Maybe he'd felt it too.

The landlord rose to his feet. "If you changes your mind about sleeping in the forest, you comes back here, see? You can have a guest room for the night. Enjoy your meal."

I don't remember what we ate. My mind was too full of the Gwyllgi. I tried to tell myself that the landlord's story was just a ploy to get paying guests, but I wasn't convinced. Jake was quiet. This trip wasn't going as planned.

It was a short ride to the forest. We wheeled the bike along a woodland path that led us to a small clearing, and we began unpacking. I pulled out two thick scarves, wrapped one round my neck and passed the other to Jake. "Keep this handy to wrap around your eyes in case the Gwyllgi shows up. Promise?"

He grinned, but he took the scarf. "I've been thinking about his name. He may be wild, but that doesn't mean he's evil. Maybe he just gets a bad press."

"Maybe," I said, "but I'm taking no chances."

A voice behind us shouted, "Hi there."

We turned and saw a figure stepping into the clearing. He waved. "Are you hoping to see the Gwyllgi?"

Jake shouted back, "We kinda hope not to."

The stranger laughed. "He's only a dog. I say, bring it on, bad boy."

He walked closer and I recoiled in shock. I knew that face. It was older but still recognisable as the face I saw in my recurring nightmare. He held out his hand. "Ryan Slade."

Jake shook it and said, "Jake and Lucy Davies."

Ryan offered his hand to me. I allowed him to shake it then snatched it away, dreading that he'd recognise me. Why should he? Little Lucinda Griffiths, who everyone called Cindy, bore no resemblance to Lucy Davies. He probably didn't remember that I existed, and even if he did, he had no idea that I'd seen him murder Tommy, but I couldn't prevent my heart thumping in apprehension.

Jake said, "It's only a legend. The dog's not real, is he? But if he were, what makes you think he'd show up tonight?"

Ryan said, "It's the autumn equinox, the night the veil between us and the Otherworld grows thin. If he is real he'll pass through the veil and I'll be waiting."

Trying to keep my voice from trembling, I said, "Why aren't you afraid? People die when they encounter him."

He shook his head. "But he doesn't kill them. They die of fright and he doesn't frighten me."

We pitched the tent as the sun was setting. Ryan sat and watched. He was still there when the moon rose and showed no inclination to move on. So much for romantic stargazing.

A cloud drifted across the face of the moon and that's when it started: a constant howl that grew louder and hurt our ears. We heard a pounding on the earth of what sounded like a four-footed beast drawing nearer at a frightening speed. The undergrowth rustled as small woodland creatures screeched and fled.

I pleaded with Jake, "Please cover your eyes." He didn't need persuading. We blindfolded ourselves with our scarves and clung to each other, too terrified to move, even to grope our way into the tent.

Jake called to Ryan, "Don't look, man. Don't be a fool."

Ryan laughed and called back, "I want to see it. I have to see it."

The beast was upon us. I felt its hot breath on the back of my neck and smelled its musky, animal scent. The pounding feet stilled and the howling was replaced by a low, angry growl. Its footsteps passed us by and seemed to turn in another direction. The growl rose to a roar and then silence fell. The pounding of the great feet began again, but gradually grew more distant.

We untied our scarves as the cloud dispersed and the moon showed her face. I looked at Ryan. It may have been a trick of the moonlight but he appeared drained of blood. I saw terror in his eyes as he held his head and whimpered, "Don't hit me. Please don't hit me." He fell to his knees, gasping for breath and then he stared at something we couldn't see, and screamed, "No, you can't be here. You're dead. I killed you. Get back into the earth where you belong." He scrambled to his feet, and still screaming, ran into the depths of the forest.

I knew what he'd felt and seen. It was the nightmare that had haunted me since I was seven years old. He'd felt the agony of every blow he'd inflicted on Tommy. He'd struggled to breathe as the sea, like a cold, gaping mouth, had swallowed him. Most terrifying of all, he'd seen Tommy's decomposing corpse rise from the earth and point an accusing, skeletal finger. My nightmare always ended when I awoke but Ryan's would end with his death.

Jake said, "I suppose we should go after him."

I shook my head. "There's no point. He saw the Gwyllgi. Maybe the innkeeper will know what to do. Let's go back there. I don't want to sleep here."

"Me neither."

In silence, we packed everything, stashed it on the back of the bike and rode to the inn. Blinds covered the windows. Those inside must have heard the beast. We knocked on the door. The landlord let us in. "I'm guessin' you covered your eyes, isn't it?"

Jake said, "We did, but there was someone else there and he didn't."

I said, "He ran into the forest. We thought it would be useless to go after him."

He nodded. "Tidy. You thought right, as it 'appens. He'll be dead by now. I'll ring the police. They'll find him tomorrow, see."

"What will happen then?"

"There'll be an inquest and the suits will say he had a heart attack. They won't mention the Gwyllgi, look you. It's what they has to do. You folks want a bed for the night?"

"Yes, please," we said together.

"Crackin'. Sweet dreams."

We lay awake and I told Jake about Tommy, about the nightmares and about my conviction of what Ryan was experiencing before he fled.

"Why didn't you tell me about Tommy and the nightmares before now?" he said. "I would have tried to help you."

"There's nothing you could have done and I didn't tell you because I felt so guilty for not reporting what I saw. I deserved the nightmares."

"No, you didn't," he said. "Ryan may well have come after you. Your parents may have needed to take you into witness protection, change your names and leave all the family and friends that know and love you. You saved them from that, and the Gwyllgi dealt Ryan a far worse punishment than the law would have done. He got exactly what he deserved. The black dog is wild but not evil."

"Thank you," I said. I fell asleep in his arms, knowing I'd never have the nightmare again.

The day after we returned home I bought a packet of wildflower seeds from 'Bulbs and Blooms,' a garden centre close to Llanmarged. I took them to the churchyard and scattered them around Tommy's headstone. "It's over, Tommy," I said. "You can rest easy now. So can I."

The End

HOW FLAT-TIRE GOT HER NAME

by Grant Balfour

"It takes a compassionate man to love a three-legged dog. And it takes a sorry son-of-a-gun to name that dog Flat-Tire."—Gamble Rogers, Oklawaha metaphysician.

Grady McKinnon was not what an impartial observer might describe as a happy man. But he did have love in his life. He had a long face, dark circles under his eyes, not much memory for figures and not much patience for the whims of employers, which meant he had a wallet that was almost as thin as his standards of personal hygiene. The one thing he had that made the rest of that cargo he'd put on himself tolerable was a dog.

The dog was a yellow cur who came to him as a pup with the name Scout, which so far as Grady could tell suited the animal's temperament just fine. The dog was his opposite in all the ways that mattered—curious where he had become resigned, optimistic where he had become overwhelmed by the tempests of life, simple-minded where he had become suspicious of strangers' motives, enthusiastic where he had surrendered to the weight of routine existence, as much as Grady had a routine. Grady was like a dock built on pine pilings where the woodworm had started to set in. Scout, she was always ready for a boat ride.

In another man, a difference so extreme in temperament would show itself in impatience, resentment, or even unkind behavior. But Grady was a sorry man, not a cruel one. He indulged that dog. And Scout, for her part, kept Grady going. Gave him a reason to keep corn bread in the cupboard instead of corn mash whiskey. Nagged him like a wife and cheered him on like a grandchild. And that dog followed him everywhere.

Not that the two of them got out too much. They lived down one of those mud tracks to the northwest of Meuse, where the Babcocks' and Deeses' cattle land gave way to mud and mosquitoes on the far side of their fences. Stands of cypress and pond apple. Red bay and water oaks. Low trees that don't mind getting their feet wet. Places cattle go in the depth of summer to cool down. Places with, not to put too fine of a point on it, a bit of a stink to them. Mud holes like these aren't part of the Everglades proper because what water there is just collects during the rainy months—it doesn't flow out into the River of Grass. Just sits and gathers a particular pungent character.

So, it suited Grady fine. And if Grady was happy, Scout was too. And if Grady was sorry, Scout did what a dog could to ameliorate the situation. It was a mutually beneficial living arrangement.

*****

One thing about Florida is that the names of places tell you what those places are. Fisheating Creek is a creek where a man patient with a rod can eat a lot of fish. Shark Slough is a slough that's shaped like a shark, with a big fin on the back and open jaws off to the side. Pine Level Campground Cemetery is the cemetery behind the cow field where the revival camp used to share the gifts of the Holy Ghost with the sinners of Pine Level, which used to be a town before the highway came through. And Ugly Tiger's Land was a strip of land that belonged to Ugly Tiger.

Now, Ugly Tiger might or might not have had a legal deed to that land. It wasn't much more than a dark patch of swamp sticking out from where the Boggy Creek Bog kind of oozed into Long Creek Branch before it flowed southwards past Fort Lonesome, Arcadia, and Utopia, through Lake Istokpoga and Audubon Corkscrew, and ultimately into Fakahatchee Strand. That made it Everglades proper, or a corner of it. Anyway, everybody knew where it was and knew not to go there, because Ugly Tiger was one of those old fellows you just didn't want to agitate. Or even see. He was supposedly an old Seminole gentleman who'd only ever left his land once, and that was to go fight Nazis, or maybe Communist Koreans, with his buck knife and a gopher rattle. That's a rattle made from a gopher tortoise shell. That gopher rattle, the old folks at the Corner Store would say, might have killed more Nazis or Communist Koreans than the buck knife did, because Ugly Tiger knew how to use it. What that meant, we didn't, in all honesty, really know; but we could imagine. And so, nobody ever really went into Ugly Tiger's Land with trouble in mind. Grady was a little foolhardy to even consider approaching the boundaries.

It was the loneliest stretch of swamp we could think of, with a healthy population of alligators, cottonmouths, brown recluse spiders, and those striped gallinipper mosquitoes big enough to pick up a quarter and fly off with it. Straight shooting, it was the mosquitoes that put the fear in us more than all the rest of that bunch. Alligators, snakes, and spiders as a general rule want to stay away from you. A gallinipper wants to get nice and close, and then invite its extended family over for dinner. More than an inch long, they came out in thirsty, black clouds, so a couple thousand would get up in your ears and eyes while the million or so rest of them were drinking you dry. The bites didn't itch so much as sting. Grady always said he didn't mind gallinippers so much, though, because at least they were big enough that you could feel them land on you before they actually set to draining you. A chance to swat was all he needed.

Of course, there were stories about other things in Ugly Tiger's Land that the old folks and little kids would argue over at Easter picnics and on the porch of the Corner Store. (About that particular name: It wasn't on a corner, that store, but Mrs. Strahorn liked the sound of it, and since she had Mr. Strahorn's ear and Mr. Strahorn had taken over the place from his Uncle Buddy who built it right where it was on the side of the Myakka Road, the name was the name. If another road ever came through to make a corner next to it, we might need to put up a stop sign, and then, the old folks said, the town would really go to the   devil.)

Now, Grady, in this particular chapter of his life, didn't invest much in tall stories and would rather be alone than avoid a few predatory insects. And he might have been a sorry son of a gun, but he never was stupid. He wouldn't be going into the deeps of Ugly Tiger's Land hunting boars or deer or whatnot.   That would be rude, legal deed or none, and not even Grady wanted to be in a position to discuss the niceties of plats and surveys with an angry veteran bearing a gopher rattle. Especially not in a bald cypress swamp where you were, by conservative estimate, a good three hours by jonboat or five by hip wader from the nearest highway or hospital. It was, as previously mentioned, a lonely place. Lonely places can be the ones where it's most important to mind your manners.

With this in mind, Grady's plan was to pole his jonboat along the edges of Ugly Tiger's Land, transporting his fishing cane, a coffee-can of nightcrawlers, a sack lunch, and that dog of his. The one we all call Flat-Tire nowadays, but back then, he called Scout. A dog can eat fish as well as a man can, if the man cares to pick the bones out beforehand. And Grady knew beyond a doubt that right around there, however many miles off the south road, right around that wetland where Boggy Creek Bog met Long Creek Branch and the marsh became true swamp, right around that invisible boundary of Ugly Tiger's Land, there were catfish swimming that grew longer than a man's arm.

*****

Other things grew, too, if the taxonomists sucking hard candies on the Corner Store porch had their information properly ordered. Gar bigger around than a canoe. Flying things the size of vultures that didn't grow any feathers. The skunk ape, which walked like a man and smelled like rotten beef. And the dogkiller.

The cracker dogkiller, some called it.

Now, a "cracker" was an old-time cowboy who brought in wild cattle with a whip in the days before fences.

And the so-called cracker dogkiller was one of those things with a name that explained exactly what it was: a creature as yet unknown to modern science that lurked out in the dark and wet places with the unnatural capacity to kill a cracker's dog. And a cracker's dog was a fierce and fearsome guardian of home and herd well capable of killing any man who dared trespass—therefore, by transitive property, that which could kill the dog could also kill the owner. The dealing of death is right there in the name.

Other attributes were strictly secondary. The dogkiller was dark of hide, but for a pale and bone-like head. It was long and slender as a serpent, and like a serpent carried itself low to the ground, yet bore rounded ears like a human being. It was sleek as an otter, ferocious as a panther, faster than a mongoose, meaner than a wolverine, and possessed of a jaw with the clamping power of a wrathful pit bull, easily able to reduce a fisherman's femur to a delectable bone jelly lightly seasoned with his cries of anguish and heart-stopping fear.

The thing, it was said, kept trophies. An alligator would pull a victim down under the water, spin until it stopped struggling, then tuck it under a log or other snag until it had a few weeks to ripen. The dogkiller, on the other hand, was said to strip flesh from bone and then keep the skulls of its victims stacked around the entrance to its lair as a silent warning to keep far, far away from that place. Or perhaps it just favored the smell of old bones. No one had ever gathered enough data to test a hypothesis and survived.

The younger segment of the Corner Store population held that such tales were hooey meant to keep favored pets from being allowed to wander too freely in uncivilized regions. The elder portion would merely grumble about this one particular hound who went too deep into a mahogany hummock until it was struck down by black lightning, or that rancher's son whose coon-hunting expedition ended with him losing his entire kennel, two fingers, and all the pigment in his hair.

Grady, as previously noted, didn't have a particular opinion on such matters, but he was not, as also noted, ignorant of the ways of the wetlands. He advanced into the borders of Ugly Tiger's Land buoyed by thoughts of outsized filets fried in corn flour but with the ballast of caution due a figure of Ugly Tiger's reputation. The dog was just glad to be there.

She had never been, strictly speaking, trained. Not as such. She would react to Grady's voice almost like she knew her own name and would respond to most simple commands by either sitting or fetching, which gave her a fairly good percentage chance of getting it right. She did love a good swim and could barely resist a chance to chase possums. So it was that when hunting for possum in the Long and Boggy bottomland, this quirk of personality was regarded as an asset, and Grady would heap praise on his canine companion in a way he'd never done with any human being. She just couldn't resist the way the naked-tailed scoundrels would run and then freeze and fall over. Like anyone would be suckered by that act. The way they'd hiss and bare their teeth, fangs sticking out in that scaredy possum grimace, that was just pure delight to that dog. Doubtless, the possum saw things differently, but they're a species distinctly lacking in charisma, much to their misfortune.

The thing is, a dog—and especially a dog named Scout—lives through her nose. There are more nerve endings in one canine snout than in two human eyes. And when Grady had poled his jonboat onto the steaming, black water that laps against the cypresses marking the outskirts of Ugly Tiger's Land, Scout caught a particular scent. Something alive was moving above the waterline.

The dog, being no fool, did not act on this information at once. No, Grady had time to shove his pole down in the fragrant muck to anchor himself in place, and time to unwind, bait, and cast his line, and to commence the most essential part of the fishing process—the just sitting part. He was almost there, almost at that perfect state of non-awareness, when Scout could restrain herself no more. She jumped overboard.

*****

It was a noisy act, but graceful. At least Grady didn't capsize. The water beneath the craft was deep enough that Scout was swimming more than running, until she found footing on these fallen cypress logs that leaned up onto a hammock. That's the name for a tree-island in the swamp, being a high-up place where you can lie down without wetting your clothes. A pale flash and the possum tore off into the palmetto thicket with Scout right there behind it, barking and howling and baying like a bloodhound.

Grady's first thought was a vulgar word that summed up his disgruntlement at having been torn out of his tranquil state. His second thought was an earthier vulgarity that reflected the physical labor he would have to undertake to get his companion away from the maledicted marsupial and back between thwarts. His third thought had no words.

He froze. What if, he thought, what if this hammock was the very place Ugly Tiger had established his home? Nobody really knew exactly where the commando-slash-hermit-slash-medicine man lived, or even what he looked like. So. Rather than yelling for his dog, which would serve to alert the potential landowner to his presence, Grady made a noise that was more like a hushed little scrub jay: "Eck-eck-excuse me?"

He exited the boat, walked onto solid ground, and made another polite scrub-jay call. Then he switched to the nuthatch: "Scout? Scout-Scout?"

The only reply was a snapping of branches in the middle distance followed by another high-pitched kind of noise. Could have been a yelp of excitement. But Grady, in that fractional moment, detected a note of fear, surprise, and pain. He imagined some Vietnam commando bear trap snapping shut upon his companion and, to his credit, he scrambled as quickly as he could toward the noise and into what he'd convinced himself was Ugly Tiger's well-guarded perimeter. But when he caught up with Scout, the dog was fine. His relief quickly segued into annoyance—a transformation most dog owners will find familiar— and then into something else.

She was wagging her tail and poking that nerve-laden snout into a hollow log in a kind of clearing in the center of the hammock. As far as she was concerned, a possum was availing itself of temporary shelter inside that log.

She hadn't paid much mind to the rock-like objects stacked around the opening. Grady did, though. He knew that a hammock was formed through gradual accumulation of free-floating silt and muck around the broad bases of a cypress stand. Rocks don't float, and so they typically aren't a constituent part of the average swamp hammock. The only stones are dropped there.

Or else they're not stones at all. Hard, pale objects in this habitat are a heck of a lot likelier to be bones. Especially if you notice the empty eye sockets.

Only one creature he'd ever heard of stacked animal skulls like that around the opening of a hollow log. The cracker dogkiller.

He gathered his wits and called for the dog, quietly, firmly, and with the authority of sheer terror.

The dog turned to Grady. She wagged her tail. She took one step toward him. Then another. And then all hell broke like thunder on that poor creature's backside.

Grady would recall it as a black-and-white streak of fur and fury that shot out of that hollow with all the speed of a nitro-burning stock car. Part cobra, part wolverine, jaws like a hyena, body like a python, ears like a child, and eyes like one of them boys who thought it might be a good idea to convert their relief checks to crystalline methamphetamine before heading north on the Interstate to see some of America's highways at velocity three nights ago or maybe four because they'd lost count, officer, why do you ask? The thing was bad news, in other words, and bad news that traveled fast.

Grady didn't think it was real. He didn't think it could be real. There was a smell to it, and a sound that was as much a rattlesnake's buzz as it was a coyote's wail. But it moved too quick to be seen, except in flashes.

The dog was twisting and howling and carrying on as she was getting hauled into the darkness of that hollow log. There was blood, less than you'd expect but more than you'd want. And Grady says he just lost it. If he could have seen the dogkiller's eyes, he'd have gone after it like you would a gator, thumbs first, twisting into those eye sockets deep as you can. But that creature was part ghost and entirely inside its den. The cypress log was too big to lift. So, Grady kicked it. And the log cracked. Just a little, just a foot or so back from the opening. The dog was still setting up a noise like an ambulance siren, so Grady kicked again. He kicked so hard the wood just parted under his feet, his body slipped between the sides of it, and he found himself seated on the shoulders of the dragon-weasel of death itself, rodeo-style. White skin, blood-red eyes, razor-sharp fangs sunk deep into his dog's left rear flank. Worse than a bear trap; these steely jaws were directed by a malevolent force.

Now, maybe things might have been different had Grady then applied thumbs to eye sockets, but he was in a bit of a panic given the precariousness of his posture. The dog's twisting back and forth didn't help either.

So, Grady grabbed the only weapon within reach. Like Samson battling the Philistines, he took up a jawbone from the pile and began beating the demon about the head. The gambit only worked halfway. The devil's attention was now turned fully away from the dog and toward him. The problem was the damn thing didn't let go. Quick as a snake and strong as a bulldozer, it reared up with Grady on its back and the dog's leg in its teeth. Next thing he knew, they were going for a ride. The dog was bleeding and howling, Grady was snarling and growling, and the dogkiller was carrying the whole mess of them forward through the underbrush. Branches were slapping him upside the head about as hard as he was clubbing the dogkiller. His poor dog was getting the worst of it.

Grady had never wrestled in high school, but he'd watched the wrestling on TV when he had one, and he credits that with inspiring his next move. He put the unnatural creature in a tight head lock and, as they traversed a fallen cabbage palm, set his boots down heel first. Grady's crooked legs acted as twin poles and vaulted himself, his dog, and the wailing demon into a loop-de-loop. The thing landed on top of him belly up. His dog's leg made an awful snapping sound beside his ear. His own head made a deep, echoing clonk as it came in contact with the palmetto, but the demon's head, still held firm in the crook of his left arm, had shifted such that Grady was pressing its eyes and nose into the mud.

As unearthly as the dogkiller might seem, it still required oxygen. Recognizing his outstanding fortune, Grady held the thing's nostrils fast against the earth and pounded it with the jawbone. The monster writhed like a rattler, but with the dog locked in its jaws, it couldn't wriggle out from under Grady's arm. Grady pushed and pounded like their lives depended on it, squeezed and slugged until his arms were ready to unravel.

And the dogkiller twitched. It wasn't a voluntary motion, not an attempt to escape. The thing was in trouble, and Grady was doing it. So of course, he had to mess it up somehow. He laughed, causing his arm to move the barest fraction of an inch.

What happened next was all jumbled together in Grady's recollection. He remembered the feel of the thing whipping southward like an express elevator through his arm and vanishing into the hammock.

He remembered picking himself up, picking up his half-dead companion, and turning toward where he reckoned the jonboat was. And he remembers hearing a hiss like a cornered possum somewhere in the neighborhood of his ankles, loud enough that he jumped like an alley cat and landed like the town drunk. His feet went out from under him, the wounded dog stayed on top of him, and his head once again came into abrupt contact with a tree root.

When he came back to consciousness, the sun had moved across the sky, the hammock was once again still and tranquil, and his dog was still in his arms, still hanging on to life. The vet had to take the leg the next day, what was left of it, but at least they'd both returned to the land of the living.

Grady swears that before he blacked out, he heard the sound of a gopher rattle. But no one pays too much attention to what Grady McKinnon says. He's the kind of man who'd name a three-legged dog Flat-Tire.

ABHARTACH

by Charles Sartorius

When their father succumbed following a brief illness, his heirs were made privy to two requests. One anticipated, the other a peculiarly outrageous revelation to his progeny, twin daughters Lyndee and Lynda. Felix Negron, an underpaid, spendthrift community college counselor, never gave any hint of this second bidding during the living years; it was only after their father's demise when his only two surviving kin were informed of the odd request via video, one he'd recorded several years earlier.

The young women, now in their mid-twenties and on their own, diligently searched in frustration for over an hour in the cluttered and dank attic of Felix's dilapidated three-bedroom home on the outskirts of Bakersfield, California to locate that old VCR of his. It had been stored up top around the time their late mother, Ana, finally convinced her reluctant spouse to purchase a DVD player. She knew anything more technologically advanced would be unceremoniously rejected. "Like pulling out nose hairs," Mom joked with her youngsters at the time. Even so, the ancient VCR lingered in the living room for several months before relegation to the attic, Felix refusing to discard the unit.

"Got it!" Lyndee hollered to her mirror image sister from across the room. The dated contraption was in a box labeled *Baby Clothes*. "I ignored it the first time around forgetting Dad never was any good with labels or organization," she quipped to her sibling.

The sisters scurried down the attic's rasping wooden ladder eager to play the tape acquired from their father's attorney, Kanesha Stuart, at yesterday's reading of the will in a dank downtown Bakersfield law office. Relatively short and indeed succinct, Felix had bequeathed his entire estate, such as it was, halved between his two girls . . . with one caveat.

"You must follow your father's requests to a tee," advised Ms. Stuart, handing over the VCR tape to Lyndee (the nearest sibling) after the will was read. "If you fail to carry out these instructions within thirty days, everything goes to the Salvation Army. Your father has authorized up to fifteen thousand dollars from his bank account to fund said requests."

"Such as?" queried Lynda.

"You'll have to view the tape; that's your father's wishes. I've already perused it and will require proof of completion via pertinent documentation within the stipulated period," the middle-aged attorney sternly advised.

After a bit of finagling, Felix's daughters got the VCR unit hooked up to the living room's old Sony TV (bought well before the introduction of flat screens), Lyndee pressing the play arrow button. They stared at a blank screen the first ten seconds before the image of their somewhat younger father appeared:

Obviously, I'm no more. I've lived longer than deserved, not anticipating outlasting dearest Ana. It's now up to you, Lynda and Lyndee - my sole surviving heirs, to fulfill my wishes.

I've only two requests. First, I'm to be cremated just as my grandparents were with no funeral. A simple urn for the ashes will suffice as it's only a temporary vessel. Second, my ashes must be spread over the grave of Abhartach located in the surrounds of Glenullin, County Derry, Northern Ireland. No variation is acceptable. None. Abhartach's resting place is located under a lone tree shading a large rock; the village locals can advise of the precise whereabouts. They might be reluctant to divulge this information; demand they do so. Use my name if you must.

Reasons for this second request are my own, not to be shared . . . for now. A sealed written explanation will be provided on your thirtieth birthday, available from the law firm at that time. You'll have thirty days beginning tomorrow to fulfill my wishes; if not completed within that period, the attorney has been instructed to donate my entire estate to a specified charity.

To my dear departed wife, Ana – I'm sorry involving our two precious offspring in this sordid affair, but I absolutely require these requests be heeded. I have no choice.

Both women stared wide-eyed at the screen as their father's image faded to black.

"What the hell was that?" queried Lynda. "Ireland? This is crazy."

"Both sides of our family tree sprouted from Mexico as far as I know," replied Lyndee, perplexity etched across her face. "I believe we're something like fifth generation Americans according to Mom; Dad never really uttered a word about our heritage, come to think of it."

Lynda shook her head slightly, reaching over to turn the VCR off. "The family's been in California for so many generations, I've never given it a second thought."

"Well, the inheritance isn't a fortune by any means, but with the house, saving and retirement accounts, and a few other assets, it's still relatively substantial – way more than anticipated . . . and to retain a little more of it, only one of us needs to go to Ireland. Since you're the one with a passport, Lynda, you're nominated."

"I can't take off work just like that," complained Lyndee's startled twin.

"You get some bereavement leave, right? I'm sure they'll let you combine that with a few days of vacation time; you can have this wrapped up easily within a week, probably less."

*****

Lynda tentatively stepped off the plane at Belfast International Airport. Every instinct in her body screamed at her to book a return flight back to Los Angeles immediately, if not sooner. Ignoring the internal alarm, she pressed on, partly due to a surprising monetary greed taking root during the reading of the will, but mostly because of a morbid curiosity about her father's furtive life. Inquisitiveness trumped caution. Deciding it best not to potentially scare herself into retreat via research into the history of the stipulated gravesite, Lynda dove into her little adventure with a blank slate. Maybe she'd change her mind once she arrived. Probably not.

After spending a restless, jet lagged night in a nearby hotel, Lynda made her way to a rental car office near the airport the following morning. The agent (after informed of Lynda's travel plans) provided a map with directions to Derry where she'd booked accommodations, then on to Glenullin explaining cell service was dubious at best out in that area; relying on her phone's GPS was risky business. "You'll thank me for the map, young lady," he said. Although both parties spoke English, it took a concerted effort for the youthful traveler to decipher that accented dialect.

"Thanks for the heads up."

"I recommend a bit of practice driving with right-hand steering," suggested the middle-aged rental rep. "There's a little used road behind our building perfect for it."

"Not necessary. After college graduation a couple of years ago, I took a three-week celebratory jaunt to England; I've already endured the pains of left-lane driving acclimation," she responded then chuckled.

"Suit yourself. By the way, I don't get many customers driving to your destination. Not exactly a hotbed of tourism, Glenullin is. Has a bit of a sordid past."

"Such as?"

"Not my place to discuss, missy. Be on your way now." With that, he turned to the computer screen. Conversation over. Lynda ambled out the door into the rental lot.

The approximate 115 kilometers to Derry may have been scenic, but went mostly unnoticed, Lynda's attention directed toward the task at hand. *A business trip*, she reminded herself more than once during the road excursion. Steadfastly single-minded, expediency was her goal.

She arrived in Derry mentally exhausted, checking into a bed and breakfast previously booked online. Lynda decided to keep conversation to a minimum with the check-in person until settled into her accommodations where she could review her plan. *That horrid plan.* She'd then return to the front desk and confirm directions to her destination.

Her Derry room was sparsely furnished, cozy, but comfortable - pretty much fitting the B&B's description on its website. Lynda decided early on in her travel plans not to text her sister until safely seated in the airport lobby awaiting the return flight home;

she didn't need the aggravation Lyndee was fully capable of supplying . . . in large quantities. Lynda's phone remained off. *Probably no cell service out in the Irish boonies*. That's what she told herself.

Unpacked, showered, and snacked, the young woman could procrastinate no longer. Since specific instructions were sparse in the video, her plan was rather simplistic: arrive at the site, empty Dad's ashes over the grave, and get the hell out of there faster than fast. She'd record the brief undertaking via a small digital camera brought along on the journey (illuminated by a compact flashlight if needed), submitting requisite visual documentation to the attorney upon returning to Bakersfield. Too creepy to record on her iPhone, the lawyer could keep the camera for all she cared. An early freaking Christmas present.

Lynda gingerly walked down the B&B's creaky stairs full of angst tempered determination. Stepping into the living room (also used as the lobby), she approached the vacant front desk. "Hello. Anyone there?" No response; she rang the small bell on the counter while repeating her query.

A half-minute later an elderly gentleman shuffled out from a rear room. "Yes, can I help you?" Not the stoic thirty-something woman who'd initially checked her in.

"Hello, I'm a guest of your B&B. Could you please look at this map I have to Glenullin? I'd like to ensure it's accurate; don't want to get lost out there," she said nervously.

"Ah; Glen of the Eagle." The old man grew somber as he viewed the map.

"What?"

"That's what it means. What business do you have at that locale?"

"I've been directed there by my late father to visit the grave of Abhartach."

Visibly shaken, he retorted, "Bad ground, young lady; private land, too. Stay away. Do you hear me? Don't go near that place!" What little color he had drained completely from his expression.

"I have no choice," Lynda responded, exasperated. "Please - my father's name is Felix Negron," Lynda begged, recalling Dad's advice. *Use my name if you must.*

"Negron, is it? By God, I thought the last Negron died there centuries ago, but I warn you still – don't go. That thing in the grave; its mother 'twere a Negron, originally from Spain she was, had that monstrosity out of wedlock . . . some say fathered by a demon. Well over a thousand years ago and not deserving of further discussion."

"But…"

"I'll speak no more of it; if you trust that map of yours then go, but we locals have nothing to do with that cursed plot. If you're smart, go back where you came from. Now!" With that, the old man about-faced, retreating to where he'd emerged.

Lynda stood there like a statue clutching the map, frightened curses exploding under her breath, the situation becoming surreal. *My dad's somehow tied up in Irish folklore?*

"Excuse me, miss?"

Lynda spun around; a young man came into view directly behind her. Tall and almost emaciated, his long raven locks were a disturbing contrast to his piercing pale eyes.

"I couldn't help overhearing your conversation. I pretty much got the same response yesterday."

"You're looking for the grave as well?"

"I'm a paranormal investigator from Germany specializing in historical vampires," he said with a slight bow. "Name's Gunther."

"Lynda Negron from California. Vampires?"

"Yes, it's said Abhartach was the first vampire, known as the *Red Bloodsucker* among the druids of the day, around the fifth century or so. Some say Bram Stoker got the notion for his famous manuscript from the Abhartach tale."

"Who?"

"Stoker, the Irish writer and creator of Dracula. As the ancient yarn goes, Abhartach could only be killed with a sword made of yew wood thrust through its chest . . . kind of like in Dracula – a wooden stake. To ensure it stayed that way, the locals buried Abhartach vertically, face first, with a huge stone covering the blood luster's grave."

"More information than I needed to know about local folktales; it was my dad's dying wish I visit the site. Now it'll be an extremely quick visit," she joked tensely, keeping the business with Felix's ashes to herself.

"My condolences. Such a strange request, but no worries. I drove there last night; heard nothing, saw nothing, sensed nothing, and recorded nothing with my equipment. I'm returning there this evening for a final visit. You're welcome to come along."

"I was thinking a day excursion would be best."

"Well, I'm motoring out to the site around twenty-two thirty, that's ten-thirty pm for you Americans. It's about thirty miles from here and I'd like to set up my equipment well before midnight."

"I don't know."

"It *is* private property, but the locals give the site a wide berth after sundown; no one will bother us, I assure you," Gunther softly encouraged, a radiant smile accenting his angular face.

No one living, you mean. "I'll think about it," Lynda replied, a hesitant tone in her voice.

"If it's a go, I'll meet you here in the lobby at twenty-two thirty."

"Okay," mumbled Lynda, watching Gunther head out the B&B's front door into the fading afternoon light.

Lynda slowly returned to her room where she weighed the pros and cons of a solitary daytime visit to the grave early tomorrow. Ultimately, she decided the journey with a companion (who knew the exact location) was the more prudent option, even in the dead of an Irish night. *Get it over with.*

After stuffing her backpack with the urn, camera, and flashlight, she attempted an unsuccessful nap as the chamber's mechanical clock slowly ticked away to 2230, an eternity.

At 2225 hours Lynda locked up her room and scurried down the stairs, pack in hand, into the lobby. There she spied Gunther, a large duffel bag hanging from his left shoulder, staring out the B&B's front picture window into the darkness.

Let's gooo!" Lynda sang to a startled Gunther.

"Ah, you're here. Excellent."

"I hope you're not planning to spend the night at that horrid place."

"No more than an hour or so, I assure you."

"To guarantee that, we'll take my car," a suspicious Lynda replied. "I trust it's not an issue." *If it is, you'll be going solo via your own ride.*

"Not at all, let's roll," Gunther cheerfully replied.

After stowing the German's duffel into the trunk and Lynda's pack on the rental's backseat, the two headed out of town, he providing directions, she cautiously navigating the dark two-lane road.

"What's in the duffel?" Lynda queried her traveling cohort.

"The usual paranormal investigative paraphernalia. If you watch any of those ghost adventure programs, you'll know what I mean."

"I don't wish to sound rude, but I'm not a believer in that hocus pocus; ergo, I've never seen any of those silly shows." Lynda, unlike her twin, was a die-hard skeptic.

"Should keep an open mind; I've seen and recorded things unexplained by mainstream science."

"Look, I just want to get our little trek over with and return unscathed to the good old USA, thank you very much."

Except for some sporadic (and curt) driving instructions from Gunther, silence accompanied the pair for the remainder of the nocturnal jaunt. Approximately three hundred yards from their destination, the rental car suddenly sputtered, then stalled. Exasperated, Lynda made several attempts to fire it up again, each time a profanity laced failure.

"I can't believe this!" Lynda roared, banging her fists like jackhammers on the steering wheel.

"Chill and pop the hood; I know a thing or two about cars; my mom's a mechanic," advised Gunther, jumping out of the vehicle and jogging around to the front.

Lynda did just that, then grabbed her backpack from the rear seat. She hopped out and slammed the door, sauntering briskly toward the open field gravesite; a full moon, peaking between the clouds, lit the faint, narrow path leading to the lone tree in the distance.

Passing Gunther, she stopped momentarily. "While you work on the car, I'll continue ahead, complete my little task and be back ASAP. Shouldn't be more than a few minutes; the key fob's in the car. If it's fixed before my return, drive up the rest of the way." *Maybe not the best idea.* Lynda shook off the thought, continuing toward the tree. During the walk, the young woman decided the stalled car might have been a blessing in disguise. She could do what she had to do minus Gunther's prying eyes. Privacy *was* important. This was between Lynda and her father's ashes.

When she ambled within twenty yards of the tree and the elongated rock beneath it, the wind began to blow. Abruptly. *Weird,* she thought. Now just a few steps from her destination, it started to howl. "Just what I need!" she shouted at the wind. Undeterred, Lynda pulled the flashlight from the pack, setting it atop the cold rock, the light casting an eerie glow over the grave. Next, the urn was in hand, followed by the digital camera. Prying off the vessel's lid she began to scatter its contents over the stone with one hand, the camera recording her endeavor with the other. *Screw the wind, I'm only coming here once.*

The squall didn't cooperate, her father's ashes blown everywhere but on that damn stone. "I tried. That will have to do," she lamented out loud to herself. "Sorry, Dad, so sorry."

As if on cue, the wind ceased. Just like that. Lynda hurriedly stuffed the camera, flashlight, and empty urn back into her pack, more than ready to get the hell out of Dodge. Turning to depart, she heard the rental's engine come to life in the moonscape. *Thank God; just another minute and I'll be locked inside the rental - and stay there until Gunther finishes with his nonsense.*

As a large cloud precipitously masked the lunar light, to her utter shock and dismay, the rental car (revving briefly), made an abrupt U-turn, and sped off back down the road, taillights consumed hungrily by a profuse nocturnal darkness.

"Gunther! Gun . . ." Her bellow slashed short by a violent quivering underfoot, the panicked woman pivoted toward the grave. The vibration was brief, just sufficient to move the heavy stone off center, exposing the chasm beneath. In less than a moment, two short legs slowly floated upward out of the rift, followed by a truncated midsection, then a hideously deformed head with stringy red hair.

Lynda, frozen in fear and momentarily mute, could only watch as Abhartach righted itself, brushing off dirt and dark sawdust-like clumps from its front.

"The wood from that wretched sword rotted away eons ago," the diminutive creature affirmed in a crackling ancient Irish voice, gazing directly up at the frightened Californian. "No blade, no death," it chortled. "And what do we have here?" Could this be a Negron? The last of my mother's cursed line?"

Lynda's muteness ended, a soul-curdling scream blared from her lungs, words not yet an option.

Ignoring her outburst, the abomination continued, "Ah, but I sense there's another. A twin perhaps. But where? I require both to complete this reunion. Gunther shouldn't expect a full reward for delivering only half, as promised in his dreams. Between us, the young German will collect nil. I've a much better payment plan in mind," mused Abhartach.

"What?" was the only declaration the horrified young woman could finally coax from her tensed lips.

"Ashes from a Negron must be spread over my grave every other generation to maintain my permanent imprisonment in this hole. Enemies erroneously believed burying me headfirst, then covering my grave with a hefty stone surrounded by thorns would keep me still. Fools! Only the ashes of your bloodline confine me here . . . but no more. You missed!" Abhartach triumphantly tipped his head toward the sky and howled, a sinister expression contorting his small aberrant face.

Lynda found her voice. "I know nothing of this; I'll be on my way now and leave you be. Please!"

"No, no, no, dear. My eternal freedom demands a replacement; must be a Negron – and only the last living Negron of my mother's line will do. Unfortunately, half of the whole is missing, but it must suffice . . . for now."

A horrified shriek was all Lynda could muster as Abhartach beelined toward her almost instantaneously, jaws sinking deeply into her right thigh's main artery. As the diminutive bloodsucker got its fill, Lynda drifted into unconsciousness, her final recollection – stuffed violently headfirst into the monstrosity's open grave.

Deed complete, the undead ancient terror pushed the cumbersome stone back into place. It now would wait, linger around Glenullin patiently. Maybe a short time, maybe a bit longer; it mattered not. Plenty of local blood to sate Abhartach's thirst in the interim.

*****

Across the ocean, the other agonized as each day passed without a solitary word from her sibling. Yet unrealized, Lyndee's fate awaited; just a matter of time before she'd go searching for her missing twin and that ancient grave . . . the living half's destiny inalterably cemented by a howling wind one Irish summer night.

THE ABURA-AKAGO AND THE ONIBI…

by Sergio 'ente per ente' PALUMBO

edited by Michele DUTCHER

"Maru de yuki to sumi to no chigai."
(Translation: "As different as black and white.")
Japanese idiom

The citizens in town would remember those days for a long time to come, although they never knew the truth behind what really occurred and what caused things to happen as they did. This is easily comprehensible, as the lives of ordinary people usually never deal with the afterlife, and most men only care about their personal problems and the worries of persons close to them. The history of 'everyday life' has always seemed to be the most appropriate way to describe events and what makes them happen, but there are some facts, some pitiless things that go on, unseen and unknown. In fact, there are more of these situations than anyone could imagine, and these bring change, suffering and death, although most of us don't even know they exist. These loathsome happenings occur regardless of what we believe to be true, or what we think should not be a part of our world.

The ***Shōō*** era – that had occurred before the present *Meireki* period - spanned the years from September 1652 through April 1655, but that time was over with now and Go-Sai-*tennō* was the reigning emperor. The formal coronation ceremony had taken place only last year, in 1656. In the meantime, the whole of Japan had been implementing the Sakoku policy chosen by Tokugawa Bakumatsu. 'Sakoku' itself meant 'closed country' in Japanese and, thus, there wasn't any trade with foreigners, with the exception of Chinese and Dutch merchants. More than that, Japanese residences were strictly monitored by the government, and many key industries, ports and mines were under tight regime control as well.

Common people were not allowed to leave the country, and anyone caught trying to get out was killed, no exceptions! Travelers who might try to come into Japan from abroad were in the same situation, being immediately seized by soldiers upon detection. Of course, such a policy had been chosen by the ruler to prevent invaders from infiltrating their borders, wanting to keep their national characteristics and national religion safely in place. Many decades would pass before the country would be re-opened to the world again.

Though it was already March, the weather was pretty good, maybe even too warm, given the season. Some people said that it was Spring before the true Spring really came, in a way. For many Japanese, the *Meireki* period was a time of economic growth and political stability, which had finally brought peace to the empire. People, as usual, produced their personal necessities and contributed a portion of that to the rulers as taxes. Banking and trade associations grew in importance; shops appeared to be almost everywhere;

there was continuous development in the arts, too; and citizens and peasants were busy working and enjoying their life. Even *haiku* poetry had come into its own thanks to the works of many writers during these years.

On the other hand, the *samurai*, who - when peace came - lost their usefulness, ended up being given special privileges such as the right to keep their weapon with them at all times - mostly a *katana* - when they walked the streets. Others, having already lost everything, tried a different path.

After all, *there were always some different paths*.

Edo had become the real center of political power by the establishment of Tokugawa rule, although Kyoto remained the formal capital of the country. The area had grown very quickly from what had been a small, little-known fishing village in 1457, and was soon becoming one of the largest cities in the world with an ever-increasing population. The urban area was laid out as a castle town around Edo Castle. The terrain surrounding that building, known as Yamanote, consisted largely of *daimyō* mansions, whose families lived in the vicinity, while areas further from the center were meant for the *chōnin* – meaning the 'townsfolk'.

The Sumida River, then called the Great River, did run along the eastern boundary of the city. The so-called 'Japan Bridge' marked the center of the commercial area, mostly known as *Kuramae,* and many fishermen, craftsmen, performers and other producers and retailers operated there. It was possible to see at any time of day people crossing the wooden Edo Bridge, always bringing goods into the city or transferring them from sea routes to river barges or land routes.

Furthermore, the northeastern corner of the town was considered a 'dangerous area' according to local tradition. It was protected from evil by a number of temples including *Sensō-ji* and *Kan'ei-ji*. Beyond this stretched the wide districts of the outcasts, who performed 'unclean' work and were separated from the main parts of the city. A long dirt path, which was a short distance north of such pleasure districts, extended from the riverbank leading along Asakusa. This section was full of wooden buildings and narrow alleys with theatres, restaurants, bath houses and brothels, all of which were gaining popularity among the common people, of course. The nocturnal view of the entertainment district from a distance was really striking, and anyone who came from outside of the town might be surprised, even astonished, as he lay his eyes on that sight for the first time. *How could it be different, after all*?

So, hundreds of citizens came and went: the women dressed in their small-sleeved kimono; the high-ranking men wearing their ceremonial robes and very wide trousers; and the commoners wearing a short coat, leggings, and straw hats. Most of these individuals commonly appeared with their belongings wrapped over their shoulders - and they happily ate, spoke, enjoyed their time and noisily filled the streets and the main squares. In fact, it was in these squares that people assembled and remained for hours at a time. Moreover, the characteristic *jôruri*, or puppet theater, offered elaborate stories of romance, betrayal, political intrigue, and tragic love that usually kept the crowds hungry for more, and most of them stayed until late in the night.

There were also illegal fights and hand-to-hand combat tournaments, which attracted even more viewers, as is always the case.

When it all started, it was a seemingly common day and the soaring temperatures of the previous hours compelled the citizens to enjoy the coolness of the oncoming darkness as they assembled for the merrymaking. It was exactly at that time that some wrestlers appeared here and there, ready to fiercely test their skills and strength against anyone who dared to challenge them. Most of these fighters were former *samurai* who had lost their *daimyo* masters during one of the previous wars and, being forbidden to join a lower class to learn a trade, had been left with very few career opportunities to choose from. Becoming a street wrestler was one of the few occupations that was considered suitable for such people, which resulted in many of these *ronin* resorting to practicing it to make a living.

As a matter of fact, after the introduction of such hand-to-hand confrontations, the general expansion of the entertainment districts had increased the problem of violence. There were widespread incidences of brawling, especially between unemployed warriors and rough commoners. The wrestlers themselves were a particular cause of trouble for authorities, as many of their activities endangered bystanders, when people were called up from the crowd to participate or bidding became too serious.

This is why the town magistrate had issued a law that ordered an end to such street-corner fighting, forbidding viewers to take part. The entertainment districts became more regulated by rules too. Of course, despite it all, some wrestlers continued their activities illegally, which attracted a lot of people, especially when night fell. And the city was really too big to be controlled everywhere. The government had to maintain some freedom, though in secret, so the citizens and the peasants could enjoy their time while they stayed within the entertainment district. As long as they didn't become involved in even worse activities, the government often ignored their actions.

Late that evening, the ring had already been set apart from the crowd by dividing it off with straw. The circle had been marked and the spectators stood around, waiting for the wrestlers to come. Bamboo branches had been decorated with many ornaments, dolls crafted from flowers, and the traditional lighting equipment had also been positioned. Many lamps had been lit to make the show easier to see – some of them having a vertical box shape with a stand for the light, while others had a drawer to facilitate the refilling and lighting process. It was all designed to make the entire area stand apart, and some people started dancing to the sound of percussion instruments being played. A few others threw fruit to drive demons out and bring good fortune in.

It was usually an elder fighter who took the task of organizing such competitions, and tonight was not an exception, as a graying man stood in the middle of the circle. He had a visibly receding hairline and was dressed in a colorful loincloth. Amidst subdued clamor, he instructed the two adversaries to approach him before starting the fight, which was precisely what the many bystanders had been waiting for. It meant that the wrestlers would be brawling soon, much to the crowd's delight.

The two dark-haired bulky men around thirty-years-old approached the elder one and looked at each other with fierce expressions on their faces. The viewers around the circle cried out and incited them, spurring them on before permission was eventually given and the pair began beating each other up with vehemence, as quickly as they could.

The list of various techniques used during such street confrontations had grown to over 250, and some of them were really spectacular, being the most loved by the viewers. On the other hand, some methods were simpler and much more efficacious, usually granting their users an easy win. The most well-known were the *Nage*, or throwing; *Kake*, or tripping; and *Sori*, or bending. Several other groupings – like maneuvering, special tricks, and so on – had been also invented to include all the remaining techniques, and the wrestlers had no qualms about making use of them…

While the fighters combated in plain sight of the crowd, something else was going on at the back of the people, in a dark corner. It went unnoticed by most of the spectators of course. One of the many lamps that had been positioned around appeared to be weaker, and it winked out at times. It was not because it was defective, and no winds were blowing at that moment that might impede it from doing the job it had been built to. There was another reason for the problem.

Unseen and unimagined by anyone, there was a short feeble presence that stood next to the lamp without moving. His lips didn't stand still and kept licking oil from the lamp holder containing the fuel. It seemed that it was this fact that affected the luminosity itself. But the one responsible for that secret act of stealing actually appeared to be more of a child-like being than a real person, as strange as that was. And it was true, though incredible, certainly.

Small creatures like him, the Abura-akago, were used to do exactly that. In reality, there had always been tales about fabled monsters lapping oil out of paper lamps. Some said that it was an unearthly infant who acted that way, and the lamps that became the objects of his interest were mostly andon lamps. It was exactly in this manner that such lamps frequently happened to have some shortage of oil for their fire, and so their brilliance completely disappeared before they were supposed to. A few said that it was due to the actions of some thieves that came at night, and that those were the only ones thought to be responsible for it all. Though, they were not.

For example, in this place, it was only the Abura-akago named Takeo who did that, although nobody could know it for certain - at least among the humans of the world of the living beings. Certainly, there were not many individuals who might state they had truly spotted him, or that might swear he even existed, though a few people claimed to have seen his faint figure in the darkness, not far from a lamp. But Takeo's unbelievable actions were unknown to most of the citizens. Of course, any witnesses who told about what they had seen were said to be unreliable, especially if their mouth smelled too much of alcohol or if speaking was incomprehensible like a madman.

Though few, there were strange recounts about these creatures. But there were so many unbelievable stories if you listened to that sort of thing. You might also hear about souls of people who had long passed away that moved along the streets when the sun went down or visited their old familiar haunts. You couldn't believe all the stories. Though a few were certainly true; with some desperate presences of the afterlife were used to be assembled near a crowded place or a square filled with many lamps, the same as outlaws followed a rich merchant along the streets or some predatory beasts came to the corpses of some dead prey to feed themselves on.

Looking like an infant, though a dead one, Takeo really loved to lick the oil out of *andon* lamps. That allowed him get the energy he needed and it also gave him great pleasure while doing it.

The fact was that such creatures of the afterlife weren't the only ones that relied on such lamps. Their existence in our world depended upon the lamps, although not on their oil.

The lighting equipment of Japan in this period looked really varied, and included the *andon*, the *bonbori,* the *chōchin*, and the *tōrō*, which were all very different from each other. While the *andon* – or the *okiandon*, as it was called if it was meant to be used inside a house - consisted of a very popular paper stretched over bamboo or wood that protected the flame from the wind, the oil of an *okiandon* was positioned in a small holder to provide the light. On the other hand, the *bonbori* lamp was usually placed in the open. All of them were commonly used during festivals in the main squares, dangling from a wire or standing on a pole. The very different *chōchin* had an oddly framed bamboo shape, and the *tōrō*, a term which was originally used in the broad sense to mean lanterns, indicated a lamp of stone or another heavy material. The last ones illuminated the grounds of temples, old gardens, and other places based in tradition, but they were also the best protected and guarded, among all the lamps in the country. For this reason, they were not the usual target of unearthly creatures such as an Abura-akago.

The *tōrō* lamps were also not the usual target of other creatures like the Onibi, as also they preferred to come out for *andon* lamps while they were visiting back on earth, usually during spring and summer. They needed some inflammable substance, so they could start their fire that might let them come to their un-life in this world for a while. It was like the modern burners on a stove that needed gas to be set on fire, as they just had to turn to something like oil, or a lamp, to ignite them here. They needed the lamps to be kept lit, and any shortage of oil in them might be a serious problem that could affect their existence in this world. So, they didn't take lightly any action that might result in a threat which could endanger all of them.

As a matter of fact, there was bad blood between creatures relying on fire and the ones that stole oil that fueled those lamps. It was rare that two unearthly monsters shared the same place in a city so large, but this is how things were that night, and this is what brought other consequences as a result, undoubtedly.

The reddish Onibi that had suddenly appeared on top of another lamp dangling nearby was a ghost that came back from the afterlife and he resembled a floating fire. According to hearsay, monsters like him were born from the corpses of humans that had stained the ground with blood, becoming restless souls after several days or months, and were resentful creatures that might turn themselves into flames. Very rarely Onibi appeared in towns, as they were commonly connected to forests or empty places, but this one seemed to be different. The newcomer had the features of a bald man apparently in his early to mid-thirties, though his traits varied widely, because offshoots of the gaseous parts of the fire that covered his body greatly changed at any given time.

As soon as the Onibi burst, his flames increased and his eyes turned to the other much shorter ghost that was nearby. The smaller one had begun to eagerly lick the oil out of the lamp as if it was milk meant for a baby. The tones he made use of were irritating as his voice was heard by Takeo. "There is not room enough here for both of us. You should move away, at once. Go search for another lamp for you to feed on! Your presence in the vicinity upsets me."

The Abura-akago was caught unawares by that unannounced coming, though he didn't fear the presence of other creatures. There were so many of them in this town: more powerful and less powerful, ancient and young, and he had learned how to live his unearthly existence night after night since the day he had been thrown into the sad unending afterlife. Takeo was now accustomed to being dead, walking alone in the streets in his new life. His unexpected appearance was no longer that of a living being, though it didn't exactly look like the image of a dead child either.

"I came here first," the infant-shaped figure objected, as if that was the simplest and most obvious thing to say. "And I've never seen you here before. Why don't you choose another place to stay and revive your otherworldly fire?"

"You shouldn't take all of this so frivolously." the Onibi said as a warning, his strange eyes turned on the other. He appeared now as large as a very tall human of constantly moving flame.

The pale Abura-akago looked at him in return, without speaking. It wasn't clear if he had really understood the other's threats and what they meant, or if he wasn't worried about them.

"You should show me some respect, as I am the soul of Iwane Atsui! I was a great warrior who died right here in this square last winter, defending my fellow soldiers against our enemies. All of us Onibi are honorable and gritty, truth be told! You should be afraid of what I might do, if I wanted to," added the flaming creature, his features increasing in intensity.

"I am not afraid," Takeo replied in a challenging tone, with no fear in his eyes. "You know, I think you are just a *hiru andon*, and I can't figure out why you don't simply go elsewhere. This is a big town and I have no intention of moving. I started coming here long before you died, years and years ago. And, differently from you, I'm not proud of how I died. I was left in this square as a baby at night by my family, never to be saved by anyone, until the cold got the better of me."

That expression, '*hiru andon*', left the angry Onibi almost speechless, as it meant 'daytime lamp', and was commonly used to indicate someone or something that seemed to serve no purpose. Now things appeared to be even worse between the two. "You infant-like stupid creature! It is your young age that makes you speak so thoughtlessly! You know nothing about war or warriors like me, you are not experienced enough, you died before growing up! Nobody remembers you and you certainly do not deserve to be respected by humans today." The words that came out of the fire that represented the center of the flaming creature's face were very hard and clearly resentful. Then he kept speaking. "You'd better leave this place before I show you how much my fire can be harmful to dead children like you! Don't you know that ghosts can suffer pain or be wounded?"

"I've been a ghost for a longer time than you, although I may appear to be only a childish presence," the Abura-akago said. *"What if I am the one who can injure you?"*

"Try it if you think you can, or if you dare!" the other sneered, his traits becoming more brilliant than before. And he also looked to be full of power now.

Takeo didn't step back, however. He knew that his own powers were much feebler than an Onibi's, as he was more accustomed to making humans move away, if he wanted to. He had found he could scare humans by crying, whimpering or sighing, as all of those things were connected to his infant-like characteristics that had stayed with him also after his passing. However, he wouldn't easily make way for this hateful newcomer who wanted to keep this place for himself.

"Get started!" the Onibi grunted. As if in accordance with his very angry emotions, flames burst from his stylized chest. He screamed and thrust both hands toward the other, releasing all that fire strength that slept deep inside to the surface of his undead being.

The blow hit the much smaller Takeo in mid-chest with unbelievable force that hurled him backwards unexpectedly. But the Abura-akago wasn't so easy to defeat and rose to his feet again, ready to fight. So, the two ghosts engaged in a violent hand-to-hand struggle in the open. There were numerous alternating lunges and shoves, incandescent arms at times flailing at the pale, ghastly legs of the child-like soul.

Then, the Onibi made a more daring move and his powerful assault overwhelmingly reached the neck of Takeo. The flames didn't enter too deeply and the Abura-akago suffered almost no appreciable effect, but he left his flank uncovered and this was exactly what the other ghost expected. He hammered away ruthlessly.

There was a sickening crack as Takeo's back was thrown against the hard surface of a stone statue that was next to the stairs of a wooden house. If he had still possessed a skull, it would have been seriously damaged. The infant-like being's eyes grew wide and his mouth opened, gasping, as if he had great difficulty breathing. Though he didn't need fresh air anymore, of course, since the day he had died of the extreme cold, such a gesture had remained in some ways connected to him even after his passing. It seemed that none of his assaults were proving to be harmful to that other fiery creature. However, his opponent wasn't capable of causing serious wounds to his ghastly body either.

The Abura-akago made a sickly gurgling noise and rose to his feet again. Then, with an angry cry, he leapt forward and moved against the flaming Onibi. The other lifted his right arm in time to deflect Takeo's attempt.

There was another movement of the fierce soul of Iwane Atsui meant to get rid of his opponent and the infant-like's shape become fainter and feebler as he tried to minimize the oncoming blows. Certainly, some blood would have streaked down his skin and dripped to the ground from his injured body if Takeo wasn't already the presence of a dead child, and his unearthly figure wasn't lifeless now. Then, immediately after, the Onibi floated backwards as his arms became less brilliant than before. *Was he possibly trying to save his energies for later? Did he ignite his body only when the time to attack came? Did he wait for the right moment?*

At that point, Takeo's heart almost skipped – as if he did really have one still beating in his unearthly features - as he saw that this was, maybe, the opportunity he'd waited for.

"So, is your opinion still the same? Do you still think you can beat me, or will you only try to stay away from me and escape my blows until the inevitable comes? Your style of fighting is untrained," the smiling Onibi sneered, making fun of him.

"You haven't seriously wounded me yet," the Abura-akago replied in an angry tone.

"But many of your powers aren't meant for battle, this has already been made clear," Iwane Atsui pointed out.

"No, but I have many other ways to defend myself, and there are different ways to win a battle, or ending a confrontation. You'll see!" Takeo snorted and glanced up intently.

So, the infant-like ghost of the dead child started running towards the base of the paper lamp that the other creature made up of flames was hovering over and drawing power from, and both his hands grabbed the incandescent holster while his lips began lapping oil out of it, as much as he could, as if it was a matter of life or death. At first, the Onibi looked at him, surprised and uncertain, as he really didn't believe his opponent wanted to face him in close combat and suffer the consequences of that mad action. Then, things were revealed for what they were, in reality, and his mind changed.

The Abura-akago wasn't trying to engage him in hand-to-hand combat, not at all! He was doing his best to empty the lamp of all the oil contained in its holster, by licking it, and also filling his stomach. He wanted to be empowered at the same time, so he could stop the fire and make the *andon* extinguish. That was also a means to leave his flaming opponent powerless once the fire had gone out, making him faint or disappear from his sight.

'So wise and intelligent of him, that child-like, inexperienced damn' dead boy!' the Onibi told himself.

Soon the holster didn't have enough oil inside to sustain the lamp's luminosity, and the light went out. The flaming creature started to become pale, and weaken, until just a very small brilliance hovered over it. Then everything was over.

"A daring move infant! Until we meet again!" were the last things he said before completely disappearing without a backward glance. And the Abura-akago knew he didn't refer to the next street fight that would take place here between human wrestlers soon, as it was another fierce battle between them two he certainly had on his mind, for sure.

Technically, Takeo had not won, nor had he lost, but he had prevented his opponent from prevailing by unexpectedly extinguishing the source of his power: *the oil where his fire came from.* And he had also made him disappear from the fighting arena which was something, of course.

So, the matter had been sorted out. *At least, for now...*

*****

It didn't take long before the next wild fight between those two creatures took place again in the same spot. Just one evening later - when another circle had been set up for an incoming brawl between wrestlers, with all the usual paper lamps placed around the circle – here they came again, ready to continue their fight over territory. What they wanted to do, in a way, was to defend their right to freely choose how they wanted to act, while ordering the other to comply with their demands. They were both headstrong about winning the battle this night, becoming the real leader of that place, and driving the other ghost away, once and for all. The struggle for territory on earth was something not only restricted to life itself, as there were souls ready to completely loose what was left of themselves in order to seize a piece of ground, and get the right to be true ruler there, at least in the current circumstances.

Darkness was slowly descending over the town and the entertainment district was full of peasants, citizens, and travelers that looked around and enjoyed their time. They ate and drank, while the many lamps lit the area and made it all more vivid and lively. The crowds were milling around waiting for the next show to start and weren't paying attention at all to what was going on behind them, the child-shaped Abura-akago made his appearance and began doing what he was used to. He approached the metallic holster of the nearest paper lamp in that place, situated far away from where the living humans watching the two wrestlers.

Takeo started licking the tasty oil out of the *andon* so as to fill his stomach, though his eyes kept looking around to see if the site was safe. His lapping of that liquid had to be artfully done, as he had to be careful not to touch the metal, because that would harm presences of the afterlife like him.

But it didn't last for long, as the other hateful ghost of the warrior soon appeared, and that short peaceful moment was unfortunately over.

As soon as the Onibi came to the square, it was immediately clear and incontrovertible that he was serious and was ready to resolve this test of his authority. The color and temperature of his vivid glowing flame seemed to be more consistent than ever now, spanning about thirty feet and coming out of the largest lamp in the vicinity. Such a fire appeared to be so powerful and energized that it might very easily destroy the unearthly matter Takeo's ghastly body was made of. Usually, no common fire on Earth might touch or damage an Abura-akago, but those were some magical flames capable of seriously disrupting what he was. So, he had to harden his otherworldly substance and fight, if he wanted to escape this situation.

'On the roof of the nearest house!' a worried Takeo mumbled to himself and moved towards that point. Then he briefly disappeared. 'I need to distance myself now.'

Of course, the angry Iwane Atsui could soon get up there, as fast and unstoppable as a flying fire moving across the air, but he had to be better prepared before he could leap up there.

The whole place was strangely still, if you just forgot about all the noises and yells that the humans were unceasingly letting out down at the circle where the fighting among skilled wrestlers continued. But from the point of view of unearthly matters - *which was what was of interest to Takeo now* – it was as if nothing appeared to be around. The infant-like creature stood alone in the threatening silence.

Then, some small movements were spotted on top of one of the many smaller lamps positioned along the stairs below. The Abura-akago focused carefully, immediately concentrating. Several human voices carried through the air as background noise kept filling the area around the ring, though these calls were of no use at all to Takeo. He was fearful of imminent attack.

And it happened.

Fire and hatred, assaults and retreats, smart moves and failed attempts, all occurred right there, during that fierce battle that was taking place on the wooden roof, with no one alive to witness it all. *How incredible it was!* The cold metal handrail Takeo grabbed at a certain time made his stiff fingers tingle and burn unpleasantly, as if it was a wild fire touching his undead skin, but it couldn't be helped, as that was his only supporting point at the moment. He fought not to fall down because of the powerful blows he was receiving.

A rare rain of that strangely warm month of March started pouring into the river that was flowing nearby. It would have been a strange sight - if any one of the living humans that stood nearby had viewed the scene. How unbelievable it would have been to look at those unearthly flames thrown from a ghost-like creature towards another presence, while all around those watery drops kept falling to the dusty ground!

The Onibi began jumping from one lamp to another, reviving the flames and thus increasing his energy. Takeo did his best to run after him and extinguish the fires inside each lamp by licking as much oil as he could out of the holster of each one. But his opponent's movements were too fast, and too continuous for him to follow.

So, every single time the Abura-akago made an *andon* stop functioning, Iwane Atsui was already taking fire out of the next lamp, so he could become powerful again, and be at full strength. That was a strategy hard to hold, Takeo told himself with regret.

The Abura-akago began to feel tired, or so at least of lack of energy. The infant-like creature should have cared more about feeding on all the oil from a single lamp instead of going here and there, always running after his opponent to rebut his moves without resting and without really replenishing himself as he truly needed. How long could he go on? How many times could he stop his adversary's attempts?

Things were getting worse by the minute, and only a very few ideas on how to prevail came to Takeo's mind. *If only he could win for real in that square!*

Then, the Onibi made another unexpected action. He broke the holsters of several *andon* just before moving away from each one, making the oil fall down to the ground below and spreading it all around. *Why was he doing that? Didn't such an action diminish the fuel he got his powers from?* There was something in Iwane Atsui's features now — some madness not hidden anymore beneath a too thin appearance of a flaming creature - and that sight terrorized Takeo. He hated the way the Onibi looked and decided he wouldn't put an end to this confrontation until his opponent had been destroyed. "*Iru dake o tori nasai!*" the soul of the man who once had been a warrior said with a sneer, which meant "Take as much as you want!"

Of course, all the oil that had been spread around was much more than the Abura-akago had ever seen, nevertheless licked up. And it was also very flammable, which was exactly what the Onibi had on his mind from the beginning.

The creature of flames moved one of his arms and simply touched the ground where the oil was. In a moment, everything burst into a wall of wild heat and the whole square was soon engulfed in flame.

It was at that moment that some in the crowd began to notice the huge fire that had ignited behind them and ran away from the ring of the fighting before anyone told them to do so. Even the two wrestlers that night stopped violently beating each other and knew that there was something more important on their minds.

Though the Abura-akago tried to do his best to get away, he didn't make it , and the powerful fire wrapped his ghastly body in flames, consuming and destroying his whole presence. Only the faint, desperate cry of a baby was what was left of him, and then Takeo simply was no more.

On the other hand, the Onibi looked victorious and passionate now, though he soon understood that he had greatly surpassed the ordinary, which had not been a wise move.

As a matter of fact, as the historical recounts reported, the first fire began in the Hongō district, and spread quickly through the city, due to the force of the winds blowing from the northwest. Not only did the flames destroy the main castle with its five-story keep and secondary fortresses in town, but also the great residences of many important noble families. About five hundred *machi* – that were local administrative units - and many other buildings, as well as rice granaries, sixty bridges and three hundred temples were burned to ashes that night. As the winds changed again, the fire spread further on, to the merchant area along the Sumida River. In the end, more than 90,000 local citizens perished, along with thousands of guards and servants.

It was one of the worst disasters ever in the country!

After most of the city was completely destroyed, there was no house, and no living men or women around who might stand and light new lamps for Iwane Atsui to get the energy he needed to sustain himself. So, the fierce ghost of the warrior had won against his opponent in that place, but his win also meant a great loss to himself. And who knew when, if ever, other oil lamps would be put in there to let flames out and allow him to be in this world again, coming out of the afterlife he had been forcibly relegated to from that moment on.

Takeo knew he wouldn't be coming back any time soon either. At least not until men's activities and new lamps would be placed in that area again. Though, he didn't doubt that new buildings and new lamps would have surely risen from the ashes one day. And he would come to earth another time…

THE END

www.ingramcontent.com/pod-product-compliance
Lightning Source LLC
Chambersburg PA
CBHW072002190726
48293CB00001B/123